CITY OF SENSORS

CITY OF SENSORS

A Novel

A.M. TODD

$| N_1 | O_2 | N_1$

CANADA

Library and Archives Canada Cataloguing in Publication

Title: City of sensors : a novel / A.M. Todd.

Names: Todd, A. M., author.

Identifiers: Canadiana 20210369523 | ISBN 9781989689332 (softcover)

Classification: LCC PS8639.O335 C58 2022 | DDC C813/.6—dc23

Printed and bound in Canada on 100% recycled paper.

Now Or Never Publishing
901, 163 Street
Surrey, British Columbia
Canada V4A 9T8

nonpublishing.com
Fighting Words.

We gratefully acknowledge the support of the Canada Council for the Arts
and the British Columbia Arts Council for our publishing program.

PART ONE: BLACK MARKET

CHAPTER ONE

"Don't answer any questions when we get out," Stingsby said. "Not on a night like this."

I nodded, straightened my tie, and stepped out of the car. Eighth Avenue seethed with spectators and reporters jostling for a better view, hemmed in by the skyscrapers lining the streets. Above their heads, the wind whipped scraps of garbage through the night. Cop cars sprawled crookedly on the sidewalks, police equipment lay scattered around, and no clear area had been given to the media, so officers had to fight their way through the crowd. This crime scene was a mess.

A reporter hovering a few feet away was the first to spot us. Her eyes widened behind rectangular glasses when she saw the insignia on my suit jacket. She nudged her colleague. "Him," she said, pointing at me. "He's data police."

They'd all seen us now, and they swarmed us, bursts of light from their cameras brightening the night. A man with a wilting moustache raised his voice above the roar of questions and threw a microphone in my face. "Sir, will you comment on last week's threats against the data police?"

"What about tonight—will you speak about what's happened here?" a woman asked.

Her question blended into the noise, cameras, hands, faces and the smell of sweating bodies pressing thick on all sides. I braced myself. A microphone brushed my face, and I quickly moved away; I'd have to wash later. I regulated my breathing, like Dr. Luong had told me. Just a minute more, then we would leave this crowd behind. And when we did, the city would slide back into view—calm and precise, the workings of an orderly network, the pulse of data-directed traffic, the sensors that monitored and recorded, the circuits of a vast system.

We passed three policewomen keeping the media at bay, liberating us from the mess. The reporters seemed willing to let Homicide do their jobs; we had been their primary targets. I wanted to wash my face where that microphone had touched me, but I didn't want to do it in front of the cameras. While Stingsby stopped to talk with an officer, I shouldered through the cops and police robots milling outside the force field that surrounded the crime scene, its blue surface flickering behind the smoke from nearby food stalls. Flung over Eighth Avenue, the semi-circular dome concealed a stretch of the street and sidewalk. The new "police tape" was more conspicuous than the old, but it did a better job shielding the scene—and the body—from prying eyes.

A detective with orange hair stood in front of the police forcefield, dressed in the plain clothes worn by Homicide. He was barking out orders to his officers, who ran around in confusion. Maclean deserved a better investigation than this.

As I approached the detective near the dome, he glanced at the insignia on my suit. "Nobody called in data," he said. "Who are you?"

One of the lapels on his shirt was rumpled; I resisted the impulse to straighten it.

"I'm Detective Frank Southwood," I said. "I worked in the same unit as Maclean."

"Fine, Detective, but no one—"

"Maybe nobody called us in," Stingsby said, approaching from behind me, "but Maclean was one of mine, and now she's lying in there on the sidewalk with a bullet in her."

"Commissioner Stingsby," the cop said. "I didn't see you."

His face reddening, he handed a scene pass to Stingsby. Blue light from the police dome stained Stingsby's white hair and long, narrow face, pooling in the deep lines around his eyes, the hollows under his cheekbones. The strain of the job had marked him. Lately, it had marked all of us. It showed on me in the red eyes I saw in the mirror every morning, in the stubble on my jaw that never seemed to go away, in the lingering scent of last night's whiskey.

"Let's go then," Stingsby told the homicide detective.

We took a few steps before the detective held his hand up to stop me. "We can let you in, Commissioner, but not him," he said, nodding at me.

Stingsby waved his hand dismissively in my direction. "Fine. Southwood can wait here." An opening formed in the side of the dome, swallowed Stingsby and the homicide detective, and sealed again.

I bristled. Stingsby underestimated me on a daily basis. I glanced around to see if anyone had heard what he'd said. That woman over there—was she laughing at me? Wind pelted me with sodden plastic wrappers, and I felt like a hollow cardboard cut-out, standing outside the crime scene like a tourist. I shoved past a police robot towards the yellow ring of a streetlamp, where I stood a safe distance from the media. Smoke, drifting from a nearby vent, refracted the light of a nearby sign for SHUTTER GARDENS, green neon blinking in the haze.

I was only here by chance. Stingsby and I had been driving back from the police station on unrelated business when he got the call. After five seconds on the phone, he turned the car around and drove the two blocks to Eighth Avenue in less than a minute. Even though Homicide wasn't my jurisdiction, Maclean had been a close colleague, and I hated the idea of leaving the investigation of her murder in the wrong hands. I wondered who would break the news to Maclean's husband and daughter. I could almost see how they would look when they heard the news, the way they'd sit there for minutes afterwards, not moving, as the world they knew ended and a new one began. I tried to push those thoughts away.

"You're not needed inside?" asked another detective walking by, a hologram-capture in her hand.

"Stingsby asked me to come in with him, but I had a call to take out here," I said, motioning towards my phone.

She studied me with tired eyes, then gestured towards the spot where Stingsby had disappeared. "Don't worry about Stingsby. He's hard on lots of his people."

"That must be tough for them."

She smiled faintly. A few strands of hair had escaped her ponytail and straggled loosely around her face, caught by the wind. "I'm sorry about Maclean," she said.

I nodded and shoved my freezing hands in my pockets. Maclean hadn't been my partner, but we'd worked together in the corporate crime unit. The detective continued towards the dome, and when a gap opened to admit her, that was when I saw the body.

Maclean lay on her back in a narrow walkway between two buildings, wearing unmarked clothes. It looked like she'd been walking away from where I stood when she was shot, then toppled backwards. Her face was turned sideways, away from me, revealing only the outline of a cheek, an ear, and an exposed, vulnerable-looking neck. I imagined what her last seconds must have been like, lying on that cold pavement. Did she know that would be it?

The body vanished from my sight when the detective disappeared behind the blue crime scene forcefield. But even after the forcefield closed, Maclean's corpse filled my head. My chest tightened, and suddenly I became aware of how dirty my surroundings were: the filthy mud near my shoes, that scrap of garbage that just blew by—had it touched my skin? My hands were shaking; I shoved them in my pockets to hide them from the cameras. Images of Maclean's body lingered.

I shouldered my way through the crowd back to the car. I moved quickly, rummaging through the glove compartment for a bottle of sanitizer, which I applied to my hands, neck, and face. My heartrate slowed and the mental images of Maclean's body faded. I sat, very still, while a holographic palm tree fluttered outside Shutter Gardens. It was already November, and the first snow was gathering in the sky, waiting to fall.

When Stingsby finally returned, he climbed into the car and pulled us back onto the road, weaving through traffic. "I'll drop us back at the office," he said. "I'm going to start looking into this."

Murders weren't supposed to be his business, but if one of his detectives had been shot, he'd be the first one in, protocol be damned. And in a city run on data like this one, nothing got done without data detectives.

"Thank God this case will be in better hands," I said. "The way that crime scene was run back there—Christ."

"This is an emergency, Southwood. Cut Homicide some slack. Maybe when you were a kid your Mom told you all your homework had to be perfect, but this is the real world."

I didn't accept that, and I never would.

"I need to notify Maclean's family," Stingsby said. "I know them well, and they'll want to hear it from me." His eyes narrowed, but he said nothing further. His gloved hands clamped tightly on the steering wheel, one vein pulsing in his neck. He and Maclean had been close, since they'd worked together before he became Commissioner of the data police.

"You think Maclean's murder was connected to any of her cases?" I asked.

The lines around Stingsby's eyes deepened; it clearly annoyed him when I asked questions about anything other than my own cases. He kept his eyes on the road and said, "Listen, Southwood, you'll keep what I'm about to tell you confidential until it's released publicly. I know you love parading around in that uniform giving interviews, acting like you're the hero."

"Sir, I don't—"

"I only tell you this because our safety's concerned—all of us, in our line of work. I don't think Maclean's murder was related to her investigations. The crime scene made it pretty clear who was behind this. They left a sign."

"A sign?"

"It was her eye. They left the glass lodged in the socket, too." Stingsby cleared his throat. "Looks like privacy fanatics."

"Jesus."

We drove in silence. Windswept streets rolled by our windows as we moved through currents of seamless traffic, sensors regulating the changes of the lights. Freezing rain had started slicing up the sky, and the streetlamps gave a yellow glow to the water on high-rise windows.

"What about the case Maclean was working on?" I asked.

"It'll get transferred. Next detective under her, corporate sector crime."

There was no need to say who that was.

Stingsby watched me intermittently while he drove. "On Monday, I'll send you everything Maclean had on the investigation. I don't think you're ready for this, and normally a case like this wouldn't go to you. The suspect's too high-profile. But with Maclean gone, you're next in line."

"I am ready, boss—I've been telling you for years. Who's the suspect?"

"August Donaldson. We think he's embezzling money from his company."

I paused. "Donaldson. That's big."

"You know him?" Stingsby asked.

"Who doesn't?" Donaldson was rich as shit, one of the most powerful corporate suits in the city. I'd met him once or twice at the casino, but I chose not to mention that. Stingsby might think I'd try to use my acquaintance with Donaldson to snoop around off the record, going behind Stingsby's back—like I had in the past.

"And you're confident there's no relation between Maclean's murder and my new case?" I asked. "Any chance the eye wound was a cover-up?"

Stingsby grunted. "It's unlikely they're related, but I'll take a look at the evidence she'd collected. Homicide will too. You just let us deal with that, alright? You stick to the data on this one, and don't run off on any of your extra missions. Your job is not to solve Maclean's murder, it's to put Donaldson behind bars for white-collar crime."

The gravity of this began to sink in. With such a high-profile suspect, probably linked to powerful networks of organized criminals, it was possible Maclean had gotten tangled up in something dangerous. I didn't accept what Stingsby said about this case not being connected to Maclean's murder. Maybe this would give me a chance to find out what happened to her. If Stingsby didn't want to investigate every single possibility thoroughly, then I would do it myself. My investigation, my methods—everything would be perfect.

We rounded a corner onto Twelfth Street and a skyscraper rose ahead of us: the headquarters of the data police. When we reached the building, Stingsby parked across the street. "Go home, Southwood," he said. "You'll start the Donaldson case on Monday. Stick to the book on this one. Follow protocol."

He stepped outside and headed towards the building without me. As he fell into pace behind two pedestrians, electronic billboards lining the sidewalk bombarded the young woman in front of him with personalized ads for student debt relief. The man behind her was shadowed by images of expensive phones. But when Stingsby passed the screens, they went dead, displaying nothing as he glided by like a spectre.

Setting out into the damp streets, I lit a cigarette to calm my nerves. That damn Stingsby underestimated me; I'd show him that. I glanced over my shoulder to make sure he was out of sight. When he'd disappeared safely into the building, I slipped into an empty street and pulled out my Sentrac portable.

"Yeah, Frank?" said a familiar voice on the line.

"Can you help me out with some data?"

"I guess, but have you heard? About Maclean?"

"Yes. I want to find who did this to her. I'm taking over the case she was working on, and I'm going to do some digging."

"Let me guess. You're going beyond what Stingsby told you again? That didn't work out well in your past cases."

"You want me to just let something like this slide? And Homicide can't be trusted to do this right—you should've seen the way they ran that crime scene. It was a goddamned mess."

"Frank, if you see a tiny speck of dust on a counter you think it's a mess."

I ignored that. "Here's what I need. August Donaldson, Maclean's old suspect. When did he last use a transfer scanner to make an in-store purchase?"

Sirens droned in the distance, and the odd laugh or cry rose above the sound of falling water.

"At 23:21 tonight," the voice on the line said. "The Indigo Palace Casino. He spent $500,000 on casino credit."

The current time was 23:40. Donaldson had just bought that casino credit twenty minutes ago. And the Indigo Palace was only a few blocks away. I'd been on the job for years, but sometimes I was still struck by the immensity of the information at my fingertips. Being a data detective in a city like this—it was one hell of a thing.

I put out my cigarette, making doubly sure the flame was safely extinguished, then deposited it in the trash. No littering. In a minute I was back on Twelfth Street, the sidewalks bustling. Voices rose and fell. I moved faster now, with intent, tracking my suspect through the city with the brutal efficiency of the data-driven traffic that wasted no time, no money. Engines whined as cars streaked by, wheels clanking on metal grates. I would find the people who did this to Maclean. Stingsby wanted me to get started on the Donaldson case on Monday. But it just so happened that tonight, I'd been planning to take care of some business of my own at the Indigo Palace anyway. And if a man went to the casino for his own private reasons, and just happened to do a little extra digging on the side, no one could fault him for that.

My trip to the Indigo Palace would look like any of my regular Friday night visits there. An off-duty data cop at a casino was an everyday sight these days, gambling being the city-wide addiction it was. But as for the extra business I'd been waiting all week to take care of at the Palace tonight—that was a private affair. That would be done discretely.

Pedestrians parted to make way for me, staring at my insignia, and a man eyed me from behind the wheel of a rusted van. Ahead, at an intersection, a stranger stood waiting to cross, the outline of his figure standing out against the blur of passing traffic. His eyes made the familiar dance, the flick to my insignia then back again quick to the street.

CHAPTER TWO

I swallowed the Acetropen in a back street where no one was watching. It would take effect in fifteen minutes, just enough time to sneak past the staff. This would be the last time I cheated like this. Just one final night would set things right at the Indigo Palace, then I'd be clean for good. This whole mess, my nights at the casino, had only started after what happened with Celeste, but tonight, I'd put all that history behind me.

I brushed some dirt off my grid-patterned tie and smoothed a wrinkle out of my uniform. I would need this uniform tonight at the Indigo Palace. Without it, I might get lost among the other guests; the place would be writhing with them—with the super-rich, simmering in their digital money, the lifeblood that coursed through the silk, cashmere, skin. Corruption grew there like fungus. My suspect, Donaldson, would be just the beginning. But as long as I had this uniform, I wasn't one of them.

At the front door of the Indigo Palace, I ascended the marble steps behind a group of well-dressed guests. The doorman held the doors for them, and they tossed him wet coats all at once, spraying him with water. Two jackets wound up on the floor.

I helped the doorman pick up the coats. "Never mind those assholes," I said.

"Thanks, Frank," the doorman said. He paused, eyeing my uniform. "You sure it's safe wearing that around at night? You don't see that much lately. With all the privacy fanatics out there."

"I know, but I can't help it—I love this thing."

I swiped the credit scanner on the wall to give the doorman a tip.

The casino writhed with bodies. Lots of suits high on Sentrac credit, drenched in digital money, dirty with it. As I made my way towards a Gemini table, it was already starting—the effect this casino had on me. The world outside faded, erasing thoughts of Maclean, of Celeste, of the empty apartment I'd come to hate without her. Even the crowds here didn't bother me. Open twenty-four hours a day, the Indigo Palace had offered me an ideal place to avoid my apartment lately. Time stopped moving at the Palace. Flashing screens turned its interior into a permanent neon dawn. All night, the air vibrated with adrenaline, a buzz that fused each customer into the currents of digital dollars. It swept you away. It was bigger than you.

Stay focused. I was here to watch Donaldson and set my money problems right one last time. I gave my hands a quick coat of sanitizer to stay sharp, but the habit felt out of place here, unnecessary in the neon euphoria.

"Add me, next round. Five thousand," I told a Gemini interface. On the Palace doors, rain-streaked glass dulled the casino lights into smudges of reflected neon, shielding us from outside, from the rest of my life. Damn, this place made me feel good. I asked a waitress for a double gin and tonic with two limes. Mixing alcohol with Acetropen wasn't wise, but I would just have one.

My Gemini interface paused while it attempted its usual facial scan. A voice chimed from the screen. "For security reasons, you must be visible to scanners and sensors in our establishment."

"Fine," I said, faintly annoyed even though I'd expected it. A data cop gets used to his invisibility.

I pulled up my sleeve and tapped the device on my wrist. My name flashed onto the screen, the corners of the interface suddenly alive with personalized ads for Mabelle's vegan lattes, grid-patterned ties, search engine data. One swipe of my fingerprint unlocked my credit.

"Excuse me, Mr. Southwood," the screen said, "there aren't enough funds—"

"I talked to your boss, alright? He's extending my credit for one more night, understand me? Check your fucking files." I glanced around to see if anyone had heard the screen. A few feet away, a woman smiled at her friend; were they laughing at me?

The machine processed in silence, then said, "My apologies, sir. Game begins in five minutes."

My drink was already empty. I ordered another one.

Stay focused. I scanned the room for Donaldson. There, across the room near the doors, a familiar man stood with his back to me. As I watched him, my vision began to sharpen. That was the first sign of an Acetropen high. My eye twitched, sweat condensing on my back. Soon my concentration would double, then triple—just in time for the Gemini game. I adjusted my position so that my back faced the entry where the doorman stood with three armed guards. A month ago I'd seen the Indigo staff catch an Acetropen user. He'd disappeared through a door at the back, where the guards dragged him. He didn't come back out.

The man across the room turned his head. August Donaldson. He'd seen me and he was crossing the floor in my direction. He emerged slowly from of the throng, a gray clump detaching from the watery mass, his figure taking shape with every step. A man in a cloud-coloured suit, about fifty, massive glasses. Reflected numbers from the casino screens scrolled across his lenses and disappeared when they passed his oversized pupils.

"Playing Gemini again, Southwood?" he said. "You ever at home lately? Got a cockroach infestation on your hands or what?"

I laughed, my chemical confidence surging. "Sure, Donaldson. Got an infestation to deal with. Tried the poison—it did nothing. Called the exterminator—nothing. Now I'm back to basics: crunching them under my shoe, one at a time."

He beamed at me. A red flash from a nearby screen turned his teeth and glasses into a jack-o'-lantern smile.

"How's your wife?" I asked.

"Wonderful."

I nodded and slapped him on the shoulder. He'd be behind bars in no time.

Grinning behind his glasses, Donaldson crossed the floor to the video poker, a recessed area below the platform I stood on, giving me an ideal view. My heartbeat thundered. Steady twitching as the

Acetropen surged through my bloodstream. My sight sharpened and expanded, while my thoughts screeched on overdrive and euphoria unfurled fast when patterns jumped, screamed from everything I saw. Colours and shapes sprang into being. Eighty-three bodies in the crowd. Twenty-five women. Fifty-eight men. Six blue dresses made an L-shape flung across the room, the shapes strong and defined.

"Game begins in three minutes," the Gemini interface announced. Soon, my screen would be flooded by numbers, raw information waiting to be moulded into comprehensible form.

One more drink. I felt amazing.

Back to Donaldson. My hawk's vision soaked up the forensic data, saw every fibre in his suit, a scratch on his watch, the cuticles of his fingernails—but then a change, his posture alert and his back straighter when a figure took shape: a woman, emerging from the crowd to pass by him. Donaldson's eyes flicked over to me, then back to her. He ignored the woman, allowing her to pass by without speaking. But when he'd first seen her, he hadn't been able to hide the look in his eyes, not from my enhanced sight. His eyes had been unmistakeable: bright, lascivious, hungry.

The woman found a gambling interface and her account appeared on the screen as she checked her balance. With the eyes of Acetropen, even from across the room I saw her name, typed in tiny letters in the corner. I made a mental note.

"Game is beginning now," my screen said. Cascades of numbers spilled onto my interface, and I began calculating probabilities. Chaos. My chemically enhanced brain struggled, strained, fought with the Babel nonsense. The screen wavered. Shook. Roaring in my ears, the backdrop of human voices became white noise cranked to a deafening volume.

I won the first game and doubled my money. Maybe it was time to quit. But a second game could make a deeper dent in my money problems.

One more game, this time for ten thousand. One more drink. Numbers flooded my screen again, and I whirled through the calculations. Soon I had the them, drawn and ironclad. My chance to win was seventy-eight percent. I'd never felt so confident. I bet everything. White noise thundered and the casino writhed with bodies, electric glows sliding along satin blazers, neon clinging to silk and skin like static. It felt like all these people, everyone in this crowd was here for me.

"I'm sorry, Mr. Southwood," a smooth mechanical voice said. "Better luck next time."

My account balance appeared on the screen: -$1,024,100.64 in credit dues. Time moved slowly as I struggled to process what had just happened, the world around me blurred. I shifted my position to make sure my body hid the number on my screen from other guests. A sudden staleness hung in the air, a reek of plastic and sweat, and the laughter of the crowd sounded sinister, like mockery.

Even with my salary, it would take years to save up the million I owed to the casino. The Palace had given me three months to pay my debts before I faced bankruptcy and possible jail time. Stingsby could see my gambling losses if he bothered to look into my data, but if I paid them within the timeframe the Palace had allotted me, there would be no grounds for a charge of unbecoming conduct.

When I looked up again, Donaldson and the woman were gone. I shoved my way through the throng and left.

The doorman called after me, "Jesus, Frank, at least change out of that uniform before you walk home."

I didn't turn my head. A man didn't make small talk with the staff when high on a drug banned in every casino in town.

Outside on Twelfth Street, traffic flowed with streamlined precision, and Donaldson and the woman were nowhere in sight. I'd lost them. I began the cold walk home. On my right, I passed the road towards the river where I'd found all Celeste's belongings, the last traces I'd seen of her before she disappeared. Instinctively, I crossed the street to avoid that road. My head still thundering with Acetropen, I passed a dimly lit sidestreet. Layers of thick, hanging exhaust masked a road to the Border, the most common gathering place for privacy fanatics, and also the city's centre for violent crime. My feet stopped moving, my eyes lingering on that road. Around me, the rain slowed, then stopped. The street I stood on led back to my apartment, a massive empty box, the hardwood floors freezing underfoot.

The Border would probably be full of privacy fanatics, staunch opponents of the very idea of data detectives, and taking a short-cut through there while wearing my uniform would put me in danger. But the Acetropen still raced through my circuits, and I felt invincible. As the adrenaline from the Gemini faded, a void was taking its place, and I was craving just a bit more risk, another peak in my high. I was craving some three-dimensional gambling.

I turned onto the side-street.

Sagging rectangles lining the sides of Fifty-Seventh Avenue slid through the edges of my enhanced sight, the world a heavenly combination of speed and slowness, a paradise of contrasts. Light fell from the electric signs of dying businesses. A stop-sign drooped into the street, crooked. The danger made everything more vivid, more alive than it had been in months.

On the sidewalk ahead, a cluster of five men grew larger in my vision. I was moving fast. Faces swivelled towards me one by one, and the men expanded into a circle fanned out around the sidewalk. "Data cop? How much fucking nerve you got, coming here like this?"

Their ring tightened until I saw their faces, adrenaline turning the specks of light on their clothes into crystals. Their eyes scanned me—under my jacket near the waist and on the forearm, looking for the scars from firing a D72—then they hesitated, wavered with fury, and pulled back.

"Gonna turn us into data now?" a man called out as they melted into the streets.

I rounded a corner and one of the men was following me. Light poured from the doorways of late-night stores. I was running. Staring clerks, used phones, brick, chemical scents of bleach. The shops bled into a blur but their mobile storefronts followed me, small robots floating around me waving their products in their hands.

"Soap!" their mechanical voices cried. "Frank, we have soap on sale! You love soap!" Robotic arms waved a hysterical greeting.

The man's presence pounded in my head. Clicking trailed me as I ran down the alley to my left, a jungle of hanging laundry and heavy breathing; no light penetrated the narrow path crowded with boxes, crates, trash, metal stairwells zig-zagging up the walls, my lungs shuddering as the sounds got closer and I spun around.

Nothing behind me but a dog streaking by a wall with green letters screaming out: FUCK DATA. My chest heaved, head spinning.

Another side-street. Rows of low rises sheltered the narrow road from the wind. Two persistent storefronts hovered by my side. "Soap!" one cried.

"Fuck off," I said.

They did. With a soft whirring sound, their neon bodies vanished into the dark, leaving me alone.

I remembered that it was cold. My rush faded into a downwards sweep, a slow dying-out. The dawn of an Acetropen crash. Soon I'd be spaced out and exhausted. As the Acetropen faded, my vision was already transforming. Weakening. I could almost see the patterns dissolve and drain into the ground, a different, uglier world emerging. The grime around me became noticeable again, the garbage bags strewn on the ground with holes ripped in them, their contents seeping out. I pulled out my sanitizer and gave my hands and face a quick clean.

At the end of the road, a light shone on a human silhouette.

"Officer," a female voice called.

A woman's face flickered in the blue light of the transfer scanner she'd just bought off a street vendor. A thin, willowy figure with the top of her head at my chin, she held the device in one hand, black hair falling on narrow shoulders. Red polish shone on her fingernails. Those red nails brought back memories. This woman was beautiful, but somehow the sight of her made me broken. She was a stranger, I reminded myself. Celeste had disappeared.

"Officer," she said again, "I think someone's following me."

I glanced around the alley. "Who?"

"Not sure who he is. Just saw the fucker trailing me back on Fifty-Seventh. Skinny guy. Looked high. Dangerous."

"I can't see him. Are you alright?" Being with this woman made me uneasy, like there was something out there in the darkness I needed to fix, but I didn't know what.

The woman fidgeted with anxious energy, fiddling with the transfer scanner she held. "But still, Officer, will you walk with me? Just back to my work?"

There was no way she should have to walk home alone in this part of town. I glanced at the street vendor, a drooping mass of flesh encircled by gadgets beaming out multi-coloured rays in all directions. One of the devices he was selling: AX-lenses, illegal binoculars with upgrades that could see through certain materials. He was leering at the woman, openly staring at the curves of her breasts underneath her clothes. I couldn't tolerate these fucking creeps.

"Of course I'll walk with you," I said.

The Sentrac scanner became an indigo torch leading us through a dark street with more garbage on the ground. "Thanks," she said, her teeth blue. "I know this is more a job for a regular cop."

"Listen, are you sure you're okay? It's a strange time to buy a transfer scanner out here in the middle of the night."

"I'm fine. Now that you're here no one will come near us." She glanced at my waist for the handle and my forearm for scars, but if there were any marks there, she wouldn't be able to see underneath my coat. "Are you carrying one?"

"No. I got nothing."

A dull ache pulsed in my temples, a remnant of my fading high. I couldn't take my eyes off this woman, even if being with her made me uneasy. We reached a road with more regular streetlamps, the odd car limping by. People avoided us and crossed the street when we approached. I adjusted my pace to keep time with the cautious plodding of her ancient red sneakers as she avoided blackened patches of gum on the sidewalk. A blind man stumbled into our path, his hands out in that posture I saw sometimes: like he was praying but with the palms open and turned up. It was sad to see him doing that when no one would ever be able to help him. What could I do, rip off a chunk of digital money and hand it to him? There was no option on a Sentrac transfer scanner for giving money to somebody in the street. That posture was a reflex, a remnant from before cash became illegal.

No aerial storefronts followed the woman—guess she didn't make enough money to be worth their time—but six of them rushed to cluster around me, chattering incessantly as they trailed us like a crowd of children clamouring for my attention. I didn't like the way they treated her like a second-class citizen.

"Even the traffic lights change faster for us, with you here," she said.

Images of my typical purchases flashed across the hovering storefronts: vitamins, hand sanitizer, women's gloves. Apparently the personalization algorithms were too stupid to realize that I would never be able to buy Celeste a gift ever again. Still, my eyes lingered on the that last image, the red gloves. When I had given them to Celeste, those tiny lines had appeared around her eyes—the sign of her real smile, not the phony one she gave her customers. That uncomfortable feeling still shadowed me, the sense that we weren't safe, that there was something I had to fix. But the images on the ads softened that unease.

I looked at the woman's bare hands. "Are you warm enough? You don't have gloves, even though it's freezing out. Here." I swiped my fingerprint on the storefront with the gloves, and it raced away for a minute, then returned with my purchase. "Put these on."

She looked bewildered. "Thanks?"

She probably thought I was strange now, but I didn't care. The purchase warmed the air around us, and it felt good, like I was helping in some way. I still had about two hundred dollars left on my credit card, just enough to live on for the next few days.

"Really, I'm fine," she said. "I just need to get back to work."

Reluctantly, I touched my wrist and turned my sensor-invisibility back on. As if wrenched from a dream, the aerial storefronts stopped in their tracks and zipped back the way we came, bumping into us as they passed. But when they left, their warm neon glow vanishing into the distance, the darkness came back.

We stopped at an intersection. I was startled by the touch of her hand on my shoulder, her fingers fanned out, then withdrawn. "Hey," she said, "you come into my diner with me, I'll give you a free meal. You know, for helping me."

She paused, anxiously studying my face, again shifting her weight from one foot to the other. Nervousness seemed to come off her in waves. She was standing close enough for me to notice the warmth of her presence. I remembered what Stingsby had told me about Maclean's eye, gouged out by a glass shard—the calling card of privacy fanatics, violent opponents of the data police. They congregated in this neighbourhood, and lately they were growing in number, murdering officers to send a message. But none of that mattered to me right now.

"I'll come in," I said. "No need to give me anything free though. I'll buy something." Maybe she needed the business.

She smiled, tiny lines forming around her eyes.

"What's your name?" she asked.

"Frank."

"Jenny." A sign with black-and-white stripes flashed in the background, patterning her figure with bars of light and shadow. "You look young for one of them. A data cop, I mean."

"Thirty-three."

The last traces of my high faded as we walked towards the Core, nearing the edge of the Border. A hill rose ahead, and on top of it sagged a dilapidated building, dull yellow light seeping from the windows and a sign blinking: SALLY LANE'S DINER. It was built on the edge of a park that stretched across the dividing line between the Core and the Border. As we ascended the hill, a view of the Core emerged on our left.

"Our diner gets a full-on view of the Forest from here," Jenny called back, pausing to look.

I stopped beside her. The Forest of screens in the heart of the Core roared and flickered like always, cycling through its chains of green advertisements: tropical vacations, Shutter Gardens, utopian films. Threads of polluted fog caught the green and extended it in tree-like tendrils. Visible behind the Forest, encircling its edges, was the giant electronic roulette wheel on the Indigo Palace.

"This is a great view," I said. "I love the Forest at night." Lately, whenever I had another sleepless night, I liked to sit in front of my window watching the ads. Sometimes they helped me fall asleep.

"Really?" she said. "I hate the nasty fucking thing. It plays nothing but ads all the time."

"Guess I never thought of it that way."

"You really like buying shit, don't you?"

I hesitated, not sure what to say. "It just seems like one way I can help."

"You gotta funny idea of helping."

As we entered Sally Lane's Diner, a man stared at us from behind a counter lined with plastic stools. His face had that sunken look, with pits in the cheeks and temples, that you saw on a lot of faces in this neighbourhood.

"That's Anton," Jenny said. "Me and him own this place."

We crossed the diner, our feet squeaking on black-and-white chequered linoleum, and Anton simply watched us, busy polishing a glass, his expression neutral. For some reason, his face showed no surprise at the sight of a well-dressed Sentrac data cop walking into his run-down diner in the Border. Did she warn him I was coming here?

The diner was colourless inside. Private overhead lamps lit each booth, and their white light painted everything in grayscale, leaving the aisles nearly pitch black. Not even the Forest's emerald glare managed to penetrate these windows.

She seated me in a corner. "You want some food? I'll make it for you."

My sleeve brushed some thick grime plastered on the table. Jesus Christ. I recoiled from the dirt, my heartrate quickening, and slid my hands onto my lap so Jenny wouldn't see the sheen of sweat on my palms.

"Just a beer," I said.

"That's all you want? You're not hungry?"

"No."

"The burger's the best thing we got."

Nauseous at the thought, I strained to smile politely. "I'm vegan."

If they had a vegan burger I would've liked to give her the business, but my hands were still sweating from the grime. She faded out of my lighted area, then reappeared behind the counter. As she wiped the countertop, her eyes darted around, the muscles in her arms wiry with the effort, dark strands of hair fluttering in her face. That seemed to be her natural state: a cloud of nervous energy, a walking solar system of fidgeting, jittering, scrubbing.

Jenny dropped off a beer which she insisted was free, then returned to the counter. Eyeing the filth around me, I tugged at the label on my bottle, ripping off a few shreds. This whole place felt wrong: not just the dirt, also the stools by the bar, all crooked so the lines didn't match up, the angles messy. And shit, I realized, it was long past the time I normally took my evening dose of vitamins. I pulled out a clear plastic bag with carefully counted and sorted pills of various colours. The latest vitamin D supplements for strong bones, the Omega-3 for dry eyes, vitamin A for healthy skin. I took them quickly when no one was watching; people had mocked me for my obsession with vitamins before.

I opened some non-sensitive files on my tablet and the dim lines of a spreadsheet fill my vision, blocking out the diner. The lines of the spreadsheet calmed me, shaping the waves and squiggles of my thoughts into neat squares. Plugging myself into white noise on my headphones, I let a blissful crescendo of static drown out clinking glass and the voices of Jenny and Anton.

"Did you hear me?"

Anton was standing in front of me, holding a plate of food. I'd been staring at my screen for so long, the spreadsheet got stuck in my vision, and a grid of lines flickered onto Anton's forehead like light filtered through blinds, but there were no blinds behind me. The squares melted into a man, who looked like an old, black-and-white photograph under the white lamp. He was tall, over six feet like me, but ghostly pale and too skinny, almost vanishing at the fingertips. His long arms stuck out at odd angles, straight hair hanging over his forehead like sticks.

"I said what are you working on, Frank?" Anton said.

Evidently Jenny had told him my name, and probably everything else I said to her, including the fact that I didn't have a D72 on me. That annoyed me.

"Is that your business or mine?" I asked.

Anton's eyes flicked to the wall behind me. The booth wall was made of glass, the outline of a spreadsheet dimly visible.

"Got the binoculars out, huh?" he said. "Who you watching on that spreadsheet tonight? Any good-looking women?" He laughed and leaned over the table with unwelcome familiarity. "Christ, Frank, just think about it. Back in the day they had to do things the old way, watching their neighbours through the cracks in the blinds, the rear window—but you data cops, you got it made. Got everything you need right there on that screen."

"I don't take it well when people say things about the data police."

"Don't take it the wrong way now. I give the corporate police a hard time if they ever come into this fucking joint, but I respect them—sure as hell I do. They're watching for those criminal types, real scary-like."

"I joined the force for a reason. Somebody needs to keep this city clean, and something tells me it's not going to be you."

Smiling, Anton sat down across from me. The overhead lamp skewed his features, and deep recessions under his brows and cheekbones seemed to stretch him and make him longer, taller than me. He put down the plate of food he'd been holding on the table in front of him: a kind of meat I couldn't place, thin lines of blood trickling out of the flesh, mingling with the mashed potatoes, the vegetables. The whole thing gave off a foul smell that shouldn't come from food. Nausea cramped my stomach. I wanted to sanitize, but I refused to give this asshole the satisfaction of mocking me for it. I shifted uncomfortably in my seat and ripped more label off my bottle.

Anton looked at the growing pile of label in front of me, smiled, and continued tugging at the meat. Juice ran down his chin as he chewed. The veins on his arms stuck out, grotesquely prominent.

"See, Frank," Anton said, "you come back here sometimes, and maybe we'll help you out. You do us some favours, and we give you free stuff once in a while."

"I'm not the type of cop that likes free stuff."

"You sure? Doesn't everyone need a little extra cash? It might look like we don't have much money here, but we do. Plenty of money. Real money."

As he spoke, the overhead glare flashed on a gold band encircling his finger. His wedding ring. I hadn't noticed Jenny's, out in the street earlier.

One more second of that disgusting meat would be unbearable. This man was vermin. I stood up, brushing a snowfall of label shreds off my suit. "I'm leaving."

"Come back sometime," Anton said. "Just think about it. We like private eyes here."

That "private eye" term bothered me. "Private" was a dig at our corporate ties, the idea that we'd privatized the police.

"Will you come back?" Jenny's question went unanswered, the sounds chopped up by the swinging door on my way out. That man—that vermin—had just brought that meat over to bother me. He must've heard me say I was vegan.

Real money? Anton's phrase followed me through abandoned streets back to my apartment, circling me like a moth. The Core was empty this late at night except for a few stragglers wandering home from casinos, their skin still bathed in the multi-coloured radiance of gambling screens. Plenty of people out there still resented phasing out cash. They droned on with the same old fucking arguments. "Sentrac Bank will have too much influence, especially now that the anti-monopoly laws have been repealed. And they've merged with the national bank. A private company with public clout, playing a role in law and order?" Those were just sentimentalists, lamenting the loss of the old days.

The pros outweighed the cons, clearly. The crime prevention alone was enough to tip the scales. And the relaxing of the bank monopoly laws had become a necessity, when none of the other banks survived the onslaught of digital bank robbing during the early cashless days. Sentrac had a monopoly on all financial data, and since the New Privacy Act, the financial branch of the data police—my branch—used that information to keep a vice-grip on crime.

The economy had gone digital. We were the new watchdogs.

And yet, even though we were the ones in the right, now Maclean was dead. One of the good ones. How would the rest of us go on after this, on Monday at work? An image of her office lingered in my mind, all her things packed up into boxes, then carried away by strangers.

I arrived home, relieved to find the clean, empty kitchen with gleaming counters, the spotless floor-to-ceiling windows, the shining—but cold—hardwood floors in my living room. But my bedroom was no comfort. Her plants were in there, arranged neatly on two shelves by the window. They were one reason why I avoided my apartment so much. I hated seeing them. And yet, I couldn't get rid of them, because I couldn't let them die.

CHAPTER THREE

I woke up feeling like shit. My body felt fine; it was the vague, unfocused anxiety that came after a night of booze or gambling. Thoughts of Jenny clung to me like a layer on my skin. It occurred to me that I hadn't been interested in any woman since Celeste.

To brighten my mood, I forced myself up and started the day with my morning vitamins, stowed safely in a kitchen drawer. The midday and evening vitamins had already been sorted and packaged up in clear plastic bags, ready to be brought to work. Next, I grabbed a bottle of pre-made vegan latte from the fridge, but as I chugged half the drink in one swig, I felt a twinge of worry. These cost ten bucks a piece. Absent-mindedly, I ripped shreds of label off my bottle, a pile of scraps accumulating on my kitchen counter. Things used to be so great before these damned gambling debts. I pulled out my tablet and looked longingly at my old spending patterns on a typical day before my debts.

Frank Southwood—Personal Account. Room service, $122. Mabelle's Coffee, $10. Vitamins, $497. Mabelle's Coffee, $10. Mabelle's Coffee, $10. Hand sanitizer, $6. Quinn's Vegan Palace, $48. White noise download, $5. Quinn's Vegan Palace, $73. Hand sanitizer, $6.

And that was all just in one day. Now, I kept telling myself to spend less, but my daily habits died hard—Mabelle's coffee, Quinn's vegan cashew bagels, the vitamins.

Despite my gambling debts, there had still been about two hundred dollars of left on my credit card last time I looked. Maybe a bit less after I bought those gloves for Jenny. A personalized ad popped up in the corner of my screen: a new grid-patterned tie. My mouse hovered over the BUY button. Click. The next ad popped up: an e-book on veganism. Yes, I definitely needed that. Click.

Click.

Click.

Click.

A few purchases later, an image of a phone came up, the letters AKATO-800 written prominently on the screen. The newest model. What had Jenny thought when she'd seen my outdated, cracked old phone last night, the AKATO-300? I dreaded the thought of her seeing that.

Click.

DECLINED.

Fuck. I must have only about fifty bucks left now, not enough for the phone. I paced the apartment, leaving a trail of label shreds on the carpet. But then an idea came. I hurried over to my storage closet and rifled through old boxes until I found an obsolete paper printer. Would it even receive signals from my tablet? It did. I studied the AKATO lettering on my phone, and it didn't take me long to find the right font on my tablet. I adjusted the sizing, then printed out an "8," perfectly sized. Clear, invisible tape was the last step, fitting the "8" right over top of the "3."

It looked impeccable.

Later that afternoon I dialled Yury's extension, hoping he'd be in the office.

"Yes?" The thin, nasal voice on the line was the same one I'd spoken with last night, when I'd called in with a data request.

"Jesus, Yury," I said, "you're in the office on a Saturday? I thought I taught you how to have a life."

He exhaled a long breath. "And by that you mean gambling?"

There was a pause. He made me feel so damn guilty about that. If I'd known he was so susceptible to addiction I never would've taken him to the Palace. I changed the subject. "I made some progress with the Donaldson case last night. I'm going to get to the bottom of this and see if I can find out more about who killed Maclean."

"Frank, all this about Maclean—I get it, right? I know you have a hard time just letting things be. And Maclean helped you out that time you almost left the force. I get why you want to do something about what happened to her, I really do."

"I don't *want* to do something. I *am* doing something."

"When horrible, meaningless shit like this happens, who wouldn't want to feel like they can do something about it, right? But the fact is, it's privacy fanatics. Stingsby says the Donaldson case has no relation—"

"So you want me to just do nothing? Just do nothing while whoever killed her is still out there?" I respected Yury because of his talent, but he had no spine.

"It just worries me, because these stunts you pull, off the record, half the time they're not even safe. Just stick to the data and get Donaldson for the petty white-collar crime shit he's been up to—don't dig deeper than you need to, try to find conspirators, and all that."

"Yury, are you helping me, or are you not?"

He sighed. "What did you find out last night?"

"Looks like Donaldson might be having an affair."

"That's your lead? It's August Donaldson. If a guy like him *wasn't* having an affair, maybe then I'd be surprised."

"You really think that's the best I can do? I'm planning to look into the woman next time I'm in the office. If she's connected to his company, she might be helping him funnel money. I've seen cases like that before. I'll need some data from you, because I'll be busy this afternoon getting ready for tonight."

"I'm busy with my own investigations, Frank."

"But you know we have such a good thing going on. You remember that time I helped you out with the Tran case?"

"Sure, but—"

"I need you, buddy." I tapped my fingers patiently on the sofa and waited for our routine to start. He'd resist me at first, but he'd cave in the end. This game never seemed to get old, even after years on the job together.

"What other preparations are you gonna be making?" Yury said. "Soon, Frank, soon I'll be reading a eulogy at your funeral after you try a few more of these bullshit stunts, and on top of that—who knows?—you might drag me into something for helping you, too." His words tumbled out between anxious sips of something—probably coffee.

"I need some predictive analytics. Donaldson's whereabouts for tonight."

"Right then. And shall I assume that Stingsby doesn't know about this, like any of the other jackass moves you make?"

"Stingsby doesn't notice any of the good work that I do, due to his unfortunate condition of having his head firmly up his own ass. And remember, what I'm doing is perfectly legal. It only goes against what Stingsby says."

"That's how you justify your own contradictions?"

I waited for Yury to cave. Traffic hummed outside my window. A few blocks in the distance, the domed roof of Shutter Gardens vaulted high into the sunlight. It hadn't been much more than twelve hours since I stood outside that building, the street stained blue by the force field around the crime scene.

"Fine," he said finally. "But for God's sake, tread carefully."

"You know I do everything carefully, Yury. That's part of why I need to do this. I can't bear the thought of this being done sloppily. Let me know Donaldson's route for this evening. I owe you."

"That's right, you do."

I ignored his bitter comment. I'd been hearing plenty of those lately, ever since I was bumped up to rank three while he was overlooked.

I hung up, marvelling at the joys of data. Sentrac Bank had so much information about patterns of client behaviours, it could sometimes anticipate where they would go before they even left their homes. People could complain all they wanted about the privatization of the police, but the many areas of cross-over between the corporate world and the data police had proven revolutionary in the fight against crime. Predictive marketing continued to hone these techniques; we put them to new uses.

Yury's response arrived soon. Based on Donaldson's recent behaviours and the fact that it was Saturday night, there was a sixty-eight percent chance he would go to the Core Club, one of his favourite haunts, sometime around eleven or midnight. And when he did, I'd be there, waiting.

Now my mood had improved. I looked forward to the day when data detectives would advance far enough to be at the scene of a crime before it was even committed, watching—just waiting for someone to slip.

When I swept through the streets that night, high from the data Yury had given me, the city was working the way I liked it: steel gears grinding, the city circuits moving cars, goods, and people with impossible efficiency. The orderly rhythms of the city would feel even better if I wore my uniform, which suited those rhythms and made them stronger, but tonight, I needed to blend in with the crowd.

Unseen by sensors, I joined the throng of pedestrians on Tenth Avenue. The air was heavy with the smell of fried food and the chatter of partygoers flocking to nightclubs, teetering drunkenly on high heels. Roving packs of frat boys eyed the women. A couple floated by me; they were eating meat, their jaws smacking up and down. Jesus. I could practically see the germs coming from those mouths. I edged away from them, regulating my breathing like I'd been taught. Sometimes I realized that I hadn't always been this way, hadn't always hated germs, carelessness, the moral filth of criminals. But now, my world had been divided into two parts: the clean and the dirty.

I lingered by a digital newspaper stand and pretended to be engrossed by the day's events, while keeping an eye on the Core Club entrance. Discretely, I double-checked my reflection in the windshield of a parked car. The Expo-Screen was working like it should; Donaldson would never recognize me. In my reflection, the stranger's eyes displayed on the top half of my face blinked back at me. I touched my temple to make sure the device was securely attached to my face, a clinging paper-thin layer. Having access to restricted DNA-linked police tech came in handy for these off-the-record excursions.

A cab pulled up. One long, high-heeled leg snaked out the back door, and a tall woman emerged, pulling a fur boa tighter around her neck. It was her. The woman Donaldson had leered at last night at the casino. The outlines of the city seemed to sharpen with adrenaline, the cold air crisper. Where she went, Donaldson might follow.

Twisting her neck, she scanned the sidewalk, then went to stand near the entrance to an alley. Minutes slid by as she waited, adjusted her boa, glanced in all directions. My face still buried in what I was reading, I wandered over to a bench a few feet away from her. Her jewelry clattered when she moved.

Another taxi rolled up. The door swung open to reveal the rectangular majesty of August Donaldson, sliding his narrow, boneless slug body out onto the sidewalk.

I barely needed to watch him show up. I'd seen it happen already—seen it when Yury gave me the data this afternoon, when the Optica mined deep layers of big data and found patterns in the nonsense. It found designs in the masses of information collected by a city of sensors. It found order in the writhing mess of human behaviour, an anarchy that seemed to obey no laws. I watched the crowd eat, bustle, and shove from far above Tenth Avenue, distanced by the lens of the Optica. There were patterns in the city tonight. Patterns in Donaldson's behaviour. Patterns in the data.

Donaldson's gaze skimmed over the street and my face without recognition. Flashing neon from a nearby nightclub turned his glasses into yellow globes, the bulging eyes of a dragonfly. When he saw his female companion, a broad smile wrinkled his fleshy face.

He glided right by me, flooding me with aftershave, and put his arm around her. "Sara. It's been too long."

She laughed and smoothed her ponytail into her scalp with a chorus of rattling bracelets. "It's only been one day, August."

"But you're wearing fur. You know I wish you wouldn't do that. You know how much I love animals, darling."

They disappeared into the alley, his arm around her waist. I waited, then slunk a safe distance behind, sticking close to the wall where a layer of shadow concealed me. As we plunged deeper into the narrow darkness, the roar of traffic and voices faded. Only the clicks of the woman's heels broke the quiet.

"Now tell me, dear," Donaldson said, "did you put through your end of the authorization?"

"Yes. On Friday."

"Good. We'll celebrate tonight."

I could almost see the dirty money on their skin: a blue slime, a euphoria that congealed on their flesh and dripped into a trail on the pavement. We slunk still deeper, and the farther we went, the more a moral reek filled the air, radiating from the haunt of the city's dirtiest criminals, a hub of human filth. As we lost sight of the main road—the mouth of the alley was distant now, very faint—the city's orderly grid receded into the distance, and a simple, soundless nothing took its place.

Her laughter pealing in the semi-dark, the woman clung to Donaldson, her fingers on the back of his neck. She said something quiet I couldn't hear. One of his slug hands slid down her back and squeezed her ass. Smoke poured from a vent, blanketing the three of us in exhaust as I stalked behind them like a scavenger, my eyes stuck on the shape of the woman's figure shifting under her dress. The thought crossed my mind that I hadn't been with a woman since Celeste. But what was I doing, looking at her? These people were filth; I needed to remember that.

I stumbled—suddenly Donaldson and his companion were right in front of me—I'd almost tripped on them, I thought—but no, they were still off in the distance; they had been all along. The smog had distorted the space between us and made them seem closer than before, all of us united in the polluted haze.

As I regained my balance, my shoes scraped the pavement. The clicks of her heels fell silent.

They stood still, their twin outlines flickering in the smoke, his arm still around her waist when his head turned, swivelled until two dragonfly eyes pointed in my direction. I remained in the shadows, unmoving.

"There's nothing there, dear," he said.

They resumed their pace. They stopped at a back entrance to the Core Club, and I slipped into a recessed doorway behind two dumpsters. Trash, food scraps, and condom wrappers littered the ground, making me dizzy with nausea—all the filth and germs in this place, so much infectious, terrifying filth—but this hiding place would have to do. Donaldson had just led me to a hidden rear door I hadn't known about. Time to make mental notes.

Donaldson entered a code, the door opened, and a bouncer let them in. With my back pressed against a steel door behind me, I watched the traffic moving through this entrance, fixing an image in my mind of everything I saw. I should probably leave here soon, but greed compelled me to stay—greed for more information. Any additional knowledge about who went in and out of this back door might be useful.

A van pulled up. A blonde woman headed from Core Club's back door towards the vehicle, her legs bare, a tight dress cut just below the curves of her ass. More women came and went, wearing almost nothing. My eyes lingered on their exposed skin shining in the half-light.

Minutes crawled by in silence. The door opened again, and Donaldson emerged with a wide smile stretching his cheeks, his lady at his side. "Just a smoke, Dave," he told the bouncer.

My eyes went to the drinks each of them held as they smoked. Small, gulp-sized bottles with a familiar orange stripe and bolded letters reading: IRON ENERGY DRINK. Those bottles of toxic waste were all the rage right now—so pumped full of caffeine you'd be up for days if you drank one. But wouldn't Donaldson want something heavier than an energy drink for a night on the town?

After a few minutes he and the woman disappeared again, and more time passed. A man in a gray suit burst outside, stumbled a few steps and stopped, doubled over. Within the next minute he'd sprayed the pavement with vomit. When he continued on his way, I saw his face and recognized him. It was the familiar haggard face of Jules Mercier, a petty white-collar criminal I'd investigated in the past.

More traffic came and went, traffic of all kinds. One drunk after another stumbled out and vanished into the alley, the artery that pumped blood in and out of a sick heart. If only the Core Club had a rear window, and not just a rear door, then I could see into that sick heart—see, without ever going inside.

A thud sounded behind me. When it happened it was very fast. The door at my back swung open and I was leaning against empty air, when hands grabbed me from behind and I was air-borne, slammed forward into one of the steel dumpsters. I smashed into the metal and crumpled into a heap on the pavement.

Cement scraped my face and I tasted dirt. I flickered in and out of consciousness. I couldn't breathe.

Rough hands flipped me over. A stranger towered over me, his eyes two circles glittering above thick facial hair. I realized I was being searched but he had a gun so I did nothing to stop him. A door creaked open. Footsteps followed, and a voice floated from somewhere: "Who the hell is that?"

"Nobody worth worrying about. Skinny little fucker, looks a bit like a rat."

As I struggled to force air back into my lungs, a new face appeared far above me: the blurry features of the bouncer from inside the Core Club. "What the fuck's he nosing around here for?"

"Probably trying to steal a look at the whores." The first man laughed and smashed his foot into my ribs.

Pain pounded beyond the thresholds of my experience. The alley took on an underwater aspect, blue-green and pulsing with pressure.

"I've seen one of his kind before," the first man said. "I caught a guy last month in this very place, dick in hand, hiding and watching the whores come in and out. Too broke even for the strip club. So he came to do his thing out here behind the dumpster."

Laughter resounded in the small doorway.

The first man hauled me to my feet and held me while the bouncer rolled up his sleeves. "You have any clue what you're fucking around with, snooping here?" he said.

I did now.

He drove a fist into my jaw. My neck snapped sideways. I sagged in the man's grip while red fell to the concrete and the drops became a cluster, then a pool. The blow had struck me low on the face and hadn't dislodged the Screen.

"Don't come back here again."

They left me lying there behind the dumpster while the blood welled into puddles, trickled over the food and plastic strewn on the ground. There were lines etched in the cement, straight lines like a grid, but the red streams ignored them, dribbled over them. The blood ran where it wanted.

After slinking home, grateful I was in disguise, I passed out. The next morning, as I crawled into consciousness, the awareness of pain swelled in my broken body.

No one could see me like this.

The thought came urgently. Images flashed in my mind of people laughing at the sight of me like this: Stingsby, Yury, Jenny. I struggled out of bed, my head pounding, and quickly closed the curtains. No one could see into my windows anyway, this high up on the twenty-eighth floor, but it still felt better.

I stood in front of my bedroom mirror. My ribs ached, but I could breathe without pain, so they didn't feel broken. There was a long gash on my jaw, sticky with clumps of dried blood, the skin around it purple. Looking at my haggard reflection, it seemed like every day the hours I spent in front of the Optica took more of a toll on my body. The curse of the data police was stamped all over me: the ghostly pale skin from being inside all day, that sagging posture from all the sitting, the red eyes from looking at the screen—"data eyes," I called them. I wasn't even wearing my uniform to distract onlookers from the tired eyes. Dark stubble grew in uneven patches, dotted with blood and pus oozing from the wound. That bald spot on my right cheek where no hair grew. This must be someone else rather than me, a comedian maybe, someone's idea of a joke. Looking at the person

standing there gave me that horrible feeling I used to have whenever one of my dates dragged me to a musical. I loathed musicals:
all those singing idiots, so openly pouring out their emotions,
oblivious to how ridiculous they looked—and the feeling I got
when I watched them was a creeping sense of embarrassment,
shame. That was what I felt now. I glanced over my shoulder to
double check that I'd closed the curtains firmly.

My phone began to beep, announcing a visitor in the lobby.

"Fuck off," I told the phone hoarsely. No way anybody
would be coming in here today.

The beeping stopped.

But in a moment, sounds chimed from the phone with
renewed vigor. "Jesus," I said. "Open a line to the intercom."

"Frank?" a voice said from the phone's speaker. "Jesus, are
you there? It's Yury."

"Not now, Yury. I have a guest here." I coughed to clear
the hoarseness from my voice and tried to speak clearly, ignoring the pain in my ribs. "She's still sleeping, so I don't want to
wake her up."

"You don't sound right."

I strained to make my voice as normal as possible. "I'm fine.
Just tired—stayed up with the guest last night."

I hung up. But a minute later my doorknob turned and Yury
swept through the front door. I must've forgotten to lock it.

"I knew you were lying on the phone," he said, the words
tumbling out quickly. "You sounded wrong. This morning, I
was about to call Stingsby. I've been texting and calling you—last
night, this morning—to see what happened at the Core Club,
and I got no answer. I thought you got shot. These off-the-
record missions might kill you, and plus they might get me into
shit for helping—"

"Yury, you fucking jackass, get out!"

But it was too late. He'd already seen me, wincing when he
noticed my face. I turned around and went into the kitchen to
cool off. While I was in there, I took my morning vitamins.

"Hey, I was just worried, right? What happened?" Yury
called from the other room.

"Just a dust-up. I beat the shit out of the first guy, but there were five of them."

When the vitamins had been carefully swallowed one after another, I recovered my composure and returned to the living room, sitting down on the couch across from Yury. I told him the beginning of what happened last night. "But after I'd been in that alley a little while, one of the bouncers snuck up from behind. He said I couldn't snoop around there, and he grabbed me, thinking he was some kind of tough guy, but I shoved him off and laid him flat with one in the face. Another guy came out, but he got the same treatment. Problem was, there were five of them."

"You're planning to press charges?" he asked.

"Those guys are going to be begging for forgiveness when they're looking at jail time."

Yury twisted his fingers together, knuckles stretching under the strain. When he spoke again, the words came out fast. "But look, Frank—you remember Detective Hernandez, a few years back? He wanted to make that big Hertz bust. Went beyond the data. Behind Stingsby's back. You remember what happened to him, how quickly he was gone? You know Stingsby, Frank, you know him, right? He comes down hard when his detectives ignore protocol, and he caught you doing it once already."

I sank back to the couch and rubbed my temples. Time for some painkillers, or some gin. Those bouncers needed to get what they deserved, but even worse was the thought of losing this Donaldson case, which might be a chance to find out what happened to Maclean.

Yury shook his head. "No. No, don't tell Stingsby. Get some synth-skin to cover up that wound, then start doing things properly. You can still lock up Donaldson, but follow the protocol. Do it with data."

He stood up to leave.

I sighed. "Anyways, Yury, thanks for helping me with the data. I'll get you back next time you need help, alright?" I meant it. Yury had helped me out enough times.

"Damn right you will."

As Yury stood there, the light caught on the bursts of silver at his temples. His eyes had sunken into pits, two watery blue circles blinking behind his thick glasses, his strings of blond hair tangled and disorderly. One spidery line extended across his forehead, deepening daily. As usual, there was a heaviness in the tired line of his shoulders, in the wrinkles on his shirt, the shadows below his eyes. The weight of perpetual disappointment clung to him. He was still a rank four detective at thirty-four. I recalled our recent trips to the casino together: one minute he was beside me at the Gemini table, and the next he was gone, the back of his shirt drenched in blue as he merged into a blinking nirvana of slot machines. And he was losing. Running up debts like mine. A few weeks ago, he'd been forced to sell his wife's investments, property she'd owned since before they were married. He didn't speak to anyone for days afterwards, didn't eat, didn't look away from his screen. I wanted to help him, but I didn't know how. I'd tried talking to him, and even begging him to quit gambling, but it was no good. The moralists were right when they complained about the prevalence of gambling among the data police—"speculative bankers," they called us. There was something about Gemini that was similar to our work, and that similarity drew us there.

Yury threw on his jacket. "Listen, Frank, what about everything that's happened with Maclean? Are you sure you're okay?"

"I feel sick thinking about it. How are you taking it?"

"Don't worry about me. I know you two worked together once on that Gura case, and I know she helped you out sometimes."

I avoided Yury's eye contact. If I stayed busy with Donaldson, I wouldn't have to think about her lying on the pavement.

"It's Stingsby you need to worry about the most," I said. "He and Maclean were inseparable. I wonder how he's taking it."

"Guess we'll find out on Monday."

On his way out, Yury paused, his eyes falling on my phone. "Seriously, Frank? That's not a real AKATO-800. Get a life, man."

★

Yury and I had a history of helping one another out. It started one night when I was at the office late, toiling like the rookie I was back then over a petty tax evasion case. As I hunched in front of my Optica in my cubicle, the elevator chimed and familiar footsteps came down the hallway. You could hear Yury coming from a mile away. His footsteps clicked on the floor about twice as fast as anyone else's; he was always in a rush, late for something, forgetting things, and wherever he went, a chorus of rustling and shuffling followed, the sounds from all the junk he always carried. Sure enough, there was Yury hurrying towards me, arms overflowing with bags, one from the liquor store in one hand, one stuffed with groceries in the other.

"I just realized the one thing I've been missing in my Tran case," he told me breathlessly. "I was in the middle of running errands and it hit me." He stopped in front of his desk, and when he shifted one bag to the other hand to pick up his phone, he lost his grip. Thuds sounded through the office as cans of beer hit the floor, rolling in all directions.

"Fuck," he said, racing around after the cans.

I picked up a beer that had rolled towards my feet and handed it to him.

"Thanks," he said. "This is going to be it, the key to the Tran case—I know it is, right? I know what I need to look for now."

Yury's legendary Tran case. He'd been struggling with it for weeks. It was high stakes, and Stingsby had given it to him as his one chance to break out of rank five and move up—it was his chance to see if he could handle the big stuff. But so far, no luck. I'd seen him hunched all day and night in front of the screen, his lips drawn into a tight line. He was probably sleeping less than four hours a night.

Yury sat down at his interface and furiously typed in some commands. A second went by.

"Fuck!" he said.

Guess that new search hadn't helped him after all.

A door opened down the hallway, and the familiar click of Stingsby's shoes came closer. He must've stayed late tonight too.

"Sokolov," Stingsby's voice said. At the angle he was standing at, I couldn't see him from behind my cubicle, and he wouldn't be able to see me, or know I was in the room. "Any progress on the Tran case?"

"Well, I followed up on a few more leads, and nothing yet, but I ruled out a few—"

"That's enough. This is a time-sensitive case. I'll give you until Monday. Then it's getting transferred to Liu."

Stingsby's heels clicked again as he left the office. Yury put his face in his hands.

The poor guy. That must have been humiliating.

"Hey," I said, coming over to his screen, "let me run me some predictive analytics on Tran and find out where he's going to be tonight."

"Data isn't supposed to be used to spy on people by following them around. That's part of our code of ethics."

My fingers flew over the touch screen on his interface. When I was done I said, "Meet me back at the office tomorrow afternoon."

Sure enough, he was waiting there for me the next day, white-faced and wringing his hands together. I gave him what I'd found last night. He darted into his chair, and his fingers flew across the touchscreen. Slowly, his fidgeting stopped; his awkwardness melted away as his face—younger and less worn back then, stained blue by the Optica's afterglow—became a mask of focus, his eyes locked on the data. He transformed the moment he saw data in front of him, his skinny, knife-like figure held taut with energy.

Hours later, he said, "Oh my God. Frank, thank you. Thank you, thank you." I'd never seen the guy look so happy. It made me laugh seeing that cartoon grin on his face, but I felt pretty good about having helped him.

When he'd finished working, I said, "Come on, Yury, let's go celebrate."

"You mean go out?"

"That's right, out. It's Saturday night." I eyed his rumpled plaid shirt and running shoes. Was that really what he wore on the weekends? "You're killing me with that outfit."

He looked down at his clothes, as though he'd never thought about them.

Within a few minutes, we'd stepped outside and I was leading us swiftly through the crowded sidewalks, Yury trailing a few steps behind.

"Where are you taking me?" he asked. "No strip clubs. My girlfriend won't like it."

"You think I spend my spare time in strip joints? Jesus. I'm taking you somewhere much better than that."

We turned onto a street lit by the red and black light of an electronic roulette wheel, turning in its endless circles on the front of the Indigo Palace. I almost never went to the casino back in those days, but this was a special occasion, and it seemed like a good place to take Yury to celebrate.

Inside at the bar, I grabbed a double gin and tonic with two limes, shoved a second drink into Yury's hand, and led the way to the Gemini tables.

"I'll just watch you play," Yury said. As he squeezed a lime into his drink, a few errant drops of lime juice exploded from the crushed lime and splattered onto his cheek.

"This one's on me," I said as I swiped my fingerprint on the transfer scanner to buy some credit.

"I guess," he said. Soft chimes sounded from the Gemini interface. A flash of red neon, and the game began. Yury's eyes sharpened, focused on the screen. The first batch of numbers cascaded onto the interface, and a hint of panic showed in his eyes—that was how it was, when the data first flooded the screen and looked impossible to understand, impossible to calculate all the probabilities; there were just too many numbers and the chaos was overwhelming; but then that moment of fear subsided, wiped away by the slow, rising elation when you began to see the patterns and realize your own power. Yury didn't look away from his screen. At the end of the first round, he bet half the credit I'd given him.

There was a pause.

"That's a win for you," said the soft voice from the screen. Green light flashed, the reflected brightness dancing in Yury's glasses. I smiled at him, but he didn't smile back. He didn't notice. He was already starting the next round.

"Hey, take it easy, alright?" I told him later that night. "You're betting a month's paycheque on one game?"

He didn't pay any attention to me. And that wasn't his last trip to the Indigo Palace.

I never quite forgave myself for that. As the months went on, a schism broke open inside him, and he became two different people: the Yury who went home after work to see his girlfriend, who came to the office every morning at 8:00 eager to work—and the other Yury, who snapped at me if I interrupted his Gemini game, who told his girlfriend he was going to my place and went to the casino. On the rare occasions when I showed up at the Palace I saw him there. He gambled and drank, but he wouldn't go anywhere near the women. They flocked to him back then, when they saw his data cop uniform or his bets flashing across the Gemini tables, all the money he threw away. But he barely noticed them. He gambled with his phone beside him, and the screen flashed constantly with the letters: NEW MESSAGE—AKSHARA CHAWLA. The guy was hopelessly smitten.

After that, Yury and I fell into a routine of helping one another out. The truth was, I liked having him around. It wasn't just his talent that I admired; there was something else too. Yury, he was what you might call "wholesome." He cared about other people, worshipped his girlfriend, helped the old man in his building carry groceries every Sunday.

Things hadn't changed much, years later. On a Friday night, you were still likely to find Yury at the Gemini tables, all but melting into his screen.

CHAPTER FOUR

Sunday night, the day after I followed Donaldson to the Core Club, I couldn't sleep. My ribs and jaw ached, and the sight of Celeste's plants bothered me. I lay awake for hours, thinking about the day I met Celeste.

It was at the seediest dive in town. I'd been shadowing a suspect who frequented the place, otherwise I'd never have set foot in there. The bar was behind a thick steel cage, and the bartenders wore bulletproof vests. Purple neon blinked from a broken sign on the back wall, dust floating in the light, and tables shook every time the subway thundered by, glasses rattling. The door to the women's washroom read: DAMES.

Sitting at the bar, I busied myself scanning the crowd for my suspect. I was working a tough case at the time, a group of white-collar criminals with a pretty powerful network, but we'd gotten a line on almost all of them. Once we found something concrete on this last suspect, that would be the last of them.

The hand on my back came as a surprise, and I turned to see a woman sliding into the seat beside me. It was her. I didn't know her, but I'd seen her here before. It was hard to miss her in this slum. She had tattoos on her neck, black hair cut jagged around her face, and red nails.

"Will you buy me a drink?" she said.

I'd been to this bar enough times to know what she was doing. "I'll buy you a drink, but that's all I can do."

"What, you think I don't just wanna talk to you?"

I shook my head. A woman like her, talking to me for free? Besides, I'd seen her doing business around here. She seemed to make pretty good money; anyone who'd taken one look at her would know why.

"I've seen you here before," I said. "It's not that I don't want to give you the money, but let's just say I'm a law-abiding type."

I bought her a drink and we talked a while. Her wrists were rail-thin and there were track marks on her arm. The jacket she'd put on the back of her chair was full of holes and made of thin, worn fabric. A bitter winter night waited for her outside tonight.

"Listen," I said after a while, eyeing her skinny arms, "are you hungry?"

"Nah. I don't want food."

I hesitated. "If you need somewhere to stay tonight, I can pay for you to get a hotel room. And a warmer jacket than that one."

She smiled. "I wanna stay with you tonight. Free. I promise."

Maybe this wasn't too good to be true after all. On the walk home, she kept shivering, and there was a wide hole in the back of her jacket. "You can't wear that around in weather like this," I said. As though reading my mind, an aerial storefront floated towards us with an advertisement for a red wool jacket. "There," I said, "just take this one."

I swiped my fingerprint on the storefront's transfer scanner and it whirled away, only to return a minute later with the product I'd just purchased, its mechanical arms holding it out to the woman.

With a shrug, she said, "Thanks." She laughed when she saw me watching her put it on. "What, you think you're some kind of hero if you buy me stuff?" She smiled, but her expression didn't look like it had at the bar; this time tiny lines formed around her eyes.

I didn't mind if she gave me a hard time. I liked seeing those little lines around her eyes. And it had been ages since any woman paid attention to me. Snow gathered on the shoulders of her new jacket, the white flakes standing out against the red. Five ruby-painted fingernails pushed a dark strand behind her ear, then hastened back to the warmth of her pocket. She told me her name was Celeste, but I knew it wasn't.

Later, she fell asleep curled on her side with one arm on her pillow, the track marks dark blotches on her skin.

When I woke up, she was gone. Half my drawers were open, clothes and junk strewn all over the floor. What she'd taken was going to cost me. Phone, tablet, and watch were just the beginning.

Fuck.

I blew off steam for a week or so drinking double gin and tonics at Gibson's Pub, a place where I knew I'd never see her. But it didn't help. I couldn't think about anything else, and I couldn't sleep well either. Every detail about her burned in my head: her jagged tattoos, so strange against her smooth skin, her small hands, the lines around her eyes when she dropped the fake smile for the real one. And did she even have a decent place to stay at night? Her clothes told me she didn't have much money, probably because she spent whatever she made on needles. And her financial situation wasn't all I thought about. There was also the way she'd looked when she sank down on my bed that night, her hair fanned out on the sheets beneath her as I followed her down.

I went to the store and bought a new phone, a new watch. Back at home, I left them in drawers I knew she would open. Then I knew where to find her.

Yes, I let her rob me. I brought her back and let her take whatever she wanted before I woke up in the morning—again and again. Every time she came over, I left new things out, then went and bought new ones so she could take those too. Was this legal? I didn't think so, even though I never really paid her. I'd never done anything like this. I'd never even had a speeding ticket.

Every night she came, we stayed up late. She wanted to look around my apartment, drink expensive whiskey, wrap herself in the silk sheets, look out the floor-to-ceiling windows at the view. She talked non-stop, mostly about music. Whenever she stayed over I couldn't sleep because adrenaline kept pumping through my system, so lots of nights I just lay awake while the sounds of her breathing broke the silence. During the days I was desperately happy, almost manic. But she never told me about most of her life, like what she did all day, where she lived, why she started using.

Besides leaving her phones and watches that she could sell, sometimes I left things I wanted her to keep for herself. Jewelry, the expensive booze she liked, red gloves—warmer than the ones she had—the same colour as her jacket. On my tablet screen, one ad after another would pop up with new things I could buy her, and my finger went click, click, click, buying one thing after another. I couldn't stop. There was a hole I had to plug with those gifts. The hole was the track marks, the parts of her life she didn't talk about, how thin her arms were. Maybe when she got these new things, it would be like that moment when I'd bought her that jacket and she'd shown her real smile. Buying all those things cost me, but I kept thinking that the more time she spent at my place, the less she spent getting high, stuck with whatever horrors she lived with.

Meanwhile, I closed in on that suspect I'd been tracking at the bar where I met Celeste. I finally found enough data to nail him, and he was the last of their little operation to be rounded up. When I brought him in, during interrogation I remember he kept such a straight face, like nothing could phase him. He said almost nothing at all, until at the very end, when he looked me in the eye and said, "You think this is the end of us, but it's just the beginning. You'll know when the rest of us find you."

I just laughed at him. The man was pathetic.

But not long after that, Celeste stopped coming by my apartment. I looked for her everywhere: at the bar, on some of the corners I'd seen her on, at all the shelters in the city.

Finally, I found all her things down by the river, abandoned in some shack, her red jacket in the dirt. I never found her again.

It couldn't be because of me, I kept telling myself. But night after night, I woke up sick to my stomach, thinking about what that slug had said. "You'll know when the rest of us find you."

You'll know.

Celeste was the only person who was close to me then. If they wanted to hurt me, they would've gone straight to her. I didn't sleep for weeks. The Indigo Palace became my refuge of choice for avoiding my apartment after she disappeared. And I suppose things changed too in terms of how I saw everything, although it was hard to explain how. Filth—everyday stuff around the office, kitchen—started to bother me more. I carried sanitizer around, wore my uniform all the time, even in my apartment. Doing those things calmed me for a while, even though the harder I tried to hold the line, the more things seemed divided, broken.

CHAPTER FIVE

On Monday morning, I woke up thinking about Jenny again. I shook my head as I sat up, trying to shed the thoughts and leave them behind in the mattress. But the thoughts followed me throughout the morning—the way she looked polishing glasses in that cloud of nervous energy, a forest tattoo moving with the muscles in her shoulder.

My ribs hurt as I got dressed, took my morning vitamins, and put on my favourite grid-patterned tie, taking a second to admire the perfect, iron-clad shape of the grid. On my way to work, early sunlight slanted between the high-rises, and pedestrians hurried down the sidewalks with the dogged determination of the morning rush to work.

An aerial storefront floated in front of me with an image of a Mabelle's vegan latte.

Swipe.

The storefront quickly delivered the coffee to my hand. That was all I could afford for now, I told myself. I probably had only about forty bucks left on my credit card. But then came another storefront, this one with a cashew-cheese bagel from Quinn's Vegan Palace, my typical breakfast.

Swipe.

That purchase had been justified, because I needed to have that bagel in hand as I walked by the fried chicken joint and glared through the window, as I did every morning, at the filthy meat-eaters inside. Maybe that glare would knock some sense into them about the animals they slaughtered every day.

More storefronts came rushing to orbit me like my own personal galaxy.

Swipe.

Swipe.

Soon I had a bag of stuff to carry. Probably only ten bucks left now.

"Sir!"

The shout rang out above the rush of passing cars. A young woman emerged from the crowd and fell into step with me, holding a digi-sign with flashing letters: HIGH PROFITS, HIGH COSTS—THE DATA REVOLUTION.

"Sir," she said, "has anyone ever told you how the data revolution has affected women?"

My breath came with difficulty; every step sent a tremor of pain through my side.

She took long steps to keep pace, the wind ruffling her neat, red blazer. "Are you aware that companies are using data to cut costs on maternity leaves? Did you know that, sir?"

My shoulders tensed. "But thanks to data, we locked up thousands of criminals last year."

"Are you aware that companies monitor when female employees stop buying birth control and watch for other data indicators of future pregnancy?" she said. "And that women have been laid off in advance to save money? And that data screening is being used to discriminate against employees with potentially higher medical costs, to save on benefits?" She took out her phone and started filming my response.

I cringed to think about how I probably looked today in front of that camera—the data eyes, the paleness, and could it detect the gash on my jaw beneath the synth-skin? "Listen, no photos of me today. Not a good day for that."

Her eyes lingered on my insignia. "Sir, the Sentrac data police are a corporate police force. Does that sound right to you? Does it sound right to have no separation between public and private industries? To give corporations an influence in law and order?"

I spoke suddenly, almost against my will. "Yes, it sounds right to me. Do you know how much crime prevention we've gained from partnering with corporations? Without us, the police would never have been able to keep up with businesses in their data collection. Don't harass me with any more of that shit!"

A few faces in the crowd turned to stare. I didn't know why my voice was so loud.

I got rid of her by going into a Mabelle's. These people didn't understand a damn thing they were talking about. We were the glue that held everything together. I'd broken the law once in my past, to help Celeste, but I still had a sense of what was right, and I knew we did good work.

That was the problem with other people, especially privacy fanatics, I thought as I bought my second ten-dollar latte from a pimply Mabelle's barista with a cheap haircut. They weren't rational. They made decisions on impulse. Me, I drew up charts to make all my decisions, weighing each option carefully and logically. Money, work, it didn't matter—I made balance sheets for everything.

I needed to lighten my mood, and the walk into Sentrac Bank would do the trick. I ascended the marble steps, passing through a shifting jungle of holo-indexes, the web of global commerce swallowing me up—the Dow Jones, the Global 8700, the RD Data Composite—and when I walked through those indexes I could feel it: the joy and fear, the hope and desire of billions. The vast network of a market. An electronic voice announced briskly: "The time is 7:59."

Time for commerce.

The doors swept open onto vaulted ceilings and a lobby as wide as a concert hall with the orchestra waiting, ready to start the music. Latte in hand, I let the elevator shuttle me up sixty-five storeys, serenading me with the soft tones of musical nothings—on the way up I imagined Stingsby was in there with me, praising me for my latest work—then the forensics department, suited employees looking sharp, greeting me with a smile, glad to see me—oh hell, now that orchestra's started up in my head, violins playing to announce my entry—then rows of tiny trees in pots, a happy sea of data detectives bustling to keep the streets safe, then my office with the doorframe and Yury sitting behind it, and hello Yury ain't it nice to be at Sentrac Bank this morning. This was my haven, made of the straight lines and sparkling white spaces of spreadsheets, the patterns of data mining, the clean, empty rooms.

But as I took off my jacket, I was struck by the quiet in the office. A few people lingered outside Maclean's office and tried not to stare at her empty desk.

Speaking to no one, I stayed in my office and initialized my Sentrac Optica. The interface conducted the standard retinal scan for the DNA-linked contacts implanted in my eyes. Within a few seconds, information appeared on my screen that only data detectives could see. A stranger looking over my shoulder would see nothing but a blank screen. The famous eyes of a data detective. The privacy fanatics stabbed them out for a reason.

"Retrieve Maclean's notes on the August Donaldson case," I told the screen. Stingsby should've sent them this morning.

I started flying through the evidence Maclean had collected. Yes. There they were: the unruly numbers. They caught my eye when I read her notes—the corners of my office sharpened when I spotted them, the angles where the walls met the ceiling popping out, shot through with electric energy—these details definitely didn't add up, errant numbers slipping from the spreadsheets, just waiting to be ground back into the grid.

"Retrieve account information: August Donaldson," I said to the interface. "Purchases from the last two weeks."

The privacy fanatics could complain all they wanted about the New Privacy Act, but the financial branch of the data police kept the streets safe, and to do our jobs we needed access to all the spending records at the hub of digital money, Sentrac Bank. One glimpse of my Optica interface left yottabytes dripping off my skin for days.

The Optica began processing deep layers of data. If things ever got chaotic, the idea of data mining reassured me. It was the patterns, the way the Optica searched for sense in the chaos of human information. That was why I became a detective. I wanted to be part of that search. I didn't mind the late nights I'd spent with the Optica, when the interface filled my office with its residue, the hazy afterglow of the screen. First the raw data, a Babel nonsense of information; then the target data, processed, normalized, made uniform; and then the mining, the ultimate step: the search for patterns in the nonsense, moulding the Babel medley into strands of sense strung out like steel wires in the sky, slicing the world into segments, into a grid.

The Optica had retrieved my data. *August Donaldson— Personal Account*. The Core Club Café, $1,340. Property, $12,050,000. The Core Club Café, $235. I skipped ahead. Lots of hotel fees, all paid late at night and within the city, even though he lived here already. H&V Fine Diamonds, $10,700.

"Save those hotel fees, and the diamonds. Group them under the subheading, 'Evidence for Affair.' Now give me purchases after 21:00, last three weeks."

It didn't take long to find what I was looking for. Candy Body Massage Oil, 23:05. Taxi, 23:37. Hotel, 23:52.

"Jesus. Save those too. Group under: 'Evidence for Affair' subhead." I fought back the vomit in my throat when I recalled the spreading teeth and bulbous glasses of that jack-o'-lantern smile at the Indigo Palace. Thank God I didn't have to take any old-fashioned photographs of Donaldson's affair. I was a digital detective. Data took my photos for me.

"Retrieve account information: Fullston Big Data Tech," I said. "Narrow to: employee salary payments, last month." I recalled the name of Donaldson's female companion from her screen at the Indigo Palace. "Check for the name Sara Figueira."

And there it was. Sara Figueira, $35,420.

"What did you find now?" Yury asked from the hallway. "There are fucking hyena eyes popping out of your face right now, so it must be good."

I looked up through my mahogany doorframe at Yury hunched in his cubicle. His desk was cluttered with Styrofoam coffee cups and garbage, his five digi-plants all but hidden by the blanket of trash. A couple of times in the past, I'd waited until he left the office and cleaned up that damned desk for him. He didn't like that, but I couldn't stand the sight of it.

Yury got up, stepped into my office, and shut the door.

"Just busy stunning the world with my excellence, Yury," I said. "As expected, I found that woman Donaldson's sleeping with in the payment records for his company. She's one of his staff. Outside the Core Club I thought I heard them talking about the money transfers they're authorizing together."

"So?"

"This might lead me to something new, something Maclean didn't even know about yet. All she knew was that he was funnelling money into a fake company, then paying himself out from there."

"Why wouldn't Maclean know about it? She was a better detective than you are."

"Maybe she didn't go beyond the data like I did. These criminals have been careful about their data trail—I had to stalk Donaldson to find this."

"I don't know, Frank. That seems odd that she didn't find this."

"True. Maybe she was just starting to find out about it. Maybe that's why someone killed her. Either way, this is gonna be big, Yury."

"You think you got something good, right?"

"This Figueira woman wasn't even involved in that little scheme Maclean knew about. Donaldson must have another outlet. He can only pump so much money into a single fake company without raising red flags."

"If there are multiple people involved in this scheme, then who knows? You might find something even bigger than Donaldson. A network, maybe." Yury sighed. "You're damn lucky to get a chance to work a case like this."

"It's about time. Stingsby should've given me this years ago. But don't worry, man, you'll get your break too."

Yury left my office and went back to his desk, the screen glazing the lenses of his glasses with soft light. His fingers moved sluggishly, plodding painfully over the touchscreen. I hated Stingsby for overlooking Yury's talent again and again. But sometimes, Yury was just easy to miss. His wispy frame seemed to shrink into the corner whenever the other detectives were around, their figures more visible, their voices louder. I took any opportunities that came up to prompt Stingsby to notice Yury's work, but it made no difference.

The day rolled on, my eyes glued to the Optica interface. I was making progress investigating the payments Donaldson and Figueira had co-authorized. Throughout the afternoon, quiet voices drifted through my doorway: snatches of conversation about the service planned for Maclean, about the fanatics responsible for her murder, about the media coverage of her death. Night fell slowly. One after another, screens went dark, and voices and ringtones gave way to silence, broken only by the occasional patter of footsteps.

I took a break and lingered outside Maclean's office. It looked the same as always: that shelf on the back wall with bright red dividers, separating the different things she kept there—digi-plants, photos of her husband and daughter. I'd often wondered why she obsessed so much about keeping things separate like that. Standing there, staring at her empty office, I remembered the night Maclean had gotten me back on track after Celeste disappeared, when I'd almost strayed from my path. If that talk with Maclean hadn't happened, who knew where I might be now?

"I'm out," Yury said from my doorway, throwing on his jacket. "Good luck."

"You going to the Indigo Palace?"

He busied himself zipping up his jacket, his gaze downcast. "No. Akshara would kill me. I'm turning over a new leaf."

I hesitated, finding myself annoyed. "You better be right about that." Why did his gambling bother me so much? He made his own decisions, and I couldn't hold myself responsible, but for some reason, I hated when his addiction got the better of him.

I went back to the data, and even though my eyes ached—they must've looked blood-red—I couldn't tear myself away from the Optica. "Retrieve account information: A. Chawla Consulting," I told the screen. "Note tag: a shell company; a second outlet Donaldson's using to funnel money, this one with Figueira helping. Implication: larger network of white-collar criminals; possibly a money laundering ring."

As the Optica dutifully recorded my words, an account appeared on the screen: *A. Chawla Consulting—Income*. I skimmed down the list of incoming payments. A sense of potential opened up as I read; every payment added to the momentum. A. Chawla Consulting was nothing like the poorly concealed scheme Maclean had already found on Donaldson, where the fake company led straight to him, the exit strategies clear and simple. A. Chawla Consulting had payments to and from all sorts of companies, the exit strategies virtually invisible, nothing obvious linking the stolen money to anyone's personal bank account. A. Chawla Consulting was just one cog in the vast machine of money laundering that cleaned dirty money with soap and bleach, blending it into a complex and nearly untraceable network.

This was big.

Big enough to kill for. My mind raced. Could this be what Maclean was just beginning to find when she was shot?

I stayed in the office a while longer that night, giving a bit more thought to the name of the fake company, A. Chawla. The name sounded vaguely familiar, but I couldn't place it. Later, I took the elevator down and hurried out into the cold, headed anywhere but home.

CHAPTER SIX

I shouldn't have gone looking for Jenny and I damn well knew it. But I'd been thinking about her all weekend, and now I was high on my big find. My footsteps hurried into a torrent, the yellows flung out by streetlamps sliding by fast—the way I liked them. After what I'd just discovered at Sentrac, it felt like nothing should be still. When I reached the Border, the street clamoured with noise and activity. Fires glowed like little islands in the dark sidewalks, burning in the grills of food stalls and thickening the air with the smell of grease. Street vendors shouted prices at passers-by.

But of course, I needed to buy something for Jenny, I realized. I couldn't show up at her place without a gift; it made me feel better to have one, like it was a distraction for her. Maybe I still had a bit of credit left. I passed the stalls of street vendors, scanning the silver bracelets and bottles of French and Italian wine—there, maybe that last bottle.

Swipe.

DECLINED.

Jesus Christ. This morning's purchases had drained the last of my credit. The thought of showing up in front of Jenny empty-handed gave me an uncomfortable feeling. I saw myself standing there stupidly in Sally Lane's without anything to give her, the bad light emphasizing my tired eyes. After staring at the Optica all day, that horrible, grating sensation in my eyes told me they were red and dry as paper.

Not long after I pushed through the swinging doors of Sally Lane's, feeling naked with nothing to give her. She was there behind the counter, her hair pulled back into a loose knot, a few wayward strands around her face. The stillness inside the diner marked an abrupt change from the tumult of the streets. Soft, whining music droned in the background and mingled with the boiling sound of the coffeemaker. Jenny's eyes darted over to me, and she shrank from the rush of cold air that swept in through the doors with me. Anton wasn't around.

After a moment, when the air of the diner had warmed me, she approached, bringing her scent of soap and cigarettes, familiar from Friday night. My pulse quickened. She was close to me. I thought of the way the streets outside would look on my walk home—it would be late then, and the city would be abandoned, dull blinking neon falling on empty sidewalks, the buildings of the Border sagging—and I knew that the only way to ease the bleakness of that walk home would be to bring Jenny with me, bring her back to my apartment and my bed where we could shut out the ugliness of the night. God, I wanted to ask her to come back with me.

"Didn't think you'd come back," she said.

"I had my reasons for coming back."

"Did Anton bother you on Friday? I told him not to harass you with that fucking meat, but he couldn't resist when he heard you say you're a vegan."

"Sure, he bothered me." I moved closer to her, still high from my success at work. "I came here to spend more time with you, but then I found myself face-to-face with the husband I didn't know you had. So yes, I'd say he bothered me a lot when I saw him."

We stood still, near enough that I could reach out and hold her if I wanted to, but I didn't, afraid to scare her off. Her face appeared in hyper-detail: the little wisps of hair on her forehead near her hairline, the black makeup around her eyes smudged on one side, faded from a day's work. Under the smell of soap and cigarettes was the scent of her shampoo. We both felt the heightened awareness of our physical proximity; at this close range I could tell she felt it—her thoughts flickered visibly across her face, little movements in the muscles around her eyes and mouth. Her hand brushed against my arm as she fidgeted, setting off a tiny charge.

A flash of uncertainty passed through her eyes, and she moved away, pulling a cloth from her pocket to wipe a table. "Lemme get this clean for you. Look at you. So neat and clean all the time. Me, I'm always leaving things in a fucking mess. Shit."

Her hand was a blur as she scrubbed anxiously. I watched her sudden awkwardness with interest. She might be trying to set me up, to lure me into some trap, but maybe she'd started to realize she was drawn to me in a way she hadn't anticipated. That wasn't part of her plan, and it frightened her. That was something she didn't want.

"Anton hasn't been well lately," she said. "But he'll be fine. Some nights are okay. He's getting better, see?"

"He at least treat you well?"

"You're pretty interested in the wellbeing of somebody you just met once."

"Yes, I am."

She looked at me, and when we made eye contact her body tensed with nervous energy.

If that wasn't the truth about Anton treating her well, I'd find some way to take care of him. Maybe I'd lock him up, find data on him if I had to. He would look a bit like he had on Friday, when the squares from my spreadsheet had lingered on his face, except this time the lines of the grid would harden into steel wires that I could pull his flesh through like a sieve.

Jenny invited me to sit down at the table she'd cleaned, then brought me another free beer. She settled across from me, her red fingernails holding a ceramic coffee cup, the narrow oval of her face visible in the spotlight beaming down on our booth. Her lipstick left a red stain on the rim of her cup, the place where her mouth touched the ceramic. I put my phone on the table, watching to see if her eyes went to the new letters, AKATO-800.

"You're sweet when you're excited about something," she said. "Your eyes get all bright and you can't sit still. Something happen at work tonight or what?"

"Things are going well at work right now. I might get a chance to help out someone who always treated me well. And maybe it's you that gets me like this too."

She smiled. "You know, you're funny. You're a data cop, and a neat freak—I mean, look at you"—she gestured to my clothes—"you look spotless all the time, you seem to love wearing that uniform, and I've never seen a wrinkle in it. And yet, you do some things that make no sense. Like parade around the Border when it's dangerous. Like come looking for me when you know you shouldn't."

"All those things are perfectly legal. And I weighed that options carefully, the pros and cons. Either I could come see you, or I could drive myself crazy waiting around and thinking about seeing you. One option makes a lot more sense."

I hesitated, then decided to take a gamble. "But you're hiding something. You think I haven't realized that you planned our first meeting? You intended to run into me near that street vendor, and you made up that story about someone following you. You want something from me."

Jenny drank her coffee without answering, her composure unaffected by what I'd said this time. In the overhead light, only her head, shoulders, and hands were visible—fingers locked in a tight sphere—the rest of her too shadowy to see. Two brown irises scanned my arms crossed on the table, searching for the scars that might be underneath my sleeves.

She changed the subject, and I let her carry the conversation away from the mysterious favour she wanted. I yielded to the simple pleasure of talking to her, alone like this, sheltered by the privacy of the booth and the warm emptiness of the diner. Sometimes while we talked, she leaned forward slightly over the table, as though wanting to come nearer to me, but she always drew away before we got too close. She tried again to get me to eat their burgers, but I quickly declined, wincing internally and reminding her I was a vegan.

"I keep on a strict diet," I said. "Vitamins are important. And each meal needs a little bit from each food group, too."

"You're pretty . . . *strait-laced*, aren't you?"

I thought about it for a minute. "Maybe. I never used to be."

"What changed?"

"Just sometimes—sometimes things happen that change your perspective, that's all. Partly it was something another cop taught me, a great cop named Maclean, who talked some sense

into me when I was drifting. Just basically there are two kinds
of people: the ones who follow the laws and the ones who
don't." Even as I said it, a pang of guilt came over me—I'd broken the law once with Celeste. But I'd had to. Her life had
been on the line. As for the Acetropen, those drugs were legal,
just banned in casinos.

"Is that why you like wearing that uniform around all the
time?" she said. "You should be careful coming to the Border
like that. Data cops, they're not liked here, see? You might get
hurt."

"Will you come to my funeral?"

"Risking your life, huh? So gambling's your thing? Like
most of the Sentrac staff."

"Sure. You play Gemini?"

"I don't gamble. A girl like me can't afford it."

I remembered all the places I'd taken Celeste to make her
happy, like Borgnino's, the best restaurant in the city, on top of
the Thirteenth Avenue Tower with a view of the Core at
night—after I pulled some strings with the owner just to get
through the doors—then Mateo Wine Bar in the heart of the
Core, or all those rooftop patios, the black lights and the music,
the aqua blue of a rooftop swimming pool, framed by the darkness of the night, the glass centrepieces and champagne flutes, a
breeze on a patio at night, and the sweep of black hair on my
neck as she rested her head on my shoulder. Sometimes, in those
brief stretches when she was clean, she even gave me the smile
that showed in her eyes.

"Jenny, have you ever had a night out in the Core?" I said.
"I can show you some of the most amazing places you've ever
seen." I'd find some way to pay for it. "You wouldn't believe
some of the places I can show you. Borgnino's—it takes a lot to
get in there, but I can get us in. I have the money. And I can take
you to Reginia's, get you something there too."

"Are you trying to attract me by showing me how much
money you have?"

"Right, that's how you see it, is it?" I bristled as I looked
down at my beer bottle, ripping off a few label shreds. She didn't

understand. It wasn't about impressing. I'd done it to help, to make her happy.

Jenny reached across the table and touched my wrist. "Don't be angry."

Her hand was warm. My shoulders softened, and I decided not to pursue it further. "Let's talk about why you brought me here," I said.

"I like chatting with you."

"When you smile at me like that, I can tell you love taunting me."

"I thought you like playing games."

"I do. Normally it's Gemini at the Palace, but there's no game quite like getting used by strangers for unknown reasons on a Monday night."

She sipped her coffee, her eyes shining with amusement.

"The thing is," I said, "I like to know the name of the game I'm playing. What are we talking about, the game of bribery? Asking your old friend Frank for a cover-up in the data police?"

"Not sure." She fingered the rim of her coffee cup, near the red smear her lips had left. That lipstick stain drove me crazy.

Through the window outside, the road led back to the Core and my empty apartment. The street seemed to darken, blackness spreading like a dilating pupil. I thought of the balance in my Sentrac account, the million I owed to the casino. I had to remember what Maclean had taught me, about the two camps people were in. And yet, my chest tightened when I thought about waking up tomorrow and not being able to buy a single damn thing. How would I even get by until my next paycheque?

"No," I said finally. "Whatever you're offering, it's not for me. I'm a law-abiding type."

"I just wanna get to know you. Maybe I like you. Keep coming back to see me."

Her fingers loosened from their interlocking web, and her palms rested flat on the table for a minute, then withdrew into her invisible body. As I got ready to leave, we stood up at the same time. Her hands on my forearm surprised me. "Will you come back?" she said.

I didn't answer, surprised by how easily I was being taken in by such a simple trick. Her face, just a few inches away from mine, was flushed from the warmth of the diner, her eyes bright with the thrill of taunting me. The steady pulse of blood came back. I remembered again the night outside and how much I wanted to ask her to come back with me. But when I studied her expression, the question died before I could voice it. Her face told me that the answer would be no, because this time she was only playing a game with me. Her gaze met mine steadily, without darting around the room like it did when she was nervous, like it had when I came in earlier. She was in control now, because she'd planned this little move and she'd expected it.

So this was the game we would be playing. When she drew away from me it was painful, like a piece of fabric ripped down the middle. The voices of other customers chattered in the distance, suddenly noticeable again as we merged with the rest of the diner, the intimacy fading. She vanished into the darkness of the aisle.

Over the coming days, I threw myself into the Donaldson case. I had a few other investigations on the go, as usual, but I put them on the backburner. The days felt long as I pored through financial data from A. Chawla Consulting, trying to find any easy trails from the fake bank account into anyone's personal finances. It made sense to check the obvious stuff first. But nothing came easily. Whoever did this was a pro.

After the long days, I was exhausted, and yet still I wanted to avoid my apartment, so I found myself showing up at Sally Lane's every other night after work, looking for Jenny. I kept my data invisibility on and took the long route through the back streets and the park. Whenever I saw her I checked her face and arms for bruises, but I never saw anything. That meat-eating vermin husband couldn't be trusted. When the two of them were in the diner together, he followed her around and doted on her, brought her coffee, water, and little pieces of cake with maraschino cherries, helped her carry things, and every so often stopped what he was doing, held her, and brushed the hair out of her face like a teenager looking at his first girlfriend. But what she felt about him was less clear. She did some strange things when he was around, things I didn't know what to make of. Once he brought her a coffee, but when he disappeared into the back she dumped it out, put the cup through the dishwasher, and poured a new one for herself. Another night she saw him walking up to the diner through the window, and made herself busy quickly, picking up a tray and disappearing into the back.

Jenny and I spent a lot of time there alone. At the end of the night, she patiently swept my label shreds off the table and my suit jacket, showering the floor with white powder and asking playfully, "Something making you tense?" On the nights when Anton was there, he acted strangely, jittering with weird energy, wired out of his mind, his hands twitching. And the pigment of his skin changed slightly, turning yellow with faint purple blotches showing on his neck. The change in skin tone was subtle—only the trained eyes of a detective would notice it—but once you knew to look for it, it was distinctive. He always wore a high collar on those nights, but I could still detect the blotches.

Two weeks passed before things came to a head at Sally Lane's.

December had arrived, the streets stained with polluted snow. Darkness fell a few minutes earlier each day, and my feet left outlines in the powder that made me nervous. When I walked through the Border, the people who lived on the streets were gathering whatever they had—coats, cardboard, blankets—readying themselves for a long winter.

"Frank," Jenny said from the aisle one night. "Will you stay with me until after we close tonight? I want to see you alone, when the customers are gone."

My blood simmered at the thought of being alone with her. She barely waited for my answer before she fled to the counter and lost herself polishing coffee cups. Tonight, I couldn't get a read on her. She was nervous but I didn't know why. She hadn't taken her eye off me all night—I'd seen her watching me from behind the counter, her gaze flicking back over her shoulder while she worked. Maybe this was the night I could finally ask her to come home with me. I'd sold all my expensive furniture and my apartment made me look like a nobody, but I'd try to distract her from noticing that. She'd be anxious at first, worried about that husband who smelled like toxic waste, but she'd forget him quick. I couldn't sit still.

Slowly, the last stragglers trickled out of the diner. My senses sharpened, and the pools of light around the tables seemed to solidify into cylindrical blocks, each of them like a spotlight on a stage. Putting away glasses behind the counter, Jenny's outline looked hyper-sharp, like a drawing from a cartoon. The absurdity of the situation struck me as she locked the doors, drew the curtains, and unplugged the OPEN sign. We'd arrived at some kind of unspoken contract, but neither of us could verbalize it. I took a few steps towards her, ready to ask her to leave with me.

The kitchen door swung open and Anton came out, holding a gun. He pointed it at me and fired.

CHAPTER SEVEN

Pain spread outwards from my shoulder, and my vision blurred, details fading fast. Jenny stood in front of me, and in the blurry mess she looked exactly like Celeste. Then everything darkened into black.

The plan that Celeste and I made to get her clean started the night I found bruises on her. We were in bed and it was too dark to see, but when I touched her side, she flinched, drawing a sharp breath.

I turned on the light. Now that I saw her without her clothes, the bruises on her body were obvious. "Jesus," I said, my mouth going dry.

She pulled the sheets around her to hide them. "It's none of your business."

"These fucking men make me sick," I said. "It's not safe, what you have to do for money."

"You think your money can fix everything, but it can't. When you see a problem you just throw money at it."

I tried everything I could think of to get her to give up that line of work. I offered to get an apartment for her, to pay for her to start a new life, but she told me that wouldn't help her, because as long as she was hooked on the needle, she couldn't hold a job, couldn't hold on to money—all of it went straight into her arm.

Finally, she agreed to let me help her with one thing. I could pay for her to go to rehab. I wasn't as wealthy as I used to be before all those expensive nights with Celeste, but I had enough money still.

Rehab helped for a while. When she got out, she smiled more and her body filled out, a soft layer of flesh hiding her ribs, her hair glossed with a sheen of health, all the tangles combed out. She started talking about music again and staying up late listening to it with my expensive headphones. But then one night she didn't show up to meet me. I went looking for her down by the river where she used to go to buy. And sure enough I found her there on a street corner, staring up at the sky with blank eyes. "I'm just so tired," she said.

Things went back to how they used to be. "Just eat this, please," I said, putting a croissant in front of her, her favourite food. "I hate seeing you so skinny." Every time I met her I bought her something to eat—if I bought her enough things she liked, then maybe she would gain weight. Her hair lost its sheen and became dry and knotted at the ends. Sometimes I tried to comb the tangles out of her hair with my fingers. After she left once, I went on a bender and woke up on a park bench, a stranger to the hours that had come before.

One night at my apartment, she cried. "Maybe there's one other thing I could try to get better," she said. "One thing I'd let you help with."

"For God's sake, tell me."

"It's a surgical procedure. I heard about it from a customer. It's illegal, but it kills your addiction. You can get in done in the black market."

"Why is it illegal?"

"It's dangerous. And also, sometimes it doesn't work. But I know it'll work for me, I know it, the customer was totally cured by it, suddenly he was like new, like magic. Really, it's like magic, I know it is."

My mind seized upon the idea. "But—how can I get it for you? If I get involved in something illegal, my job—"

"You've been paying a prostitute."

"Don't call it that."

"Why?"

"What would I do if I lost my job? I'm nothing without it."

She nodded, her eyelashes casting dark semi-circles of shadow under her eyes, deepening the purple circles of exhaustion.

"Fuck," I said, "I hate seeing you like this."

"And there's the price, too."

I was low on money. Even if it weren't illegal, how would I pay for it?

Things got worse. Celeste got thinner, her wrists like twigs, and she got more desperate for money; soon she had to find more and more customers. One night she showed up with bruises again.

In the end, I found a way to get the money. I wasn't proud of it. But I didn't have a choice.

After Anton shot me, I woke up with my hands tied to the arms of a chair. Around me was a blur of smoke and red light. My head felt full of sand, my shoulder stung. Anton must've shot me with a tranquilizer. Slowly, my senses picked up fragments of people—faces, arms, hands—behind the haze. My pockets had been turned inside out.

I strained to focus. I was looking at the barrel of a Russell. The woman holding it sat across the table watching me, her face unfamiliar.

"Who are you?" I asked hoarsely. The ropes sliced deep into my wrists.

"Haru," she said. "Been watching you for a while. You're working for me now."

She put the gun on the table, and her dirt-crusted fingers pulled out a cigarette; her lighter blazed and died. Lipstick stained the filter.

Under the tight ropes, the circulation had drained from my fingers. I wanted to try and move but I couldn't bring myself to, not when the pistol still lay in front of her. This was turning out to be more fucking dangerous than I'd thought. The smell of smoke suffocated me.

"You start working for us tonight," Haru said. "You made your choices already. Made them when you came here, night after night. Made them when Jenny asked you to stay 'til they closed and you did."

My fingers had lost feeling. I could barely see through the red light and coiling smoke. Anton lurked in the background behind Haru, loading clips into a Holt-FR. I scanned the door behind Haru. Locked with fingerprint ID. Next to it sat a massive man holding an automatic.

The quiet extended. Overhead, the thick blades of a ceiling fan circled and propelled the smoke into spirals. The fan chopped up the red light coming from above, and the shadows cast by the blades turned the room into a wheel of spinning red and black, like the roulette wheel on the Indigo Palace.

Haru extinguished a cigarette and said, "Guess he's not dealing."

She dropped an old-fashioned photograph onto the table. Me, leaving my apartment. She pulled out another. Me, walking into Mabelle's with Yury. The last one she put down more slowly than the others. It was me, in the back of a bar talking to a man with a shaved head and a tattoo on his face. I stared at the last one, my pulse pounding.

"Lotsa people know you," she said. "You try to back out, we release what we got on you."

She nodded at the muscle near the door and he started an audio clip on some device. My own voice came through the speakers. "Listen, Aaron, I need some money. What I'm thinking is, you help me out, and I help you. Understand me?"

"Didn't know you were that kinda cop," said the voice of the man with the face tattoo, the one sitting with me in the photo. The realization of what these criminals were doing to me, what they had on me, had now fully taken shape in my mind. It was an ugly realization, one I wanted to push away and never look at again. Sweat dripped down my forehead.

"A black market surgery—I need you to pay for it," my voice said in the clip. "You pay for it and keep it quiet, then I help you. Right now you're looking at potential charges for tax evasion. But if you help me out, I'll make that file go away. You avoid jail-time. Are you dealing with me or are you not?"

"I could be interested."

The man with the automatic stopped the clip.

"It's not just an illegal surgery," Haru said. "It's bribery. Corruption. You'll be doing time for this."

The orderly haven of Sentrac, its clean lines and sanitary spaces—they were melting in my mind, as if acid had been poured on them. I would lose my job. My big Donaldson case would never be completed. I wouldn't get a chance to find out what happened to Maclean. Pain shot up my arms from the ropes on my wrists, my knuckles ash white and numb.

Haru looked over her shoulder and nodded at Anton. "He's still not dealing."

Anton raised his gun to my head level.

"I'll do it. I'll do what you want." I sounded like a child.

Anton lowered the Holt but watched me closely. The ceiling fan spun steadily and sent its shadows in circles around the room.

"I told you I'd fucking do it," I said unsteadily. "Untie me."

"Just lemme untie him," Jenny's voice said. With a knife, her shining ruby fingernails cut the ropes. I'd barely noticed she was in the room. My hands stung as the blood leaked back into them. I jerked away from her touch so she wouldn't feel the shaking.

Jenny sat down calmly beside Haru, her knees tucked into her chest, chin on one knee. She had her own Russell but she didn't point it at me; it lay untouched on the table. Haru sat across from me wearing a faded denim jacket, black hair falling on its tattered shoulders. Wine-coloured light fell softly on her skin, on her long lashes. Her face was unreadable, and her eyes were sharp, dark wells of intelligence.

"Frank, it's not all bad," Jenny said. "You help us, we make it worth your while."

"I don't want your dirty money." But even as I said it, I knew I didn't have forever to pay my gambling debts. Wincing, I ran a hand over the deep dents in my wrists. Filled with stale air that reeked of nicotine, this room must be festering with disease. Germs danced in the air, multiplying, copulating.

"What do you want me to do?" I asked.

"Small tasks for now," Haru said. "Maybe you pull some strings at Sentrac. Maybe you get us information from their records. Been looking for a man on the inside for a while, but it had to be the right one."

I couldn't bring myself to answer. I wasn't meant to be a fucking criminal. Law and order had some meaning to me. I'd broken the rules once to help Celeste, but when it came to the big things I had a sense of what's right. I knew I did.

Haru watched me from beneath thick bangs. "For your first job, we need to borrow those fucking eyes of yours. It's only them can see the data we need. You go into Sentrac. You look up data. You memorize it. Then you report back to me. Don't record it. First thing, you look up the company Sentrac pays for their security tech, their firewalls. How much they pay their IT maintenance teams, when, how often."

That was only the beginning of a long list she gave me. It would take days to memorize all this. I knew better than to ask questions about why they wanted this information. If they had ambitions for some kind of cyber-attack, they were wasting their time. A ramshackle organization like this, just these four crazies here in this room—they had no chance to take on Sentrac cyber-security. It would take a huge operation and some of the brightest minds in the world to even attempt that.

"You got the smarts to cover your fucking tracks when you're retrieving this data?" Haru asked.

"I know how to cover my tracks."

In the pause that followed, Anton sat down, lit a cigarette, and poured himself a glass of acidic, pungent-smelling liquid. That must be what he was on whenever I saw him at the diner.

Jenny stood up and put her gun in its holster. "Let's go downstairs to the bank, Frank. I'll show you the money we're offering you. We can make you rich."

She disappeared through a door while the others remained where they were. Trailing her, I stole a look at Anton on my way out. He didn't even see us leaving. The drug had silenced him, and he'd all but vanished into the corner, smoking silently, a spectre enveloped by tendrils of smoke. His hands were already jittering. Misted with milky dullness, his eyes were doors that opened onto empty storage rooms.

"Mind if I escort you down, bud?" asked the man by the door. The end of his gun pressed into my spine as I followed Jenny through the door. "Don't mind the gun. I didn't like the look of you when they brought you in. Something wrong with your face. Not a good face."

I glared at him over my shoulder. His gold teeth flashed behind dense facial hair. The man was a landscape, all hills and valleys of muscle, his chest a carpet. His grip, gold rings on every second finger, could snap a spine.

We entered a metal stairwell that extended down into a basement. Above the stairs hung a wooden sign, green paint proclaiming: THE EDGE OF DATA. VERGE OF THE REAL.

I followed Jenny down the staircase, the man behind me. "So you think you make a lot of money at Sentrac, right bud?" he said. "I know. But let me tell you, this stairwell"—he thumped one of the walls with the side of his fist—"it's got a kinda magic to it. Fairy tale stuff. You like fairy tales? Once you walk through it: nothing. That's what you have. That's your money. But maybe that ain't a fairy tale, it's the truth." He laughed wildly.

As the stairwell zig-zagged down, each stretch doubled back on the last one, a small landing in between each flight. Moisture, dust, and the narrowness of the space choked me. Automated lights turned on and off, one at a time, when we passed. Images of bleeding eyes spray-painted on the walls drifted by us as we descended. The symbol of privacy fanatics. I thought of Maclean.

"So you're them, then?" I said, pointing at one of the bleeding eyes. "Privacy fanatics?"

The man laughed, jabbing the gun harder into my spine. "Some folks call us that."

These eccentrics might be more organized than I'd thought. It was rumoured that the networks of privacy fanatics ran wide and deep.

Four storeys down, we reached another door. While we descended, I'd been forcing my brain back into shape, calming myself by counting the flights of stairs in case I needed to get out quickly. Now I'd know exactly how far down I'd come. If you count something, you can control it. Every Sentrac detective knows that.

Jenny looked up at the man behind me and waved him away. "Fuck off Cedric. I'll take him into the bank on my own. He won't try anything. He values his life too much."

Cedric grunted and left us reluctantly. I followed Jenny through the door and stepped into a vast vault.

The vault smelled of alcohol and a dusty scent of things unwanted and untouched for years. Gold and platinum were stacked in peaks of bright metal, and light fell on deep layers of dust, on pyramids of gleaming metals. Behind them were tall shelves and a vast space that overflowed with piles of artefacts and other stray objects strewn across the floor, shelves stacked with things along the edges of the room and erratically throughout the centre, and some of the things not organized at all, just heaped up in random piles, too many to count: guns, paintings, belts of automatic ammo, arcane machinery, cigarettes, coloured stones, crates of strange liquors, a car, a statue. And those were only the things I recognized. Some were completely alien, forgotten things from the past.

I stopped beside Jenny and stared, like I had two weeks ago when we stood watching the Forest outside Sally Lane's. A porcelain bust tilted sideways, a box teemed with fabrics, silk strands fluttered in an indoor wind. A narrow path snaked through the centre of the piles, between towering shelves and deep layers of dust. The stairwell we took to get here was like a low-tech time machine, taking us generations into the past.

"What is it?" I asked.

"The bank."

Not much of a bank. But I didn't have time to worry about that right now. Now that the adrenaline and survival instincts had faded, the reality of what had just happened sank in. I paced the vault, avoiding the junk strewn all over the ground, covered in' dirt and dust. Goddamn the filth of this place. The filth had seeped into me, tainted me.

"Fuck, Jenny, this isn't right. This is not who I am."

"Isn't it? You've done it before. Bribery."

"That was different—I had to fucking help someone whose life was on the line. No, I don't do things like this. You know how I see things, Jenny! The two camps: the ones for the laws and the ones against them. How could you pull me into this?"

"There was no 'pulling.' You knew what was happening and you kept coming back, because the truth is, you know you have to pay your gambling debts. Yeah, we know about those. Or else what happens—jail? Losing the job you love so much? You made a choice to get involved in this."

"Goddamn it, Jenny." I kicked a small box near my feet, a loud clatter filling the vault when it hit the wall.

"Somebody's got a temper."

If I couldn't get out of this, I would have to make a vow to myself now. This was the last time I did anything like this. The second I had enough money to pay my gambling debts, I'd be out. Then this would all go away, erased from my life like lines on a chalkboard.

Setting out ahead of me, Jenny called over her shoulder, "Lemme show you around. This is a hell of a lot of money. That gold over there's worth a hundred times what you made in your whole career. That bronze artefact, not much less."

The black market had died out. That was what the media told you. The stories that circulated about the underground were fantasies told to pass the time. The whispers told of an underworld full of strange people with weird fetishes for all kinds of things. I'd always seen them as creeps, fit to be locked up whenever we could find them. More irrational types—the world was full of them.

Jenny approached a three-foot-tall pyramid of gold and picked up a small rectangle. "Ten thousand real dollars," she said.

"Wait a minute. Is that the money you're giving me?"

"It's the only real money," she said, her voice soft and reverential. Turning a rectangle around in her fingers, she held it up to the electric light, and tiny gold specks blinked in her dark irises. The gold seemed to absorb and project the light simultaneously. "This is what you want, anyway. When we trade with this, no one watches. No data. No trace. Doesn't it fascinate you?"

That gold did draw my stare like a screen in a dark room, but I ignored it and said, "Listen, this is important. I don't want that money. If I'm compromising my principles and going through with this, what I need is cold, hard Sentrac money in my fucking bank account."

She lowered the brick again, a slight frown tightening her brow. "You can buy anything you want with this in the underworld. Any kind of property, any object, any service. Drugs. Black market tech. Sex. Weapons."

I paced the area near the door. "That's not going to cut it, Jenny!"

My mind began to churn, working quickly. I hated the thought of accepting this dirty money, but it was either that or jail and job loss. A change of tactics might be in order. I needed Jenny to trust me if she would ever give me any information. I sighed, pretending to let the frustration drain out of me, then approached the table where she stood and stopped close beside her. She didn't move away. I brushed one of the loose strands of hair from her face and let my fingers linger for a second on her cheek. Her eyes turned up towards me, and they grew sad at the touch, a sadness that might have been loneliness. I didn't blame her. It must be tough being stuck with that hopeless junkie.

"So," I said, "this 'money' down here—is there any way to convert it to Sentrac money?"

She diverted her eyes to the gold again. It made sense for her to tell me as little as possible, but I think she was feeling the pull of whatever we had between us. She was starting to trust me.

After a pause she said, "There are ways."

"I'm listening."

"But you should never convert. It's against the code, see? The code of the black market."

Quiet stretched through the vault. "I see how it is. So people do convert. Just discreetly, of course."

She didn't answer. We stood still and let the warmth and closeness of our bodies continue to sharpen the air between us. In the heaps of stuff around us, textures and colours seemed to intensify, outlines jumping to define every shape.

"If you wanted to tell me more about converting," I said, "I wouldn't let the others know."

I watched her gaze track from me to the piles of things, until her eyes got stuck on a pyramid of gold and she stared, fixated, at the towering triangle. It cast a shadow on her. Then, as if the sight of that pile had changed everything, her face grew cold and she turned away and set off into the maze of piles, her red sneakers scratching on the cement.

"Converting's fucking wrong," she said. "You convert clean money to dirt, and you kill what we're building down here."

"Where are you going?" I called as I followed her, sighing.

Heaps of junk drifted by as we walked, and jagged objects stabbed blindly, strange overhanging claws. Avoiding a shelf of dusty paper books, I turned left, right, then right again. A man made of paint strokes watched me from inside a frame. I stopped. Rocking gently on its axis, a map of the globe barred my route; two separate paths curved around it, splitting into a fork.

I looked left, then right. "Jenny, which way'd you go?"

Fear came over me. All this weird junk. A mannequin torso. A gold chain. A clock and a swinging pendulum and the terror, the germs on the silks sliding over the surfaces, the chaos, the mannequin arms and TV set and the pot with the skeleton of a dead plant sticking up like long, fleshless fingers.

"Which way, Jenny?"

The steady drone of robotics had started up in the distance, a soft shuttling sound that became louder as a plain blue cube floated towards me from behind the piles, louder as the cube snaked around a clock and into the clearing I stood in, louder as it floated straight towards me.

I ducked. Dirt and dust choked me, but the thing was gone; it had floated off into the piles, its robotic engine fading into the distance.

"Over here." Jenny's voice drifted from the path to my left.

Swerving through the maze, drenched in sweat, I followed the sound of her voice until I reached a clearing, relieved at the sight of another human body. She was bustling around and arranging stray things, the ends of her long hair trailing on the muddy floor as she stooped to pick things up. We'd arrived in a meadow carved out by the rusted skeleton of a car and a circle of shelves and boxes. The towering heaps cast long shadows on our clearing.

"That blue square just about took my fucking head off," I said. "Are you keeping some kind of robotic weaponry down here?" I pulled out my sanitizer and started cleaning off the dirt crusted on my elbows.

She laughed. "That's what you're afraid of? That's not a weapon. It's just a goddamn art piece. Mid-century. Watch out for it when you're walking down here—it doesn't have any sensors to detect humans, see?"

I took a few steps towards a sofa. The fabric was ripped and stained with brown patches, chunks of foam spilling from the rips like an open wound. I backed up a few steps, then stood around awkwardly. "No human sensors? It just floats around at random?"

"Completely random. That's the point of it."

"What kind of point is that?"

"Somebody like you wouldn't get it."

"I take pride in being one of those people that don't get it. That cube thing is completely irrational. Anyone ever get crushed by it?"

"Plenty of urban legends about that. That's partly why it's so infamous. It's worth a lot. That's why we keep it."

Silence, and the smell of deep layers of dust. As I watched Jenny flit around the clearing, my panic faded, replaced by the familiar sense of dull need that had been thrown over me like a net since I met her in the street. She moved as though she knew I watched her, her eyes glancing over to me occasionally and that smile back on her lips.

"You make me crazy, you know that?" I said. "Every time I look at you."

That only seemed to delight her further.

"I shouldn't even be down here. Look at the power you have over me."

"No one made you do this."

"Anyway," I said, "tell me more about converting."

"You don't convert. It's a betrayal. If other traders found out, they'd kill you. Sentrac money is dirty."

"Why's it a betrayal?"

"Because this money, it's what we believe in. You buy something down here, it's a political act. Every time. No matter what you buy, even if it's just some fucking trinket. That's why we got all this stuff down here. We trade anything. Everything. Every time you use our money, you show you believe in the project. This money, these things make us free. The purchases are untraceable. And every transaction you make down here, that's one less transaction you make with Sentrac money. We're building towards our own independent economy. Someday, it'll replace yours."

"Replace ours?"

She said nothing, arranging a stack of silver bricks.

"You're free down here, you say?" I asked. "Sure, as long as you've got your machine gun ready to protect your property, because if someone steals it there sure as hell won't be any police or legal system coming to help you out. But let's get back to those traitors you mentioned who want to convert. They try to sell this stolen stuff for Sentrac money, or what?"

She continued tidying up the mess in the clearing. "Too risky. Looks strange if you sell a bunch of expensive shit you never bought in the first place. To convert safely, you need the help of powerful people."

"Powerful people?"

"The businessmen, the suits, the corrupt cops. Sometimes the fuckers want Chems. You smuggle it to them secretly, and they got the resources, skills, and laundering networks to get you Sentrac money safely. But traders shouldn't be helping them. You risk exposing others, you betray everything we're building here, and you help out those white-collar slugs."

"Chems, those are what your lovely husband is always on, I assume? Is that why he smells like toxic waste and gets those patches on his skin?"

"That's Ruz. An elite Chem. Famous in the underworld but almost impossible to get your hands on. There's only a few got access to it."

"Lucky Anton. So, if trafficking to these white-collar suits is so bad, then why are people doing it?"

As she cleaned the powder buildup off her pistol, an emotion came over her face. Was it anger? She frowned and cleaned the gun with a sudden strange energy, one bare shoulder jolting, long hair shaking down her sides.

"Well?" I prodded.

She jerked the pistol back into her belt, red patches spreading across her cheeks. "Maybe some people don't have any fucking choice, Frank. You don't know shit about it."

What had I said to trigger such a strong reaction? Intrigued, I stood and waited until the red drained from her cheeks again. I knew I wouldn't be able to get any more information from her that night.

When Jenny escorted me back to the red room, Anton still lurked in the corner, a silent spectre.

"We'll be in touch soon," Haru told me, her face floating in red smoke. "When we want you to come back with your report, you'll know."

The blackmail was no idle threat, I thought as Jenny walked me up the metal steps. Their level of organization was convincing. At first it had seemed they were just eccentrics, but when I saw that eye on the wall I realized they were privacy fanatics. They operated outside all data in a mammoth network, running wide and deep beneath the city like vast, undiscovered veins of minerals. The stairwell led to the back kitchen of Sally Lane's. We must've been underneath the diner the whole time. Leaving through the back door, I re-emerged, alone, into thick fog. Keeping my sensor invisibility switched on, I took the path through the park.

The mist thickened, and ice coated my jacket in a cold sheath, blending with the dark thoughts that wrapped around me like a shroud. Maybe this mist should thicken until it erased me, wiped me right off the earth. It was what I deserved, a filthy criminal like me.

Fog hung low and heavy between dark skyscrapers with yellow squares of light. The world shrank to a white enclosure that obscured the pillared faces of the stock exchange, Sentrac, and PW & Anderson Financial. Skidding on black ice, lone cars crawled along their careful journeys, dim outlines in hanging mist. I passed the Indigo Palace. It was open, as always, but its marble steps were abandoned. The holographic ads were still running—they stayed on all night—and a pair of blue, three-dimensional figures squirmed through the fog, writhing with excitement when their imaginary slot machines flashed out a jackpot.

CHAPTER EIGHT

I was corrupt.

When I got home my heart was beating so hard it hurt. I ran to the kitchen sink and scrubbed my hands with dish soap. But there was still dirt under my nails, residue left over from the dirty things I'd just done. I grabbed a dull butter knife and started gouging under my nails. It did nothing. Nothing could get the dirt out. I dug harder with the knife, kept digging until my nail bent backwards, kept digging until I heard a snap.

A burst of pain, and then blood trickled from my finger. The nail had broken right off.

I threw the knife across the room. It left a dent in the wall, sliding downwards with a clatter.

This was not who I was.

Moving quickly, I grabbed a pen and paper, leaving a trail of red droplets from my finger. The charts had always helped me make all my decisions, and they would help me with this. Using a ruler, I made sure the lines were perfectly straight. Blood stained the paper. On the left column I wrote, *Sell them out—Pros*, and on the right column, *—Cons*. Under *Pros* I wrote: *Put the fanatics behind bars where they belong, do the right thing, make the city safer, avoid risk of even worse jail time than the blackmail.* Under *Cons*, I wrote *blackmail, gambling debts,* and *she goes to jail.* My eyes lingered on that last entry. Somehow this fucking chart wasn't working like it usually did; it only made things muddier.

I ripped up the paper and burnt the shreds with a lighter in the sink.

This would be the last time. My vow to myself would be upheld. Never again would I do something illegal, not even a parking ticket. The second my gambling debts were paid, I would pull out of this little agreement. More than anything, I wanted to talk to Maclean right now, like I had that night she set me straight. She had a way of saying things that made a lot of sense.

That night I lay awake, the emerald glare of the Forest shining through my windows. A new ad started playing. It was that familiar clip again—the ad for Chem Connect with a green background and a brunette with fake, spherical breasts smiling at her phone, then a man with his phone out too, wearing a dress shirt with no tie and leaning back, relaxed, his clothes and body language oozing money. That man's wealth reminded me of my old self, before Celeste, before the casino. As I lay there, my life seemed to spread out in my mind. Childhood in the Core. Video games. College, and data detective training, then Sentrac, repetitive days sliding by, filled with Sentrac spreadsheets and numbers, all those women, back when I was younger and just wanted one-night stands—Chem Connect matched us, inspecting thousands of chemical profiles and body scans, a mass of human data, the search engine spinning until it found a chemical match and told us where to go; we followed the directions like machines, joints moving with motorized motion, flanks, cheeks, and teeth turned into titanium, wires almost poking from our flesh; we shuttled through the city to an apartment, then shuttled back again through data-directed traffic into the shower. The rhythms of a single-cell organism, set to a mechanical heartbeat. All those petty little concerns and repetitions of an ordinary life. But when Celeste disappeared, that ordinary life disappeared too.

Celeste survived her surgery. The track marks on her arms faded, and clean, healthy skin replaced them. She got a job at a hair salon, and she still invited me over to her new apartment, even though she didn't want me to leave things out for her to steal anymore. She started listening to music again, and even started making her own on her tablet, which she sometimes let me listen to. Every day, I checked my phone for texts from her— first thing in the morning, at work, on lunch, before I went to bed. I couldn't concentrate at work. I wanted to see her all the time, but I was afraid I might crowd her.

But then, two weeks went by and I didn't hear from her. No response to my texts or calls. I stopped by her work, but they told me she'd missed her last two shifts. Next, I checked out her apartment—she'd given me a key because I came over so often—but the place was empty and silent, nothing there but her plants; she was obsessed with them, the window cluttered up with leaves, vines, and a white, flowering orchid. But when I got closer, I noticed that the leaves on one of the vines had sagged and wilted. I touched the soil. Bone dry. I watered the plants for her. They were dry, but I could still save them. I remembered what Celeste had said about the surgery, that sometimes it doesn't work.

With all my will power, I forced my feet to carry me towards the river. Hunched in the falling snow, I kept my hands in my pockets the whole way, but they still felt cold. All of me felt cold.

The path wound downwards to the river, descending into the darkness, into the hiding place of the destitute and desperate, the ones who had lost everything. Shadowy fingers lingered along the sides of the path, huddled around makeshift fires, hooded and shivering. A woman with bare legs eyed me from a street corner. I scanned face after face, searching. But none of them were her.

I asked everyone I passed if they'd seen someone of her description, but they shook their heads. Finally, a tired-looking woman asked, "She was wearing a red jacket?"

"Yes, exactly. Jesus, have you seen her?"

The woman pointed to a building down the path. "I saw her go in there."

"Thank you. Thank you so much." It wouldn't be too late to fix this. Even if she slipped up once, she could come back from that.

Inside the building, I found all her things. The snow, falling through the broken window, had thickened on her discarded red jacket, which had been left on the ground and covered with dirt. There were two bags full of stuff in there: everything I'd bought her was there, jewelry, clothing, books, just scattered around, like she'd left in a rush, like she hadn't been able to take anything with her when she left this place. Why had she brought all her stuff here? Where was she planning to go? And why had she left everything so suddenly?

You'll know when the rest of us find you. That was what that criminal had said in the interrogation, that stupid piece of shit. Those words burned in my mind.

On the sleepless nights that followed, I paced in circles through my apartment, cleaning it over and over, thinking that might help me sleep. I pulled some strings to get a meeting with that fucker at the prison, but when I asked him about his threat, he wouldn't say a word to me, just sat there behind the glass, laughing. I couldn't go to work for a while. In the weeks that followed, when I wasn't at the Indigo Palace, I made the nights less long by meeting women off Chem Connect, even though I had no interest in sleeping with them—I just wanted to buy them things. I still had a good chunk of money left from the bribery deal I'd made—not all of it had gone to fund Celeste's surgery.

I took one of my dates to Reginia's. "What about this? You want this one?" I asked, passing her a crystal hairpin. In the background, the salesclerk's eyes lit up. I'd already bought this woman a pearl necklace and a bracelet.

"Yes, exactly, a beautiful piece," the salesman chimed in, hovering around us.

"Maybe," my date said. She held the hairpin, but her eyes looked dull and bored this time. When I'd bought her the first two things, she'd smiled and her eyes had brightened. I wanted that brightness in her eyes to come back. The sight of it disappearing made me cold again.

"What about this, then?" I said, grabbing another necklace and thrusting it in front of her.

"I don't think so," she said. There it was again. That blankness in her eyes.

"This?" I seized another one. "Or this?" My arm moved so fast I knocked a sign off a glass case.

She looked alarmed. "I'm fine. Just chill out."

The blankness in her eyes. I couldn't stand it. I felt like a string being stretched, threads fraying off one by one.

"Are you okay?" she said, staring at me.

The string stretched a little bit tighter. That deadness in her eyes was in the air too, thick and stifling like cigarette smoke, making it hard to breathe. I made up an excuse and left the store.

"But sir, there are so many more delightful pieces left to explore!" the salesclerk called after me.

Not long after, I found myself at the Indigo Palace. My newest habit.

About an hour later, I left the Palace, drifted back towards the Core, and settled on a park bench to smoke a cigarette. Maclean walked by, her heels ticking methodically with her confident stride. This must be on her route home from Sentrac. She moved with impossible grace, even though her small, compact figure was built for power. As always, she'd pulled back her sleek black hair with one streak of gray. Her face bore the first traces of middle age, the lines around her mouth deepening when she smiled.

When she saw me, she stopped. "Another night at the Palace?" she asked.

I said nothing.

"I've seen you before, heading home from there at all hours of the night," she said, sitting down beside me. "Got another one?" She gestured towards my cigarette. I handed her one.

"You know," she said between puffs of smoke, "there's counselling available for us as part of our job package."

"I don't need counselling."

"What happened? Did you lose someone?"

"No." I appreciated Maclean trying to talk to me, but because of Celeste's former line of work, I didn't want to make my relations with her common knowledge.

"I'm here to talk if you need me," Maclean said. "Stingsby wants you to come back to work eventually. He's giving you some time, but he won't wait forever. You know Stingsby, he doesn't make a lot of space for . . . feelings." She paused, looking up at the sky as she exhaled. "And I'm getting concerned. About you."

I chuckled. "Well, thanks for being concerned. Honestly, I think you and Yury are the only ones in this city that give a damn about what happens to me." There used to be one other person.

"It's just," she said, "with all this gambling, I'm seeing something that worries me. Something I've seen before. Did I ever tell you about slash and line?"

"Slash and line? What, those Chems that were so popular years ago?"

"That's right. I saw plenty of cases back in the day involving the trade in those two Chems, but there was one thing you always had to remember about them. Never mix them."

"And if you did?"

"I saw it for myself once, on a case. We busted a Chems lab, but when we went inside, we found a guy inside on the ground with half his tongue burned right out of his mouth. He'd mixed slash and line."

"Grotesque. Half a tongue gone?"

"Burned off by the acid from the combination. That case stuck with me for a while after, it really bothered me. Took me a long time to figure out why. It's because what that man had done, mixing two things that shouldn't be mixed, spoke to something bigger. When it comes to us, and what we do, we need to be really clear about what camp we're in: the good one or the bad one. A cop should always be one of the good ones. And we should never mix those two categories. See, there's us—you, me, Sokolov, Stingsby, the other cops on our force—we're out to make the world make sense. But then there's the privacy fanatics, or the people we put away, the ones that try to destroy everything we build."

I felt myself getting tense. "What are you saying about me?"

"You're starting to look a lot like one of them rather than one of us."

"I don't look a damn thing like one of them."

"You need to keep things clear. Separated in your head. Use your instincts, your moral sense. Just remember slash and line. You keep them separate."

Later that night I stayed up for hours, thinking about what Maclean had told me. The things she'd said had been obvious enough, and yet something about the way she'd said them had affected me. It must have been her certainty. She had no doubts in the world about who the good and the bad were—and as long as she knew that, everything else fell into place. Somehow, hearing her say those things with such certainty made them true.

The next day, I went back to work. I knew which camp I wanted to be in.

The night after my deal with the traders, thoughts floated through my head about Maclean's talk with me.

Slash and line. One camp or the other. And tonight, I had just changed camps.

CHAPTER NINE

The next morning, an elevator—normally crowded with employees sipping coffee and reading the news on phones, but empty this early—shuttled me up to the forensics department, my mind still disordered from the events at Sally Lane's. Everything felt hyper-sharp and tinged with the strangeness of sleep deprivation. Taking nervous sips of coffee, I nodded at the secretary and slouched down the hall towards my office, haunted by the fear that my deal with the traders was somehow visible, my guilt imprinted on my face. Why was the damned secretary here so early? It was 6:00 AM. I needed to get here before anyone else to memorize Haru's data.

Fuck, it was weird being paranoid at Sentrac. This was supposed to be the place that calmed me. The office didn't seem right today: the rows of trees looked a little bit crooked, a streak of dirt on the floor near my chair, the wrong song playing in the background. Oh God—everything in my office was out of place. I adjusted my digi-plant until the edges of its square pot aligned perfectly with the corner of my desk. A quick sanitary wipe removed tiny specks of dust from my keyboard.

"Initialize the Optica," I said, glancing through my doorway to double-check that the cubicles were still empty. Early in my career, I'd figured out how to erase all the searches I'd logged afterwards, but if a colleague walked in while I had the data open on my screen, I'd have some explaining to do. But closing my office door would be unusual and draw more attention.

"Online," said the electronic female voice of the Optica.

To make sure no one could hear, I typed my commands. *Retrieve data for Sentrac expenditures.* I ran a search for the word "security."

Heltatech Cybersecurity—$23,070, November 2.

Heltatech Cybersecurity—$53,881, October 12.

Heltatech Cybersecurity—$7,209, July 20.

Since Sentrac was making frequent payments to that company, they might be in charge of our firewalls. *Retrieve data for Heltatech Cybersecurity: Expenditures. List only employee salary payments.*

"You want anything, Detective?"

I jolted with surprise and turned towards the doorway. The secretary stood leaning against the doorframe.

Thank God. He didn't have the eyes. My screen would be blank to him. But in my mind, I pictured what he must've just seen: my tense face as I jumped from the surprise of seeing him. He stared quizzically at me through round glasses, his jaw flapping up and down as he chomped on his morning gum. How could this guy even look himself in the mirror wearing those ugly orange ties every day? Men with no style were a pet peeve of mine.

"I'm going to Mabelle's," he said. "You want anything?"

"No." I winced mentally at my own voice. My attempt to sound relaxed had come out forced.

"Right," he said and left, still chewing gum loudly.

This job for the traders might give me high blood pressure at an early age. Back to the Optica. *Corroborate this list of Heltatech employee names with Google searches. Check for links between the names and the terms "maintenance" and "monitoring." Start with the company website, social media, networking websites, personal websites.*

The results appeared almost instantly. Soon I had a list of Heltatech employees whose job titles were "IT Maintenance Manager," "Systems Monitoring Assistant," and the like.

Check Sentrac financial data for any Heltatech employees on this list receiving hourly wages. With luck, a little more digging might help me figure out how often Heltatech did routine checks and updates on its security systems. I managed to make some progress before Yury arrived early for the morning. As soon as his familiar shoes squeaked in the hallway, I quickly closed my searches and wiped them from the Optica's memory.

"Hi Frank," Yury said as he took off his jacket.

Something in his voice made me pop my head out of the door and ask, "Someone give you candy this morning or what? You're in a good mood."

He smiled but didn't say anything. His watery blue eyes looked distant, the lines on his face a bit less deep. That happy look had been in his eyes a lot lately, especially in the morning when he first came into the office.

Yury studied my face for a minute. "You, on the other hand, Frank—you look terrible, right? You get any sleep at all last night?"

"Just another one of my guests last night," I said, turning away and returning to my desk.

Call up my notes on Donaldson, I told the Optica. I'd spent the past two weeks looking for the exit strategies from A. Chawla Consulting—any obvious methods the criminals had used to get the money from the A. Chawla account into someone's personal account—but I'd found nothing. It was all too well laundered, their networks too vast. Time for a new strategy.

Retrieve background account information: A. Chawla Consulting.

My eyes skimmed over the phone number associated with the account, but I got caught on the address. 8032 Henrikson Avenue, in the Borough, a popular vacation villa just outside the city.

I knew that address.

It was as if my chair and desk had been turned upside down and hung from the ceiling, while data tumbled from the Optica to the floor. I glanced out my door at Yury, who had his back turned to me. *Search the Sentrac database of employee information, including spouse information.*

And there it was. The Optica had found my "A. Chawla." *Akshara Sokolov, née Akshara Chawla—wife of Yury Sokolov.* I'd known the name sounded familiar. It was the same one I'd seen lighting up the screen of Yury's phone every night at the Palace before they were married: NEW MESSAGE—AKSHARA CHAWLA.

I sat for a long time, staring at the Optica's answer. Beyond my doorframe, Yury's fingers crawled over the touchscreen of his interface. Bouncing one foot, he exhaled a heavy breath of air. His gambling addiction had brought him to do desperate things for money before. That address on Henrikson Avenue was the location of his vacation cottage, one I'd been to with him once for his bachelor party.

The Optica never lied.

And yet, it had only taken me three minutes to find this trail. Using your wife's maiden name for a fake company was the oldest trick out there. A financial data detective, who knew the system inside-out, would never leave a trail so clear. I checked the data once, twice, three times; I couldn't stop checking it, as though certainty was always around the corner, evading me. Yury—no way he could've fucked up this badly, he couldn't have, I wouldn't let that be true, because fuck, I had to admit, the guy actually meant something to me.

A deep, resounding voice sounded down the hallway, followed by quick footsteps. My fingers fumbled to close all the windows on my screen. I typed a command: *Erase all searches and notes on Sokolov and A. Chawla Consulting.*

A shadow fell over my desk. Stingsby stood in my doorway, his long, thin frame covered by an unbuttoned trench-coat as he made his way into the office for the morning. "How's the Donaldson case?"

"It's coming along, boss."

"Got anything new?"

My mind raced, my bones grinding as Stingsby's presence flattened me. "Nothing new. Just gathering more evidence about the funnelling scheme Maclean had gotten started on."

He grunted and leaned against the mahogany, arms folded. "I suppose I shouldn't expect too much, since you're out of your depth on a case like this. You got enough to put him away?"

"Listen, I'm handling this, alright? I think I have enough. Over three million stolen."

"And that's all you've got?"

"If there's anything else, it's too well hidden." Sweat dripped down my spine. If Stingsby knew what I'd found, Yury would be looking at serious jail time.

Stingsby's eyes were fixed on me. "Let's get things moving then. Try to make up for all the time you've already wasted. If you've got enough then you've got enough."

I needed to think fast. How could I buy myself more time to look into this situation with Yury? "Well, it's almost enough," I said. "But it looks like I'm going to need co-operation with other departments."

"What, you can't nail him just with financial?"

"It would help if I had some GPS tracking and surveillance footage."

"For God's sake Southwood, you know how slow those clearances are going to be." White-collar crime cases could stretch out for months.

Stingsby hesitated. He came into my office and sat on the corner of my desk, his small round eyes downcast. "Remember your last investigation, Southwood?"

"Sure, boss."

"You had plenty of evidence to lock up Miller, but you overreached."

"Well, I wouldn't call it that."

"You reached too far trying to find conspirators. We didn't have enough. You need things to be perfect. Anyway, I'm sure you remember it all. Wound up wasting my time and yours."

"I had something good there—"

"Think of this as an opportunity not to make the same mistake. Stay on track. The Donaldson case involves a lot of money but it's dead fucking simple. Finish collecting the evidence Maclean was already gathering, then close the case. Get GPS and surveillance data if you need to, but don't go chasing people down alleys again."

I bit all back the things I wanted to say. When Stingsby spoke, you shut the fuck up and did what he said. He stood up to leave.

"Wait," I said. "Has Homicide found any connection between the Donaldson case and Maclean's murder?"

Stingsby looked down and busied himself with his phone, but not quickly enough for me to miss the flash of pain in his face. I wondered how the conversation had gone when Stingsby went to notify Maclean's family.

"No connection," he said brusquely. "You heard what I said at the crime scene, Southwood. Privacy fanatics."

Stingsby vanished, halogen gleaming on the black metal handle of his D72. Even though I saw the weapon regularly, the sight of it reminded me of the superstitious stories people told about the ghosts of people shot by a D72. I recalled a conversation I'd had once about the ghosts with Yury.

"Yury," I'd said one afternoon, "you believe in those ghosts people always talk about, the ones left after someone's shot by a D72?"

He shrugged, dumping sugar into his coffee. "Who knows? What else happens to people shot by a D72? Matter can't just become data. It has to become something else, something physical."

"Sure, but when you're shot you become part of the police records, the ones registered automatically when someone fires a D72. And plus, there's the scarring on the arm of the person who fires it. That's the material trace."

"Numbers in police records aren't things. They're not made of matter. Now the scars, though, that might be it."

"And a ghost is a thing?"

He shrugged again. "But really, if you think about it, we're better off now. We must be, now that we have the D72. I can't even watch those old movies, the ones with the old guns. It's disgusting. All that mess, right?"

"Hey, you talked to Stingsby today, right?" Yury asked on his way out for the evening. "How'd he seem? How do you think he's dealing with it all—Maclean's murder?"

"Hard to say, but I don't think he's taking it that well. There was something in his face when I mentioned Maclean. He hides it like a pro though."

"You know, I saw him the other day over there by the coffee, right? He poured himself a cup, then afterwards he started pouring another one—but he stopped halfway through, paused for a second, and dumped it out. Remember how he used to pour coffee for Maclean all the time, so he'd have an excuse to go into her office, usually to ask for her help with something? I think he was on autopilot and started pouring a coffee for Maclean without even realizing it."

"That's horrible."

Yury finished buttoning up his jacket, ready to leave. "How about your case?" he asked. "Find anything new today?"

The question gave me a little burst of fear. "No," I said without making eye contact. "Nothing new today."

CHAPTER TEN

A few days later, I stayed late at the office after Yury left work, watching his data unfold in real-time.

Yury Sokolov—Personal Account. The Core Pharmacy, $60. Beef Time Burgers, $15. The guy needed better eating habits. Bad eating habits were another thing I couldn't stand in a man. Street meat, steroid meat, supersized meat—all of it was terrible. I ate complete meals, always in properly small portions: wholesome, holistic, rational food. I thought a lot about vitamins. Each meal should have a bit from each food group. Sometimes people laughed at me for my eating habits. "You hardly eat at all," one of my colleagues had said. "You're already so skinny." Better to hardly eat at all than to eat like vermin.

Back to Yury's data. Steven's Beer and Spirits, $31. Cross City Supermarket, $37. Sixteenth Street Flowers, $34. Then a stretch of down-time with no purchases. He must be at home, giving his wife the flowers he'd just bought. An hour slid by.

And there it was, right on cue at 20:15. The Indigo Palace Casino, $15. When it came to addictive behaviours, predictive data analytics worked even better than usual. With that amount of casino credit, the poor bastard would be betting miniscule amounts at the slot machines—cents, really. That was all he had.

The moment I saw that purchase, I threw on my jacket, ready to head to Yury's apartment. But before I left, I took a minute to review the predictive analytics I'd run earlier that day on Donaldson. AUGUST DONALDSON—ESTIMATED ARRIVAL AT THE INDIGO PALACE CASINO: 21:00. I'd have to carry out the first part of my plan within an hour, in order to get to the Palace by the time Donaldson arrived.

On the walk to Yury's I glanced at my reflection in my phone screen, making sure I looked sharp and trustworthy, like I should. I was on my way to Yury's place in the guise of a friend, an honest, trustworthy friend, so I needed to look the part. A gray herringbone suit and freshly shined oxfords did wonders for a man's credibility. When snooping around the apartment of a new suspect, a detective better be well dressed.

"Sorry, no salesmen allowed in here," the concierge said when I entered the lobby.

"Jesus, I'm here for a friend," I said. "Suite 302. Yury Sokolov."

I rapped on Yury's door. A slim, professional woman appeared in the doorframe, dressed in a satin blazer with her hair pulled back into a knot. She had a narrow waist and long legs, a graceful curve where her neck met her shoulders, small hands and glasses with black rims. It was easy to see why Yury had fallen so hopelessly for her.

"Oh, hey Frank," she said.

"Evening, Akshara," I said, flashing her a smile. I wondered if she'd notice the teeth—I'd had them whitened with the latest technology before I went broke. The more charm I had tonight, the more likely I'd be able to get some answers.

She squinted at me. "Yury's not here."

I feigned surprise. "I thought he might be out, but he forgot to turn his phone on after work, so I figured I'd stop by."

"He always forgets to turn it on." She exhaled sharply. "He's out at the pub with Liu. Watching the game."

"Is he?" It was a damn shame when a husband lied to his wife. I leaned against the doorframe, careful not to wrinkle the herringbone. Had she noticed the new suit? "Think he'll be back soon?"

"He should be back soon. You can come in if you like, wait for him here." Akshara opened the door all the way, and light flooded the corridor.

"I wouldn't want to put you out."

"Oh Christ, Frank, just come in."

Smiling faintly, she led me to the couch, then flitted around the apartment and whisked away some loose clothes and empty glasses. The room smelled like flowers, and on the coffee table stood a vase filled with the blue lilies Yury had just bought her. Their apartment was small and intimate, every corner cluttered with Yury's collection of digi-plants. Holographic leaves clustered overhead. On the wall, a digital frame flashed through a series of photographs: Yury and Akshara wearing touristy hats and smiling in front of a castle somewhere, Akshara playing video games with her nieces, Akshara and Yury in their wedding clothes, holding hands under a stone archway.

"You going out later?" she asked, scanning me up and down as she finished tidying up. "You look nice."

"Maybe." I knew the suit was working well. I gave her another smile. Looking as sharp as I did right now, I'd be able to learn something from her for sure.

She disappeared into the kitchen, and I quickly began my visual search. A faded couch with tiny rips in the fabric. Dents and scrapes on the legs. On the wall was a blank space framed by a square of scuff marks: the spot where their entertainment system used to be. Akshara's phone lay on the table, an ancient model of the Akato with scratches on the screen.

This was not what I'd expected.

My eyes lingering on the old, ripped fabric of the couch, I remembered Akshara back when she married Yury: a sharp businesswoman who drank Mabelle's every morning, carried an eight-hundred dollar bag, and wore heels and expensive suits, always tailored at the waist with a crisp white blouse underneath. She was six feet tall and walked with authority, turning plenty of heads on the sidewalks of the Core.

She came back into the living room carrying two drinks.

"You remembered my drink of choice?" I said. "And the two limes, even?"

"Would I ever forget?"

I glanced at the can of soda water in her hand and said, "What, you won't have a drink with me?"

Only her eyes smiled as she sat down beside me, the couch shifting with her movement. "I have my reasons."

"That's not like you."

She laughed.

"How's data trading?" I asked.

"Good. It's a bull market right now. Everyone's making money."

"Good money, huh? That doesn't surprise me. You're one of the best data traders at the firm. I always thought so." That wasn't a lie. "You must be making a killing."

Akshara remained silent for a minute, swishing the bubbling liquid around in her can. She glanced at the scuff marks around the empty patch of wall. "I make money," she said slowly. "But I never seem to have any." She put her drink down with a sudden clank. "You'd know. You've seen Yury at the Indigo Palace, I'm sure."

I hesitated. "Sure." Something held me back from asking any more questions. The look on her face made me feel terrible. Damn Yury for fucking up his life like this. If I'd known he was so susceptible to addiction, I never would've brought his sorry ass to the Indigo Palace in the first place.

After a few minutes, I stood up. "Thanks for the drink, Akshara. I think I'll catch up with him tomorrow." I needed to hurry if I was going to carry out the second half of my plan tonight.

I hadn't found what I'd been looking for in Yury's apartment. A few days checking out Yury's data had revealed nothing concrete—but if he had a hidden, well-laundered source of income I hadn't been able to find, it might've shown in his apartment.

Within ten minutes, I'd swept through the streets of the Core, climbed the steps of the Indigo Palace, and stepped into familiar blue neon. A Friday night at the Indigo Palace. You had to fight your way through the crowds. Above the Gemini tables, the chandelier refracted the light coming from the ceiling. As I crossed the floor, I let my fingers trail over my favourite Gemini table, numbers shifting on its smooth surface. The euphoria of Sentrac money hung in the air like it always did, adrenaline blending with the buzz of giddy, intoxicated chatter, but tonight, the euphoria didn't touch me. I stood apart from it, shut off from the currents of digital money. Unlike in the past, the crowds of the casino bothered me tonight. I regulated my breathing.

Near the back of the room at the electronic slot machines, a familiar figure sat with his back to me. Yury didn't notice me when I walked up, the spinning reels of the slot machine reflected on his glasses. His finger hovered over the touchscreen.

I clapped him on the shoulder.

He jumped and spun around. "You scared the shit out of me."

"Oh, did you think I was your wife?" I said, taking a seat beside him. "I just went to your place to look for you. I heard you're out watching sim sports with Liu."

His eyes widened. "And what did you—did you tell her where I am?"

"How would I know you were here?" The lie came off smoothly. "I came here to gamble."

He nodded, shoulders slumping with relief.

"Yury," I said, "did I ever tell you you're a fucking jackass?"

"What?"

"When are you gonna stop lying to your wife? Get your shit together."

He looked away, and his posture sagged a bit, but his hand remained where it was, hovering puppet-like in front of the gambling screen. The lines on his face deepened every day, but here at the Indigo Palace they seemed softer, fading just for the night.

I checked the time on my phone. 21:12. The three-way convergence I'd planned—between me, Yury, and Donaldson—should happen any time now. A quarter of an hour passed. Then the glass doors of the Palace swung open. Freezing air rushed inside, and Donaldson appeared in the entry. The events began to unfold exactly as planned, the precision and perfection of my plan giving me a rush. Everything was working perfectly, as it should be. I cleared my head of all distractions, ready to watch Donaldson and Yury closely. Any subtle behaviours in their interaction could be a hint about whether Yury was in league with Donaldson.

The crowd melted to make way for Donaldson, dressed down tonight in a sports jacket and dark denim, his rectangular frame gliding slowly as he stopped to greet familiars and shake hands. His presence transformed the crowd. Currents of recognition darted through the casino like a static charge: the familiarity on a man's face near the door, a glint of insider knowledge in the eyes of a woman at the Gemini tables, the handshake of a nearby suit, his white teeth shining, the incisors too long. Donaldson's presence spread like a plague, sending out tendrils of corruption, power, dirty money. My whole body itched to stop that infection from spreading, to contain and control it, to cleanse the crowd. But an ugly thought crossed my mind: was I any better?

Donaldson continued his steady progress through the casino, headed in our direction.

"What are you staring at Frank?" Yury asked.

"Who do you think I'm staring at?" I said, studying Yury's face to gauge his reaction.

He turned his head in Donaldson's direction, but his eyes breezed right past him, seeing nothing. "Who?"

Donaldson was only a few feet away now. Refracting the neon, his sports jacket rippled with his movements, the fabric smooth and tailored. A smile split his face when he saw me, dents forming in the skin around his eyes. I wished he wouldn't look at me like that, like he recognized me. Like I was one of them.

Donaldson's familiar fleshy handshake. "Southwood," he said, smiling.

I shook his hand. "Donaldson," I said, watching Yury when I said the name.

Yury's shock was well concealed, but detectable, just visible in the slight widening of his eyes. Shock wasn't what I'd expected.

Donaldson's teeth sparkled as he beamed at me. "New suit?"

"Might be." I gestured in Yury's direction. "You must know my colleague, Yury Sokolov? He's a regular here."

Donaldson's eyes scrolled to Yury, squinting. "Don't think we've met," Donaldson said. He offered his hand. Yury shook it, his shoulder tense. It was the handshake of strangers.

"Never met him, huh?" I prodded. "He's here almost as much as us. Now that's dedication."

Donaldson laughed, the fleshy dimples back again. "Well, Sokolov, if you're a gambling man then you're in my good books. I'll see you again. You know I love my friends at Sentrac."

When Donaldson leaned in close to clamp a hand on my shoulder, the smell struck me: a familiar chemical scent on his breath, hidden under the stench of aftershave. I looked closer at his face and noticed the yellowish hue of his skin. He wore a high, buttoned-up collar, like Anton's, but my trained eyes spotted a hint of the purple blotches showing just above his collar. Donaldson's neck looked just like Anton's had night after night at Sally Lane's. I remembered what Jenny had told me a few days ago. "That's Ruz. It's an elite Chem, famous in the underworld but almost impossible to get your hands on. Only a few people have access to it."

In Donaldson's pocket, there was a familiar bottle with an orange stripe: IRON ENERGY DRINK. The same one he'd been drinking outside the Core Club.

Donaldson vanished into the throng of bodies. Yury spoke quietly under his breath. "You're fucking insane Frank, insane. What do you think you're doing, anyway?"

"Nothing illegal, Yury," I said, an edge of tension in my voice.

"You might get charged with conduct unbecoming if Stingsby knew. What are you doing fraternizing with your suspect like that? Since when do you know him?"

"I just see him here sometimes. And the guy's infamous. What, you don't know him yourself? How come you didn't recognize him when he's always here?"

"I only know his name and not his face, and when I'm here—right, when I'm here, Frank, I'm a professional who tries not to fucking chat with criminals, something you might want to try out yourself, right?"

"Yury, you know I can't stand it when things aren't done right. No loose ends here. I have to do this investigation right. How do you think I found out about Donaldson's affair? Saw him here with her."

"You better quit doing this kind of thing and be quick about it."

"There can't be any fucking loose ends, alright?"

I left the casino more confused than when I arrived. Unless Yury was a damn good actor, this Yury lead was taking me nowhere. I needed a new lead, and I knew where to find it. Someone in the underworld was converting their money secretly, selling Ruz to Donaldson and his cartel, disguised in those IRON bottles. The strategy they used to pay out this dealer might lead me to other people in the laundering network, more cogs in their machine. I needed to find out who that dealer was.

My feet moved a little more lightly on my walk home. Maybe Yury didn't do this. That meant something. That meant a lot. And maybe, if Yury was being set up, I could help him— yes, I thought, my mind racing now that it had caught onto a thread, that was right, I could help him, and maybe that would mean I was still doing something good in this city, that I wasn't just a dirty cop doing what dirty cops have done for generations, letting the filthy money and the darkness wash over them until they drowned in it. Maybe helping Yury could cancel out my deal with the fanatics.

Did the world work that way? Could I cancel out my bad actions with good ones, like two sides of a scale, two platforms hanging on fragile strings, shifting in a delicate balance?

If I help Yury, I cancel out the rest. The thought sounded good in my head, so I repeated it.

If I help Yury, I cancel out the rest.

If I help Yury, I cancel out the rest.

If I help Yury, I cancel out the rest.

Soon, I couldn't stop thinking it. It sounded true the moment I thought it, but then it began to fade, becoming more and more uncertain until I thought it again.

I walked home that night with that phrase in my head, playing in endless circles.

CHAPTER ELEVEN

After work on Monday, I crossed the street and stepped into my favourite after-work watering hole, Gibson's Pub. The scent of beer and the cedar wood panelling swept over me, its familiarity bringing comfort.

"Hey Frank," the bartender said from behind the beer taps. "Gin and tonic?"

I nodded and swiped his transfer scanner, leaving a generous tip. Alex knew my drink of choice, and he never forgot the extra lime.

With the bittersweet taste of gin and the buzz of drunken laughter in the background, the pressures of life faded. Gibson's Pub was a refuge. So many nights after work I came here, looking to put off going home to my apartment just a little while longer. The low ceilings, the panelled wood floors, the screen playing Sim Sports overhead, even the eccentric stuffed badger hanging on the wall—all of it warmed me. Suddenly it seemed very true and certain that my business with the fanatics would be concluded quickly, my gambling debts paid and my ties with criminals cut for good. Just this one last bit of dirty work, then I would be clean.

As I squeezed the second lime wedge into my drink, my eye caught on a man with striking white hair slumped over a pint, a few stools down from me. His thick eyebrows stood out in a long face with high cheekbones. Underneath his brown trench coat, he wore a data police uniform.

"Boss?" I said tentatively. I'd never seen Stingsby here, not once. It was strange to think that Stingsby ever drank, ate, slept—human acts that showed signs of need or frailty.

He turned towards me abruptly, as though surprised by my voice, and his eyes became defensive like those of a fearful animal. His back was curved in a slouch, shoulders turned inwards in a protective shell. I hardly recognized him. The varnish of professionalism had disappeared.

When he saw me, he drew himself up, straightening his back. "Southwood," he grunted, and turned back to his pint.

I hesitated, then picked up my drink and moved down a few stools to sit beside him. "You alright?"

He didn't answer. From the corners of his eyes, two lines fanned outwards in a V-shape, and his skin, flushed from the alcohol, looked dry and worn. I sipped my drink without speaking, astonished. Stingsby ran the financial data police without hesitation, compromise, or the slightest hint of emotion. Despite his stupid habits of underestimating me, he'd earned my respect over the years because of his competence. Seeing him like this made little cracks form in my vision of Sentrac. It didn't feel good.

He swallowed the rest of his beer. "Another," he said curtly to Alex. As he raised the new beer to his mouth, liquid spilled over the edge of the glass and trickled into a stream on the bar.

"I went to see Maclean's family today," he said. "To see how they're doing. I went in there, Southwood, I went in there—into Maclean's house, into her kitchen—and I saw that girl just sitting there, that six-year-old girl that looks just like Maclean, sitting there completely lost, staring out the fucking window and not saying anything. She barely speaks lately, her father said. She's gone quiet. That girl doesn't have a fucking mother."

I stared down at the squeezed lime wedges straggling between the ice cubes in my already empty glass. "Christ, that's terrible."

"She's gone quiet," he repeated. The phrase hung between us. Both of us focused on our drinks.

Stingsby turned to face me. "It's the fanatics, Southwood."

A few heads turned towards us as Stingsby raised his voice. Behind the bar, Alex watched us over his shoulder.

"I could've done something," Stingsby continued. "I didn't stop—" He looked away. "I didn't stop them. I should've shut down that filth after they killed Lawrence. We've had years to crush them. We failed."

"You can't blame yourself for Maclean's—"

"We fucking failed."

My thoughts began to quicken. If Stingsby found out I was working for privacy fanatics, it would hit him on a very personal level. My chest tightening, I glanced at the door while my mind searched for an excuse to escape.

"There are more and more of them every day," Stingsby said, taking a long swallow of his drink. "We'll see more attacks like this. It's not going to stop."

"No. No way. We'll shut them down." Could I make an exit now without looking suspicious?

Stingsby grunted. "Let me drink in peace."

I left as quickly as I could.

What was I doing? How did I get so deep into this?

When I got home, I rushed to the kitchen and scribbled up a chart that showed all my actions, all the key decisions I'd made at different points, each one with a complex list of pros and cons. Surely these charts must mean that I'd made the right choice— the logic, balance sheets, they spoke for themselves.

As always, I burned the lists, watching the flames erase my secrets. Later, I dreamed about those little bits of paper stuck to my skin, and when I tried to peel them off, a layer of flesh came with them.

CHAPTER TWELVE

The next day arrived, a warm afternoon for December, and the sun softened the snowdrifts as I walked to Sentrac Square on my lunch break. The Square was as busy as always, filled with parents pushing baby carriages and suits on their lunch breaks, their coffees and cigarettes in hand. Deep underground, the subway sent vibrations through the pavement. I crossed the gleaming cement and shouldered through the crowd to an isolated area at the back. I needed space to think about A. Chawla Consulting and how I could help Yury. On my right, the Forest loomed up thirty storeys tall, a shining universe of green dreams. Sentrac Square was the centre of the Core, and the Core was the centre of the city.

Squinting from snow's reflected glare, I sat on the edge of a fountain, frozen over for the winter, and glanced at the digital clock in the middle of the Square: a cube crowning a massive marble pillar. Blue numbers beamed out the time in all directions.

My stomach dropped when a massive figure in a pinstriped business suit emerged from the crowd and ambled in my direction, passing through the shadow of the clock on his way. It was Cedric—Haru's muscle, the man with the automatic in the red room. On his head, a crust of gel reined in the tangles. He held a Mabelle's cup, just like any other suit from the Core. I quickly scanned the nearby crowd for familiar faces. Someone I knew could easily be in that crowd. This was crazy.

Sipping his coffee, Cedric sat on the edge of the fountain a few feet away. His dress shoes shone in the winter sunlight, freshly polished. He pulled out a phone and held it as if speaking into the mouthpiece.

"Jesus Christ," I said in a low voice. Copying him, I put my phone to my ear as well.

"Hey bud," he said. As he raised his hand to drink, gold rings glinted on his fingers.

A woman in business attire stared at me from the middle of the Square, near the clock. I recognized her from the monetary policy department at Sentrac. Quickly, I brought my Mabelle's cup to my mouth to conceal my face. "You have any idea how dangerous it is for us to talk like this, Cedric? There are people I know around, and I've got a lot on my mind right now, so make it quick."

"So you're a vegan, bud?"

"What? Get to the fucking point." I glanced back at the centre of the square again, eyeing the woman from Sentrac.

Cedric took his time, sipping his Mabelle's and baring his gold teeth in a smile. "We're in no hurry here. Did you forget who's in charge in our little partnership? Thought you could avoid us, huh?" He laughed, and the booming racket turned a few heads. "So, bud, since you're a vegan, is that why you're so skinny like a little rat, with those red eyes?"

"I keep a healthy diet. Have you ever taken a vitamin in your fucking life?"

"Have you ever been to a gym?"

"Those places are completely obsolete." Gyms were disgusting—not just the germs, but also all that loud clanking metal, the sheer stupidity of picking things up and putting them back down again over and over. Relics from a past age.

"Hell, Frank, you'll learn," Cedric said. "You're gonna love it down in the markets. It's simple. Real men have real money." The huge man took another long sip of Mabelle's. "You finish memorizing the data?"

"Yes. If I do a job, I do it well, and on schedule. I don't like loose ends."

"Report to the bank tonight. 22:00." Pleased with himself, Cedric put his Mabelle's on the bench and smoothed a wrinkle out of his pristine business suit. Sunlight danced on the pressed, pin-striped wool.

I stood up and started walking back towards Sentrac, putting my phone in my pocket.

★

I arrived at Sally Lane's two hours earlier than I'd been asked. It would be better to get this meeting over with quickly. Jenny met me outside the back door and told me to wait outside until she went in and punched in the code to unlock the vault. She didn't want me anywhere near when she punched in the code.

After waiting a few minutes, I entered a dimly lit kitchen that reeked of grease and took a few steps toward the basement door. The rustling of clothes moved in quickly from behind me. Hard metal pressed into my back. Whoever they were, they had me.

"Who are you?" a female voice asked.

I thought fast. If this woman was in the back of Sally Lane's, then odds were she was another trader.

"I work for Haru," I said.

A pause. "Turn around slowly."

I turned to face an unfamiliar woman in her thirties, dressed in a tight, long-sleeved black shirt with a high neckline. As she took a few steps backwards to look at me, she moved slowly, with precision, but beneath those careful movements was a tension waiting to be released. Her cheeks were high arches with copper freckles, and two identical sheets of red hair curved over her shoulders, hanging from a razor-straight part that divided her scalp in half like a deep ravine. Something about her seemed out of place here. She was so well put together, she would look more at home in a library or museum rather than this filthy criminal haunt. The precision, the carefulness of her appearance drew me in. It was like looking at a kindred spirit.

As she studied my face, her expression remained cold and unchanged. And yet, her shoulders relaxed slightly and the tension dissipated. She might not have wanted me to know it, but it looked like she recognized my face.

"Your purpose here?" she said. She spoke precisely, pronouncing each syllable slowly and perfectly.

"I can't answer that."

She put her gun away and pushed back a red strand that had fallen into her face. Her fingers left the hair perfectly arranged, the ends cut in a straight line. On her forearms, identical tattoos had been drawn with painstaking symmetry.

"You're a trader?" I asked.

She looked at me without saying anything.

"You don't look like one," I said.

The tiny lines around her eyes shifted. Her breath was tinted by the familiar acidic smell of Ruz, and there were faint blotches on her neck, just visible above her high collar. This woman might be significant, if very few people had access to Ruz. She picked up a bag she'd left lying on a counter, swung it over her shoulder, and left out the back door.

When I got to the red room I found Anton, and sure enough, he was busy packing up two crates of plain glass bottles. His face was sunken and skeletal. "Don't show your face in this joint early again," he said. "Come here at the time you're told to. Wait here for Haru."

"Was that your toxic waste dealer up there?"

He ignored me. As he transferred the bottles into the crates, I caught sight of a bracelet lying with the pile of things he must've just traded for. It was made of bronze and strung with bright, multi-coloured beads. Hideous, but exactly the kind of knick-knack Jenny loved.

Anton saw me staring and shoved the bracelet into the crate with the bottles. "You fucking prying again, that it?"

Lighting an R&M, I backed off and sat down in the corner far from Anton, hoping the distance between us would deflect some of his aggression. He didn't intimidate me, but I didn't want to bother with his bullshit. It made me tired.

"But you pry—that's just what you do ain't it?" he said. "From the moment you walked into the fucking joint, that's been it. That's what you been doing. You think you got a right, a right to see everything."

"You brought me here."

That incensed him further. His face flushed. "That's right we did. And it was a mistake."

He left, carrying his crate full of Ruz. His aggression didn't surprise me. When he said it was a mistake to bring me here, he was right. He'd have to be a complete fool not to notice that something was happening between Jenny and me. When the two of them made their plan to lure me into their bribery scheme, neither of them could've foreseen the consequences. It had made sense to send Jenny out into the street to hook me in—if Anton had approached me I would've told him to fuck off. But Jenny was supposed to be just acting. What came next—that wasn't what they'd had in mind.

I wondered how Jenny would react when he gave her that bracelet. He gave her things all the time. During the past weeks at Sally Lane's, I'd gotten to know their routine. Anton ran the diner during the day, and he was often absent in the evenings, when Jenny worked alone at night, jittering from the coffee she drank constantly and smiling at her regulars when they came in. She seemed to like doing a good job running the place even though it didn't mean much to her. When someone thanked her or complimented the food, she'd smile at them with genuine pleasure. Later in the evening Anton would come back, probably from trading, reeking of cigarettes and dressed in a stupid long black trench coat that made him look even thinner than usual. And when he came back he almost always brought Jenny some trinket he'd picked up trading. He came in one night with a bright purple scarf, exactly the type of thing Jenny liked. When he handed it to her, she gave him a smile that looked forced, kissed him lightly on the lips, and put it around her neck. But when she turned her back to him, her smile disappeared and she looked tired. After Anton left for the night, she took off the scarf and put it on a shelf behind the bar with a few other forgotten trinkets he'd gotten her. Anton appeared devoted to her, but each gift just made her look wearier and more drained than the last one. "You give me too much," she'd told him once. Anton had just laughed, as though she was joking, and brought her another coffee. I didn't fully understand it, but there was something dark between them, some burden that hung over them and weighed Jenny down. Sometimes it looked like it might crush her.

The door to the red room opened, and Haru came in. She gestured towards the table. Stacked in a pyramid, thirty gold rectangles blinked at me with their metallic glow. On top of each brick were letters and numbers: GOLD, followed by the weight.

"That's thirty thousand," she said, sitting across from me. "If you completed the fucking job right." Peering at me from under her bangs, she watched me inspect the gold, one hand behind her head, a Vintage in the other, and her feet up on the table. Beside her, an ashtray overflowed with lipstick-stained filters.

I repeated the data to her.

When I finished she said, "Fine."

She nodded towards the bricks. I pulled them towards me, and they were so cold to the touch that I winced, as though the money had burned me. It was what I deserved. This money was dirty.

"You're damn lucky we gave you anything at all," she said.

"I delivered on my end. When I do something, I do it right. You can expect that from me."

Loose flakes of dirt drifted from Haru's boot sole onto the table. "You and me, maybe we're in business together, but don't forget, you work for us. Not the other way around."

The blades of the ceiling fan spun, the motor jerking unevenly, and as the shadows circled like a slow-moving wheel, my thoughts cycled with them, forming a plan. I thought about the woman I'd seen upstairs with that chemical smell on her breath. I picked up an old-fashioned playing card lying on the table and fiddled with it idly in one hand. I'd need to gamble a bit now to get what I wanted.

"I want some of these Chems all you privacy fanatics like so much," I said.

Haru took another drag of her Vintage. "Why?"

I paused and looked down, feigning a look of reserve, even embarrassment. "Is that your business? Why do you think I want them?"

"You planning to become a Chems addict now?"

"I'd like to see you try it—dealing with the shit I've had to deal with since you fanatics showed up." The edge of stress in my voice sounded genuine. "If some criminals knocked you out and blackmailed you into doing God knows what, and now you've got to put your freedom on the line every day, you might want something to take the edge off, am I right?"

"You can't be trusted enough to meet any other traders yet. Not a slippery motherfucker like you."

I shook my head. "Listen, I need *something* to get me by, alright? I've got no Sentrac money right now, not a damn cent. You gave me this other money, I want to spend it."

Haru was silent.

Time to shift gears. This was an opportunity to make a more aggressive move. "Let me guess. I buy Chems from that nice lady I met upstairs on my way inside, the one who dropped off bottles for Anton and left with a bag clanking full of money."

"I forgot you have no fucking understanding of privacy."

"You brought me into this operation. I'm going to learn more about it eventually, if I'm working for you. If I'm your corrupt cop then I'm one of you now."

She didn't reply.

"I want whatever Anton's always on."

She snorted. "A clown like you would never get your hands on that."

"You'd be surprised what I can do."

"I ain't giving you any fucking information I don't have to."

The shadows of the ceiling fan spun while the smoke thickened and dispersed. Haru wouldn't tell me anything unless I pushed her. I forced myself into a relaxed posture, pulling one elbow onto the back of my chair and leaning back. This next bluff would be a risk, but if there was one thing I knew how to do, it was gamble, grapple with Gemini numbers, mould the data into shape, and calculate risks and probabilities.

"I've been doing some thinking," I said. "I've realized I have more power in our little partnership than you'd like to let on. You need me for something big. Something way bigger than the bullshit jobs you've been sending me on."

"That so?"

"You took a monumental risk bringing me down here. You asked me for information about the firewalls. You pay me a lot of money to keep me happy. You need me badly and we both know it. You won't use that blackmail unless you absolutely have to. So I get to make a few demands."

"You don't make demands."

My mind worked to negotiate the tactical dance, a rush rising like the smoke that floated upwards, until the fan slashed it to pieces. "The amount of resources you used to keep me under surveillance like you did—it was extensive. And your friend up there, the Chem dealer, she knows about it. She didn't say so, but I could see it on her face. She recognized me. She already knows who I am, and probably that I'm your corrupt cop, so you may as well take me to her."

Haru's face looked focused, reading me for cues. "She won't fucking sell you what she sells Anton."

"Why?"

Her eyes remained fixed on me, but she said nothing.

"If you want me to keep getting you the data you so desperately need, then tell me," I said.

After a pause, Haru said, "Ruz takes incredibly rare materials to produce. She only serves that in house, at trade meets. The scarcity of Ruz makes it legendary. It helps her bring people in, just to get a taste of it. While they're there, they'll buy her other products."

"How does Anton get his paws on it then?"

"Not your business. He helped her out once. They go way back. That's how she thanks him. What she really gave him was a filthy fucking addiction, but hell."

"Can anyone else produce it?"

"No. Only she knows the recipe and has the materials. If anyone tried to replicate it—" Haru drew a finger across her throat.

"If I can't have Ruz, I'll buy her regular stuff then. Take me to her." The more information I could find out about this woman, the closer I got to finding whether she and Donaldson were linked.

Haru adjusted a leather band on her wrist. "No. Not now. You do good work for us, then maybe I'll let you talk to her.

Tonight I'll give you another job. You earn our trust. In the meantime you get your drugs from Cedric."

I studied her face. It was hardened, resolute.

"Let's go talk to Cedric," she said.

We descended a few storeys, opened a door, and entered a large space like the one on the bottom floor, this one mostly empty. Jenny had told me that this was the stairwell for an old underground parking facility. Sally Lane's had been built over the remains of a ruined high-rise apartment complex, and they'd never gotten rid of the infrastructure underneath.

Haru led me to a room near the stairwell. Cedric's curses floated through the open doorway. We stepped into an enclosed area filled with shining heaps of metal, a coffeemaker, blue ceramic cups, and a vast collection of guns. The enclosure he was using for his bank account looked like a space that had been intended for purchasing parking tickets decades ago. In the corner, the old machines still stood gathering dust.

Cedric glanced over his shoulder when we came it. "Came to check out my bank account, bud? I'm just trynna fix this damned coffeemaker."

"I told you to get your coffee upstairs in the back of the diner," Haru said.

Glass and plastic clattered as Cedric fumbled with the machine, his muscles stretching the fabric of his shirt. Behind his beard, his face glowed red. "Goddamn fucking shit."

Silver, platinum, and gold bricks lay heaped across the room in massive towers. One of them reached the roof. "Looks like it pays well being a filthy criminal," I said. "That all your money?"

"Only a fraction of it, bud."

Shoving my hands in my pockets, I reached for the three straggling pieces of gold I'd brought, turning them over in my fingers. I was poor in two ways now, instead of just one. The money still felt dirty, but I also remembered how good it used to feel walk through a crowd of aerial storefronts when I had money—all that swipe, swipe, swipe, or the click, click, click of online shopping. That feeling I got after each purchase was impossible to describe.

"The lackey needs Chems," Haru said.

Cedric pulled out a handgun: a Holt-FR like Anton's, but a smaller, more compact model. "First you'll need this, now that you've got some money, bud. Gotta keep it protected. This Holt-FR is a good basic savings account—decent theft prevention. You want the smart shells, too. Something tells me you've got no aim." He stood up and slapped me on the shoulder. "Every man for himself down here. Every man for himself."

"Don't have much of a choice, do I? With no banks, someone could rob me anytime. How can you people stand it, having no rules like that? And how much for the gun?"

"Fourteen hundred, if I throw in the smart shells."

Rough. I reached into my pocket and handed him two gold rectangles in exchange for a handful of coins.

"Guess what, Frank?" Cedric said, beaming at me and lighting a joint. "You just bought that and nobody recorded it. And just think about it, bud. You don't trust me. I don't trust you. But we do business. Beautiful."

"So what? I never trust anyone I do business with."

"All those fools up there trust somebody, bud. They trust the bank. Sentrac. Every time they exchange some of their make-believe money, they trust the bank to be keeping it all straight-like, keeping track of everything, see what I mean? Us, we don't need that. You know you got your money because you got it right there in your fucking hand, not because Sentrac says so."

He handed me the Holt, still smiling broadly with gold teeth shining. "See bud? I just handed you a fucking *thing*, Frank, a real thing. This is barter. It's how things used to be."

"I'm just here to get this money and then get the hell out of here."

"So you say now, but you'll be surprised how quickly you change your mind. Trading, money, spending—it feels good. Even an uptight motherfucker like you would like it." Cedric handed me a few bottles. "I'll give you three bottles for now. This came straight from Kay. It's no Ruz, but it's one of the best in the markets."

"That's all you'll sell me?"

"What, you need more than that?"

I glanced at Haru and saw that she was still watching me. Better not push my luck. I couldn't let on that I planned to convert my money by selling these Chems. I said nothing and paid Cedric for three bottles.

"Bud, before you go, take a taste." Cedric poured us three small glasses of clear liquid.

"Chems are wicked addictive," Haru said. "You got an addictive personality, detective?"

"No, I don't need a taste," I said. It was disgusting to think of poisoning my body with that toxic waste, unknown effects spiralling out of control in my body, spreading like a disease.

Haru's eyes narrowed. "I thought you wanted these Chems for yourself."

"Sure, I do."

Cedric held up the glass again.

Jesus, and that glass didn't even look clean. Unsteadily, I reached out to take it.

I swallowed the liquid in time with the others. It blistered my mouth, swept down my esophagus and almost peeled off a layer of my stomach lining. I coughed uncontrollably. "Jesus, it would be hard to get addicted to that toxic waste."

Cedric grinned. "Sure it is, bud."

The deep thuds of Cedric's laughter trailing us, we returned to the stairwell. Haru shook her head. "Too many goddamn clowns hanging around this joint. First it was just him. Now there's you, too."

It took about five minutes for it to hit me, but when it did it was quick. While I finished stashing my extra stuff in the vault, under Haru's supervision, the bottles started to clank together as I held them, little tremors running through my muscles. My mouth felt dry. By the time I reached the stairwell my thoughts were humming like music notes, my head buzzing in a night made strange by the unknown chemicals circulating in my bloodstream, delightful chemicals that brought confidence and warmth. With each step I climbed, one of my worries faded. My data eyes and paleness melted away, and I looked good, tall and strong but not like Cedric or those men in the gyms—a superior, modern version of them, clean shaven with none of that ugly muscle. My money problems disappeared: soon I could buy vitamins and Mabelle's coffee again, a gift for Jenny, a new suit. And Jenny, she was probably waiting for me in the diner right now, ready to tell me she was leaving that junkie to come home with me. I lingered on that thought as I pushed my way through the back door of Sally Lane's into the cold.

Shivering, I walked around to the front of Sally Lane's. But as I rounded that corner, things started to feel different, less confident and certain. One lone square of yellow broke up the darkness: the window of Sally Lane's, framed by tattered blue-and-white curtains. Through the glass, Jenny was faintly visible, sipping coffee with one elbow on the counter and her chin resting on her hand, her hair pulled back and her fingernails painted red. She didn't see me. I could sense the warmth of the scene behind that glass. I was only a few feet away from the front door, but something stopped me from going in, and I stood, hesitating, outside the window. My head felt heavy from the unfamiliar drug. The glass on the window, dirty and opaque, made Jenny look vague and distant, her edges fuzzy, as if I saw her from far away. That glass marked the distance between us and made it insurmountable. Those tattered curtains looked like the frame of a watercolour painting, the scene inside pleasing but unreal, stuck in its distant reality of paint strokes and canvas. My confident vision of myself started to dissolve, leaving something ugly in its place, a shivering, naked thing with fragile limbs. Jenny wouldn't want to see that.

I turned my back on the warmth of that yellow light and slunk off into the park, my high now edged with a vague sense of dissatisfaction. The park was abandoned, branches sagging low over the sidewalk, long shadows swaying across the path. The trees rustled with shifting leaves. Dark thoughts filled my head like white noise, blending with the soft sounds of the leaves. I shouldn't be getting involved with Jenny anyways. What had I done, getting entangled with these fanatics? I needed to keep things separate like they should be. Slash and line. Never mix them.

Slash and line. The words became a chorus as I walked, repeating in my head with every step.

Slash and line.

Slash and line.

A wave of anger came over me, anger at the fanatics for getting me involved in all this. This deal with the fanatics was the last dirty thing I'd ever do.

When I reached the edge of the park, my muscles tightened. A man was following me. The faint sound of shoes on pavement came from behind. A quick glance over my shoulder confirmed it. One lone, tall shadow trailed me about twenty feet back.

I altered my course and turned towards the river, towards a path I knew had no surveillance cameras. A reflection in a dead screen offered me another glimpse of my stalker. A stranger. Large, blond, and dishevelled.

I sped up. He sped up too. I turned onto an isolated sidewalk that wound down to the river. An overpass arched ahead, and below it, a dark path. I was carrying the Holt I'd just bought.

The roar of traffic became the sound of rushing water as we reached the river. Hedged off by a half-collapsed fence, a twenty-foot drop led to muddy water with a fast current. I walked under the shadow of the overpass and let it swallow me, then slid into a recessed area behind a pillar. I waited, the Holt in hand. The Chems numbed my fear, and I felt empowered and alive, "slash and line" still thudding in my head.

The steady scratches of his shoes. Then the noise of his breathing filled the underpass. Beside the pillar, a dim outline of a man appeared.

I charged him and smashed him in the jaw with the handle of the Holt. His body slapped against the asphalt and I was on top of him in a second, pressing the gun against his forehead. His jaw had been slashed open. I didn't recognize his face. A tattoo on his arm: a cluster of concentric circles, blue and red. That sunken face, the reek of Chems on his breath—he must be one of them. The fanatics. The ones I was supposed to have nothing to do with.

Slash and line.

Suddenly I hated this man. I pressed the Holt hard into his forehead with a hand that trembled with anger, my fingers ash white. My head crackled with chemicals.

"Who are you working for?" I asked.

No answer but his gasps. Drops of blood and saliva congealed in his blond facial hair. My emotions raced wildly, amplified and warped. I took the barrel from his forehead and smashed his face with the gun.

"Who?" I said. My hand shook like an engine, the gun against his forehead again.

"I'm not the law," he gasped. "I'm another trader."

That confirmed my suspicions. He was talking now, but that didn't matter. He was one of the privacy fanatics, the ones I shouldn't associate with.

I gripped the Holt backwards and brought the handle down onto a finger, crushing the bone.

His yell echoed through the overpass. "I fucking talked!" he said. "I gave you what you wanted!"

That didn't matter. The more I hit him, the less I was like him, one of the privacy fanatics. His eyes bothered me—they reminded me of mine, that pale blue-gray colour. In fact, his whole face looked like mine. I raised the hilt of the gun over his next finger. Metal met bone with another shriek of pain. I raised the gun again, sweat sliding down my forehead.

Raised voices drifted from behind us, and sirens whined in the distance. People were congregating on the path behind us.

I shook with rage. As if from outside my body, suspended from the overpass above, I watched myself stand up. The gun was in my hand. I stood there. His breath, the only sound between us, shuddered and rasped.

The voices behind me grew louder.

Slowly, I put the gun in my pocket and left the overpass, shaking the blood off my knuckles. I made my escape by cutting through the bushes that bordered the water. The river washed the red from my hands.

At home, I went straight into the shower and let hot water wash off the dirt and blood. It should've felt good, but it didn't.

The water seemed to strip off layers of me, the shell of my exterior, leaving something ugly underneath—that shivering, naked thing with fragile limbs, the one Jenny wouldn't want to see.

I got out and quickly put my clothes back on, as if to cover something up. I silenced my thoughts with white noise, letting the soft, empty sounds fill the quiet.

CHAPTER THIRTEEN

A few days later I made my way to Sentrac Square again on my lunch break, Yury plodding beside me. He chattered incessantly, but I barely heard him. It would be a serious violation of data police protocol to do what I was about to do right now.

We arrived at the Square and headed to the isolated area at the back, the same spot where Cedric had approached me. The emerald aura of the Forest shone on our right as we sat down on the fountain. I scanned the fountain, the nearby marble pillar, and the crowd gathered in the distance for watching eyes.

"Why are you so tense right now?" Yury said. As he stared at me, his glasses reflected back in miniature the numbers on the giant clock.

"I know about A. Chawla Consulting."

Still he stared blankly. Foliage flooded the Forest and the light stained his face with green residue. "I don't get it," he said.

Neither did I. Right now I shouldn't even be talking to Yury. I was risking my job. But the fact was, Yury was like a brother to me.

"A shell company under your wife's maiden name," I continued, reading his face. I'd already made my decision that I thought he was innocent, but a little more probing to see his reaction couldn't hurt. No loose ends. "The official company address—your vacation address. The phone number—one of your wife's old numbers. And there's more evidence that points towards you too. You've been helping Donaldson run his laundering network."

He didn't speak.

"I found A. Chawla Consulting when I was investigating Donaldson. It's a fake company he and Sara Figueira—that employee he's sleeping with—used to funnel money together.

But the information for that shell company leads me right to you."

"Frank."

"What?" I said, eyeing the crowd.

"I didn't do this." He stared at me from behind two shiny semicircles, the lenses of his glasses. He looked simple, like a child, all his layers of complexity shaved off: a man, reduced to a very basic thing. On the Forest, leaves waved weakly.

"Are you lying?"

"No, I swear! I'll swear by anything you want. Just pick a thing—pick it, Frank—pick it. Oh God, I'm the fall guy. Anyone can see it, can't they? Right? What kind of a data cop would leave a trail this obvious, right? This is a frame. Why'd you come to me first? You know I'm innocent. You must know."

"Jesus, Yury, it's just—the Optica never lies, that data never lies. And the Optica is telling me that you're the guy. You've got debts. You had to sell Akshara's property, her savings."

By the end of the next minute, I regretted bringing that up. There was something unbearable about the sight of a thirty-four-year-old man weeping.

"Listen, I'm sorry I mentioned that," I said. "I don't like seeing you like this. This whole thing is fucked."

"What's going on?" he said. Images of attractive women swayed on a green background in an ad for Chem Connect on the Forest; the men followed, bright-eyed, with their phones out. They faded into images of green apples dancing ecstatically with the caption, STAPLES AND BASICS.

"What if someone else finds this?" Yury said. "Did you tell Stingsby?"

"No, I didn't tell him, but if it's not you, then he needs to know—"

"No, no, don't tell him, please. No one can know about this until we've got something on the real culprit. They'll lock me up for this." He put his head in his hands and muttered almost incomprehensibly into his fingers. "There are so many things, Frank. So many things. Things I thought about, things I did, didn't do."

"Fuck, Yury, you aren't making sense, and it's scaring me. Look, together we're going to get everything under control again, alright? I agree that the line leading to you was too neat. It does look like a frame to me. No data detective would leave a trail like that."

He gripped my shoulder, his watery eyes wide. "You believe me? Oh God, you have to believe me."

"Yes, I believe you. Based on some investigating I've already done, I've made my decision. I've checked out your data. I've been to your apartment. Everything about it screams that you're broke. And I've seen you interacting with Donaldson. You didn't seem to know him."

"You've been following me? Looking into my data, around my apartment?"

"I needed to know for sure you were innocent. You know I can't stand when things aren't certain. I had to be certain, Yury, I had to be."

He clung to my arm, his fingers clasping my sleeve. "It does-n't matter. Thank you. Thank you. You've gotta help me, help me find whoever's setting me up."

"This puts us both in a lot of risk."

"Yes." His hands went limp and returned to his lap. "Frank, I can't go to jail. Akshara's pregnant. Just over three months. We were just about to start telling people."

"Jesus." A loose assembly of birds gathered near the Forest, then scattered. No wonder she'd refused to have a drink with me the other day. And maybe that was why Yury had been so happy lately at the office.

Yury put his face in his hands. "Why would Donaldson frame me? I don't even know him."

"It might not be Donaldson that framed you. This might be someone else in his laundering ring. He doesn't know you and he'd have no motive to frame you. To clear your name, we need to find out more about the network, find more of the people in it."

"And the exit strategies in the fake bank account? Could you trace how the money went from there to somewhere else?"

"No. It's too well laundered. Tech purchases, liquid assets that are easy to transfer, and other exits through what looks like a massive network of money laundering. These bastards know what they're doing."

Yury stared at his hands. "You think whoever set up this frame is part of something big? That's what we're up against?"

My eyes looked back at me, reflected in Yury's glasses. "It's big," I said.

Since I'd decided to trust Yury and work together with him on this case, I'd have to let him in on my new lead. "I do have one lead to go on. Donaldson's laundering network might involve some of the city's underground drug lords, too. Someone from the networks of privacy fanatics is selling Chems to Donaldson's network."

"How did you find that lead?"

I shifted uncomfortably. "For the time being, that's my business, not yours."

"So what are you thinking then? That finding Donaldson's dealer could help us learn more about his network?"

"If I can find out their identity, I can search their data and try to find the exit points they've been using to get paid out by Donaldson's cartel. The more people we know who've been paid out of this network, the more we'll start to see patterns. That might lead us to others in the network, maybe even the one who's setting you up. If we can find someone who might have a motive to frame you and some data against them, then we might start building a case to save you."

He nodded. He was pale and seemed to shrink like the melting snow behind him. "Tell me what you find. I'll start taking a second look at A. Chawla Consulting. Holy shit, I've gotta clear my name. My kid might be ten before I meet them." Wiping his face with his hands, he hastened back the way we came, ads for the Indigo Palace streaming behind him on every screen he passed.

Part Two: Babel

CHAPTER FOURTEEN

"What happened?" Jenny asked. Her large eyes were unfocused, the lids heavy with sleep.

"You fell asleep," I said. This wasn't the first time she'd drifted off leaning against me. Sometimes we went down to the meadow in the vault and wound up spending time there, talking, smoking, or watching her ancient DVD player. Sometimes she let her guard down and allowed herself to fall asleep with her head on my shoulder or chest. I didn't blame her. There was only so much loneliness a person could take.

"Hm," she said dreamily, but didn't move away. My shoulder and right side were warm with the heat of her body. The smell of her shampoo encircled us.

She glanced at my face and smiled. "You're giving me that look again."

I didn't answer. My pulse beat quickly.

"It's that desperate look you get sometimes," she said. Smiling, she ran a hand over my chest, my shoulder, the back of my neck. Her face was close to mine, her breath warm. But then she withdrew her hand and pulled away. She laughed with nervous excitement.

When I recovered my composure enough to speak, I said, "You're taunting me again."

She just smiled.

"This is hell," I said. "It's been hell every night we spend like this. If you leave Anton—"

"I can't." She stiffened and edged towards the other end of the couch. As she moved her body away, her warmth faded. She buttoned up her jacket and shoved her hands into her pockets.

A machine droned in the background. It was the blue cube, that piece of robotic art built only to float in never-ending, aimless circles. Concealed by a cloud of smoke from the R&M she'd just lit, Jenny busied herself with her possessions. She fiddled with one of the balls from her collection of old sports equipment and started cleaning it with a cloth. Everywhere she went, a cloud of clutter trailed her. In the diner or the vault, she was always surrounded by all that old stuff she collected, by three multi-coloured scarves around her neck, by those strange trinkets she collected on a shelf in the meadow—old-fashioned paper photographs in frames, antique glassware, ceramic tiger figurines. I wished she wouldn't keep all that junk around, cluttering up the space in between us and getting in the way.

"Why can't you just leave him?" I asked. "You're unhappy, anyone can see."

For a minute she remained as she was, still and unmoving. She was about to speak.

"I shouldn't talk about it," she said abruptly.

She withdrew into the things again and started cleaning the ball with redoubled intensity. All those belongings clustered around her like Saturn's rings, ready to shred anyone who got too close. Her core was hidden, buried beneath layers of clutter and lies. I played through a fantasy in my mind: a pile of all that stuff thrown onto a raging fire and melting away, nothing left in the room but the two of us.

Behind us, a makeshift wall hemmed in our clearing, made of a table heaped with silver, a marble bust, and a box of textiles. One of the fabrics had been blown loose by the air from the ventilation system, and now it fluttered back and forth, a transparent gauze suspended between us. Through the gauze her figure was nothing but an outline, but periodically, when the fabric drifted, I saw her clearly.

Jenny saw me looking again and said, "You're still giving me that desperate look."

"It's a pretty desperate thing."

"It wasn't supposed to be like this. It was just supposed to be a trick. To lure you in."

She moved on to counting some of Anton's money, piled up in large stacks beside her. She always helped him with his stash, kept his accounts, counted his money, repaired things, cleaned them. And whenever she held his stuff, her hands moved very slowly.

The fabric shifted again, and the space cleared between us. "If you left him, we could have a better life," I said. "We could get out of here, out of the Border. I could show you a new life in the Core, things you've never—"

"I don't want your money!"

"Jenny, calm down. I just want to help. I want you to be happy."

"Oh yeah? Your last lover, is she the one you helped with your money? And where is she now?"

I said nothing, suddenly short of breath.

"The one you got the illegal surgery for?" she said, her eyes bright with anger. "Did your money help her? Did it?"

Ugly silence grew between us.

I stood up and took off into the maze of piles. I didn't even know where I was going—anywhere I would be alone, far away from Jenny after what she'd just said. Stopping in a clearing, I lit an R&M to calm down, but my hands still shook.

"I'm sorry," she called after me, the anger gone from her voice.

I didn't answer.

In a minute she appeared in the clearing. When she saw my face she said, "Fuck, I really hurt you. I'm sorry." She sighed. "Lemme explain. This stuff about the money, there's a whole history to it. I don't want to feel like I'm in debt to anyone. Not after what happened with Anton."

She started pacing in a small space between a shelf and two piles, and she seemed fixated on the piles, staring, as if an invisible threat lingered amid the clutter. Light came from behind the two towers and cast twin shadows over her. She pointed up at one of the heaps. "That's how much I owe Anton," she said, pointing at the pile. "I owe him so much, it's big enough to be a huge heap like that. That's why I can't leave him."

"What, you owe him money?"

"Not exactly. Maybe."

She turned and pointed at the second pile. "Then there's you. You wanna buy me things too. You want to throw money at everything."

"Does Anton tell you that you owe him? Does he make you do that shit for him all day—clean for him, wait on him?"

"He doesn't ask me. But the code does."

"What's the code?"

"The traders' code. When someone helps you out, you owe them. When someone wrongs you, then you owe them too, just in a different way."

"But—"

"I owe him, Frank. I help him because I've got to. He's gotta work at the diner all day. He never had to work at the diner. Not before. Not before what he did for me. I owe him, see?"

I stared at the space that separated my feet from the edge of the shadow covering Jenny. By my shoe was a hollow semicircle of darkness with thin black lines inside it: the silhouette of a bicycle wheel, lying on top of the pile.

"Three years ago," Jenny said, "me and Anton, we'd been together a year. Everything was new, intense. He'd do anything for me and all that. He was healthy then, and big, like Cedric. Had some money, too. Sentrac money. He was working a pretty good job, owned a place, had investments. But when we got together, he got into Chems, and eventually he got into trading with me and the others. He helped Kay that one time, and then he got hooked on the Ruz—that was the 'gift' she gave him.

"But one day the cops found data on me, see? They had me, for fraudulent transactions with Sentrac money, from when I sold stolen stuff from an armed robbery. I got desperate and I needed Sentrac money, so I converted. Don't tell the others."

"They don't know?"

"No. I might die if they did. Only Anton knows."

I remembered Jenny's flushed face, her inexplicable anger that night in the meadow when she'd first told me about converting and the reasons why people did it. She must've been angry at herself then.

"I was looking at ten years, ten fucking years in prison," she continued. "You know they come down hard on fraud with Sentrac money, on people that don't fit those imaginary patterns they're always looking for. But Anton, he offered a bribe. Two million in Sentrac money. The cop, he was a crooked fucker, and he took it. All of Anton's property, investments, everything he had."

"I would've done the same thing if I were him."

Jenny paused to collect herself, eyes downcast, then took a long breath and continued. "Never tell Anton I told you this. It'd destroy him if he knew. If he knew I told a fucking private eye, at that. His paranoia—it's insane. After the bribe, he fell to pieces. He was scared all the time, terrified Sentrac would come after him. It's not like trading, where we work off the grids. He'd left a trace. And that trace, it was a sliver shoved into his brain just a little deeper every day. He took more and more Ruz. It took over him stronger than ever. He lost his job."

"What happened—it doesn't mean you owe him anything. He made a choice to do what he did. You can still leave him."

She was still looking off into the clutter, as though out of impulse, searching for some vague threat. But the only things out there were the giant heaps of money and things and the shadows they cast on the pavement.

"And on top of that," she said, "the bribe wasn't even enough for the fucker. I had to do something else for him too."

"What?" I dreaded the answer.

"It's not what you think. I had to do something else. But I don't want to talk about it. Now Anton works at the diner every night, flipping burgers, getting high and trying to stay outta jail."

"You don't owe him anything."

Slowly, she emerged from the shadow, but inky globs of it still seemed to cling to her. "You're not a real fucking trader. You don't understand the code. I owe him."

Jenny went back to the diner then, leaving me alone in the vault. Guess she trusted me enough to do that, though the others wouldn't be happy if they saw me here alone. My cigarette had burnt into a stub, so I lit another one immediately. My hands were still unsteady. What Jenny had said about throwing money at things bothered me. In my mind, I saw the smile lines around Celeste's eyes, the night I bought her the red jacket, and her stuff lying abandoned in that shack, covered in softly falling snow.

I wandered over to my stash of Chems, picked up one of the bottles, and held it up to the light. Should I take another shot?

I poured myself a glass and swallowed it.

CHAPTER FIFTEEN

It took some time for me to earn Haru's trust enough for her to let me deal directly with Kay. Meanwhile, Yury hung in the balance, white-faced and drinking heavily, avoiding his wife. Seeing him like that made me drink a few extra gin and tonics myself. He kept busy trying to find whatever he could in the data while I worked on Haru. He was afraid to tell Akshara what was going on, paranoid that the stress would hurt the baby. Akshara had been ill lately, suffering from complications in the pregnancy.

"We won't ever have to tell her," he said once, looking at me with desperate eyes, "because we're going to find the person responsible. Then this will all go away. This is going to go away."

I played nice in front of Haru. She gave me small jobs similar to the first one and I did them right away, no questions asked, no complaints. No loose ends. The jobs I did for her were dirty, but at least they would allow me to help Yury. The scales could still be balanced. Haru wanted a lot of information about the Sentrac security systems, and every time I repeated information back to her, I had no idea what happened to it. She'd listen, then disappear into one of the other basement levels in the bank, three locks sliding into place behind her. She paid me for the work I did and I kept building my stash of Chems by trading with Cedric, though I'd need to deal with Kay if I had any chance of getting a supply big enough to make a dent in my gambling debts. I kept my Chems scattered throughout the vault and made sure the others saw me drinking them, so my stash would look like it was for my own use.

By observing the traders, I learned more about how the privacy fanatics operated, mostly from Jenny. In the vast, intricate circuits of the black market, all kinds of illegal, strange, or forgotten things changed hands every day: Chems, weapons, stolen tech, valuable artwork, clothing, even basic things like food, soap, and repair services. Like Jenny had said, to buy something with real money was to show your support for the project, for the semi-mythical state of independence the privacy fanatics believed they were working towards. It was all bullshit to me, but the fanaticism had a tight grip on them—the culture, the mentality, the quasi-religion of it all. They weren't just in this to do crime. They were a society, and one with some kind of agenda. Tightly knit groups like this one worked together to execute heists and keep property secure in banks across the city, banks I would never see or learn the location of. Trade, an almost sacred practice, was the point of contact between them, the glue that held the underworld together. Discreet methods of transportation had been developed to keep trade moving, shuttling bodies and goods safely between locations.

And finally, Haru agreed to take me to a trade meet with Kay.

Late on a Friday night, the stealth van snaked through the icy back roads of the Border. Chunks of slush clumped on our tinted glass and melted into streams, and snow-covered sidewalks crawled through the edges of our headlights. Printed on the glass of my window, the letters SEILPPUS OTUA LAER obstructed my view. The odd pedestrian drifted by behind the letters, bent under a snow-umbrella. If they had watched us very closely, they would have realized that the traffic sensors weren't responding to our van. When we passed a glass skyscraper I glimpsed our reflection: our windows revealed back seats with no passengers, the outlines of equipment and cargo dimly visible. A stranger sat behind the wheel.

"Frank." Jenny's voice came from the front seat next to Anton. "Look over there. That's where Anton and I live."

A disintegrating low-rise with peeling paint, all the windows dark but one. Some of the windows had been boarded up, and days and weeks of garbage were heaped on the front lawn, waiting to be picked up by a trash bot. But garbage day was on Thursday. Today was Saturday.

"Can't you call the city and get them to repair your trash sensors?" I asked.

"We try. The fuckers never come."

"I can't stand seeing the city do such a shit job. This is supposed to be a smart city."

Jenny laughed. "This is the Border, Frank."

I averted my gaze from the apartment and stared at my hands. Tiny repositories of dirt were beginning to collect under my fingernails. I couldn't get rid of them no matter how hard I scrubbed. That bothered me, so I repeated a thought to calm down.

If I help Yury, I cancel out the rest.

If I help Yury, I cancel out the rest.

If I help Yury, I cancel out the rest.

The air smelled of acid and thickened into a polluted haze as we entered the Stack, the city's industrial district. The densely packed cylinders of an industrial laser crouched behind the window of a factory, SHEET METAL beaming in emerald letters above the window. A hard-working robot shuttled back and forth outside an e-commerce warehouse, its clawed arms full of rainbow cargo boxes, wheels cycling like clockwork.

We turned onto the grounds of a massive factory complex. Holographic diagrams flickered behind grimy windows, blue lines with a thousand parts, guidebooks for construction. Empty of humans, the property bustled with mechanical workers plodding through their slow, efficient existence. A narrow service road led us away from the rest of the grounds and into an abandoned area of the factory complex. The van rolled to a halt in front of an isolated cement warehouse. Stepping outside into pungent air, we approached the building.

Haru knocked on a metal door and it swung open. A woman with a shaved head and a snake tattoo came out. Noise and cigarette smoke poured from the open door behind her. She recognized the others, nodded, and let us in.

We stepped into a pit of heat and flesh, a crowd swarming in air thick with smoke that curled overhead, through the webs of aluminum pipes on the ceiling. I breathed in sweat and acid. The warehouse clamoured with laughter and voices shouting out prices, the noisy skirmishes of barter. This place made me sick, the clutter, the heat, the reek of sweat. A man, shoving towards the crowd, brushed by me and left a sweat stain on my shoulder.

I jerked away from him and withdrew into a hidden empty alcove near the door. With a bottle of sanitizer, I started swabbing down my shoulder, my hands. This place was full of oversized men like Cedric, filthy criminals, all that sweat-stained skin, and they were probably eating meat, too! What was I doing here with these people? What had I become? More sanitizer.

"An uptight, strait-laced fucker," Jenny said, appearing suddenly from the crowd. "That's you, isn't it?"

I quickly hid the sanitizer in my pocket, but it was too late. She ducked down and wiped her palm on the floor, then held that hand up near my face, black filth smeared across it. She was playing another one of her games with me. I wanted to recoil from the dirt, but I didn't want to move away when she was standing this close—unusually close, pressed right against me, her stomach against my waist and her breasts against my chest. I hadn't been with a woman in so long. Her breath fell gently on my face, every dent and line in her lips sharply visible. A thin sheen of sweat shimmered on her forehead. The room was sweltering.

"It's just dirt," she said. "Just think of this place like one of those Gemini games—you like those. You can find that here, that thing you're always looking for. And there's something else you like here. Money. That's what this place is about. Don't give a fuck about anyone else, just get as much dirty money for yourself as you can." She grinned at me, her face flushed, one drop of sweat sliding down her cheek.

She slipped away, leaving me alone in the alcove. I pulled out my flask of Chems and took a long swallow, then lit an R&M and let the burn of the nicotine in my lungs soothe me. This money was dirty, and yet as I scanned the room, with all that merchandise piled on the tables—cigarettes, guns, Chems, jewelry, even everyday stuff like food and clothing—something about this place began to remind me Reginia's, my favourite department store, where I swiped my fingerprint on one scanner after another. I thought of when I'd bought those gloves for Jenny, the way my purchase and the glow of the aerial storefronts had warmed us, and the cold darkness when the storefronts had left.

On a nearby table, a man was selling a watch. I could see myself wearing that. I wandered in his direction.

Swipe.

I handed the man some money in exchange for the watch. It wasn't actually a swipe, but I liked to think of it as one. As promised, the purchase warmed the air. The crowd bothered me less.

There—surely that perfume would be perfect for Jenny.

Swipe.

Swipe.

Swipe.

Swipe.

I felt alive for the first time in a while. The bag I'd brought was overflowing. Trade pulsed through the warehouse like a heartbeat, spreading euphoria with it, running through the hands exchanging goods, through the staggering excess of gold, food, liquor. Money moved swiftly here, like it did in the Indigo Palace.

I shouldered my way to a table heaped with multi-coloured bottles and squeezed into a seat next to Haru. Two women haggled over a gun at a table on my left. A huge man across from me set out his cigarettes in whatever space he could find. His back was thick as a tree trunk, hands smudged with dirt.

Time for commerce.

"How much for 1000 R&Ms?" I said.

"Six hundred."

Swipe. I handed him a brick of gold in exchange for the rectangular cigarette cartons and some change—cash and metal coins, the metal cold when I handed it over, the paper cartons smooth under my fingers when I took the R&Ms. I wanted more.

Three packs of cigarettes were set apart from the rest, VINTAGES scrawled across the package in glimmering gold font. Haru smoked that brand. "What about the Vintages?" I asked.

"You can't afford those."

"How would you know? How much?"

"Five hundred, one pack."

His laugh drowned out the chatter as he watched me pack up my supply of cheap, sad R&Ms. Let him laugh. I'd be smoking those within weeks, after I did a few more jobs for Haru.

A woman handed me a small glass filled with gold liquid. Haru jabbed me in the ribs. "That's Ruz," she said in in a low voice. "Drink it or there'll be a bullet in your head. When someone offers you something at a trade meet, it's rude as hell to refuse."

The liquid gold went down like water. Nothing like the harsh taste of the Chems Cedric gave me. Heat spread outwards from my stomach. In a few minutes another glass arrived. My vision wavered. We drank in unison. Kay must be loaded with money if she could afford this kind of hospitality.

The night rolled on and fragmented into a thousand pieces. The fanatics drank, traded, and most of all, they talked. A thin, middle-aged man beside me told two other men about the day the data police came to arrest his wife. A woman told the story of a trading partner killed by a D72. Two other women started a debate about the latest tactics to avoid data. One of them pulled out a sensor-cloaking device and they argued about its advantages compared to other devices. They fought in raised voices, pointed fingers, and slammed their glasses on the table, but the tension never boiled over—it couldn't, not on a night like this when the air was filled with the sounds of comradery, the bond of a shared enemy, a shared project that united the underworld.

The Ruz hit me hard. It rose up in the body like an orchestra tuning before the music started: first the small disconnected sounds—the twitches in my fingers, my face—then the steady swelling into the thunderous noise of music, into my vibrating jaw and the hammering in every distended vein under my skin. Everything that moved bled into a stream. Blue trails shadowed two pairs of hands, shadowed the money and the jewelry they were exchanging, desire spilling from them like fountains.

No wonder Donaldson always had that fucking jack-o'-lantern smile on his face.

Moments flooded by as sensations fell upon me in layers. A man hollered for a better price near my right ear. Someone passed me a tray of food and I picked up some unknown chocolate thing and ate it. It better have been vegan.

I needed to find Kay. I was here to help Yury—I had to remember that. I made my way unsteadily through the crowd, an arm jabbing my ribs, flesh jostling on all sides. And then, in the narrow space between two bodies ahead, a familiar figure emerged, half-hidden by the limbs, shoulders, and faces crowding between us. The smooth half-oval of her face seemed to hover there, disembodied. Her one visible eye, cold and blue gray, was fixed on me.

I shouted over the noise. "Can I have a word with you tonight? I'm looking for some of your products. Got a few questions about them too."

The space between us cleared, and Kay came into view, her copper freckles imprinted on red, flushed cheeks. Her skin and eyes shone with the Chems coursing through her, and blotches showed on her neck. And yet, the glow of the Chems only made her look more elevated, more composed. The neat arches of her eyebrows, the elegant line of her shoulders and neck, the two identical red walls of hair hanging over her shoulders—all of it spoke of order and neatness. There was chaos in this vault, in the seething hell of bodies and sweat and smoke, but she moved through it effortlessly. She was the gravitational centre of this universe. A universe of mess and sweat and dirt.

"Meet me in the back room near the entrance. Bring your money," she said. She turned and disappeared into the crowd, tattoos shining on her upper back, framed by a deep V-shape of black velvet, the back of her dress.

Someone handed me another glass. More acid slid down and I vibrated steadily. I was a hawk watching the scene unfold from the ceiling, perched in the overhead beams. Blood hammered in my veins.

The roar of voices faded as I headed to the front room to meet Kay and shut the door behind me. There was sudden quiet. A small, hot space with stale and heavy air.

"Sit," Kay said, gesturing to the chair across from her. She was lounging behind a table holding a Vintage in one hand. Her image floated before me, the outline of her black dress flickering, all her edges blurred except her gold jewelry, still sharp as razors.

Instinctively, my eyes checked the chair for dirt and stains. A small trail of cigarette ash marred the seat of the chair. I brushed it aside with my sleeve before I sat down.

Adrenaline began to calm the roaring chaos of sensations and sharpen my focus. I could think again, though sluggishly. I needed to ask my questions quick, before my window of opportunity closed.

"Tell me more about Ruz," I said. "Any way I can get more of it from you?"

She smiled calmly. "I want to know more about you instead." Her words seemed to float between us, each sound perfectly formed.

"There's not a lot to know. I'm a simple person."

She folded her hands on her lap with unnerving neatness. On her forearm was a tattoo with straight lines that intersected at neat, geometric angles. The image reminded me of a Sentrac spreadsheet.

"We're not that different, are we?" she asked.

"Something tells me we are."

"You like things to be just right, don't you? I saw you brush away that dirt when you came in. You like things neat. So do I."

"That sounds like me, but not like you. That doesn't seem like something traders like."

"Why?"

"Just seems like you're in love with all this chaos. This anarchy."

"I hope you'll come to see things differently, when you learn more about us." She paused and extinguished her cigarette. "Why do you want Chems?"

"Why do you think?" I shifted uncomfortably in my seat. Her eyes, green with swollen black pupils, watched my expression closely.

The room pulsed with heat. A drop of sweat dripped down Kay's collarbone and ran down the skin between her breasts. There were tiny particles of food there, scattered on her chest and on the low neckline of her dress, the remnants of whatever she'd eaten earlier tonight. How strange to see those crumbs mar her perfect appearance, the hair sleek with every strand in place, the pink lipstick without the slightest smudge, the clean, long rectangles of her fingernails. But even with those crumbs on her chest, I couldn't look away.

"It's rude to stare," she said.

I needed to stay on track. "Look, can I get my hands on any Ruz or not?"

"No. Ruz takes incredibly rare materials to produce. I only serve it in house, as you've seen."

"You give it to Anton. I saw you going to trade with him, that first night I saw you. I saw the bottles he was putting away."

"He's the only one. There's a reason, but it's a story you don't need to hear."

"You sure no one else can get their hands on it?"

"Positively. Now let's start dealing."

I hesitated. Just a little bit more of a push. "A person could make a lot of money selling that Ruz to Sentrac money bigwigs above ground."

She said nothing. She didn't look at me, turning instead to her bottle of Ruz and pouring herself another shot. But I had seen it. There was something in the tightly drawn muscles of her face, in the slight narrowing of her eyes—some thought or feeling that she didn't want me to see.

Kay swallowed another glass of Ruz, and in a few seconds she'd recovered her composure and smiled again, flashing her straight, white teeth. "I don't need to tell you what will happen to you if you try to convert your money," she said calmly. "Someone's already told you about the penalties for converting. I can tell."

"They're pretty strict penalties for such a small thing. Just converting one kind of money to another."

"It's anything but a small thing, you see. Do you know how the markets got started? What they mean?"

"It's just an easy way to do crime. Let's not get confused here—you're all criminals. You might say this means something more, but at the end of the day it comes down to crime."

"And you? Are you not a criminal yourself?"

"Never mind me," I snapped.

She held a shot glass of Ruz delicately between her thumb and one long, slender finger. Her eyes shone with concentration as she spoke carefully and weighed every word. "When this city became a data city, the underground markets started. At first, it was like you said—people searching for a way to do crime in a digital world. But over time, it became more than that. A culture rose up. Beliefs. We started trading things beyond drugs and weapons. We started building towards our own independent system."

"Not much of a system. Now the city of sensors up there, in the real world—*that* is a system."

"We live life like it used to be, pre-data. The data revolution empowered corporations. They're the ones who hold huge amounts of data. Phone companies, search engines, banks. They semi-privatized the police, because the police couldn't operate half as efficiently without getting their hands on that data. So now, we have hybrids like you. The corporate police."

"I see you know who I am."

"So when we meet down here, when we drink together, trade together, socialize as we do, we're absenting ourselves. We're building strength and we're building numbers. We believe in real money, real things. The rest of you can keep your holograms, your digi-plants, your make-believe money."

"You know how many guns it takes to take care of your money when it's all physical? When someone can just pick it up and take it? When you've got no real banks?"

She lit another cigarette without answering. She ran her fingers idly over the bare skin of her neck and collarbone, drawing my eyes there again. Behind her shoulder, the white paint on the wall was marred by long, gray streaks that extended downwards like fingers from where the wall met the ceiling. A water stain. The paint in the discoloured areas was rough and uneven, morphed by the gathering dampness that was probably leaking mould into the air we were breathing.

"What about your next best product, then?" I asked, forcing myself to ignore both the stain and Kay's attractive figure. "Your next best Chem. I've got eight thousand. How much will that get me?"

"About three crates full of Chem-7."

I picked up the bag I'd brought and dumped out my gold on the table between us. Her gaze flicked over the money, then back to me.

"That's a lot of Chems," she said. "You planning to drink all that yourself?"

"Eventually."

"I'll be watching you. To make sure." She gathered up the money I'd brought and put it in her own bag. "On your way out, there'll be three crates waiting for you."

Swipe.

Kay extinguished her Vintage. Her lips glistened with the gold acid from her last drink. Her entire body vibrated; her teeth chattered. My eyes caught, for the first time tonight, on a tattoo on her upper arm: a cluster of concentric circles. The same one I'd seen on the man who'd shadowed me in the street.

My gaze jumped from Kay to the water stain behind her. I could almost smell the mould leaking out into the air around us. Time to get out of here.

"Thanks," I said. "I like you. You're rational. And you're competent as hell. We'll deal again sometime."

I stumbled back to the main room. A few drunks were sprawled around, one passed out with his head on the table, another in the corner. I looked at the neck of the man on the table. He had the same tattoo as the one on Kay's arm. So did the man in the corner.

I found the others, and it was a quiet drive back. My head ached steadily as the Ruz faded into a nasty hangover. Cedric sat in the back polishing his K-Lode, a compact automatic, and Jenny fell asleep, her cheek against the window, cushioned on Anton's jacket.

"Oh, and by the way, detective," Haru said, "don't get any fucking ideas into your head now that you got those Chems. Death's the price for converting any of Kay's products into Sentrac money."

"Sure it is," I said. There was a hell of a lot of big talk about that around these parts, and yet I knew for a fact that somebody, somewhere, was doing it.

"Don't believe me, huh? Then you're a damn fool. Kay killed her own lover because he converted. She'd been with him five years. Gave him access to the Ruz, shared it with him. But he got into some Sentrac money troubles. Had some debts. So he converted and she killed him. The story's infamous in the markets. She made 'im into an example. For her, its principle over anything. There's no one down here who believes more in the importance of independence than she does."

"When did she kill him?"

"Long time ago. Four years or so."

Too long ago for him to be Donaldson's present dealer. I recalled the strange expression on Kay's face when I'd asked her about converting, the one she'd tried to hide from me. I hadn't been able to place it at the time, but now I realized that it may well have been sadness. What I'd asked her had reminded her of that old lover.

This lead was taking me nowhere.

Intuition told me that Kay was too principled to be involved in this mess. I fixed my eye on Anton in the front seat, driving the van. He was the only other one who had access to Ruz, and when I saw him packing away those crates from Kay they'd looked pretty big, even for an addict. It might be time to start looking into a new lead.

CHAPTER SIXTEEN

"I haven't made much progress on that last lead."

Yury's fist came down hard on my coffee table, sending waves of gin and tonic slopping over the sides of his glass. "I'm fucking counting on you, Frank! Who knows how long we have till someone else finds this!" He swallowed the rest of his drink, the fifth one he'd had since he got to my apartment half an hour ago. Wrinkles fanned out across the fabric of his shirt, and the muscles in his face were drawn tight, his eyes red and narrow.

"Just be patient, Yury. You know I won't stop until we solve this—until this investigation is perfect, fucking perfect. And do you think I like seeing this happen to you?"

"Can't you at least tell me what went wrong?"

"I tried to get information out of the suspect, but she didn't reveal anything. I couldn't find out her real name and identity, so I couldn't look into her data."

"Have her followed then!"

"Thing is, I suspect she might not be the one trafficking Chems."

"Why?"

"I can't tell you much about it, but I have my reasons."

While he poured himself another drink, his face flushed from the liquor, I stood up and paced my apartment. In the corner of my living room, a holographic plant fluttered in a fake wind as the light from my windows dwindled steadily. Chill seeped through the glass.

"What about your end?" I asked. "You find anything new looking into A. Chawla Consulting?"

"No. I've been working on it, working on it all the goddamn time, but there's nothing concrete."

Sipping my gin and tonic, I stood staring out glass walls at a coral reef of electric lights. Green apples danced on the Forest.

When I turned around again, Yury's face was in his hands. "I barely sleep lately, Frank, I barely sleep—there's just so much data to get through. If we could just find this person, whoever's trafficking Chems to Donaldson, or any more of the criminals in this laundering ring—any of them—then we'd have a better chance—"

"Don't worry, I've got this. I won't let any lead go uninvestigated. And I might have one other lead for the Chem dealer."

"Who?"

"There's one other suspect I know has access to this special Chem that Donaldson has. And this new guy—he's sketchy as hell. I'm going to start asking some questions."

"How do you know about—"

"Don't ask about that." My shoulders tensed. "I've got everything under control, alright? I'm just going to some extra lengths on the side to solve this case—all done with good intentions—I'm doing this to help you, dammit." He hadn't asked me to explain myself, but I still felt like I needed to for some reason.

"What are you so defensive about, Frank?" Yury took anxious sips of his drink. His speech was starting to slur. "Sometimes I don't know about you. I just don't know."

"What are you talking about?"

"Maybe, you, you're . . ."

"What?"

"Maybe you're corrupt."

I stood where I was, my muscles tight again. On a screen behind Yury's head, a live Gemini match was playing, and the numbers spun in torrents, erratic and irregular.

"You've got this information out of nowhere, all this knowledge, and then—and then you've got all this new shit in your apartment, like this liquor that we're drinking—well, you didn't pay for any of it. None of it's in your Sentrac account, none of it."

The Gemini board whirled through the next set of data. The numbers spiraled but there were too many possibilities to calculate, too many variations. When I sat down across from him, I moved slowly and carefully.

"You looked into my data?" I said quietly.

He swayed a bit, drinking more, "That's right."

"You fucking jackass!" Suddenly I was standing again, towering high above him, his figure small below me. Somewhere in the distance, the Forest blazed as light burst from a fresh ad, and a wave of green washed over us, staining us the colour of plant-life.

"Alright!" Yury said, cowering and shrinking into the sofa. He seemed to regret what he'd just blurted out. "Alright. I know you're not corrupt. I had my suspicions for a little while before, but now I know you're not."

"Unbelievable." The second I had paid my gambling debts I was getting myself out of this mess.

"I just wanted to make sure I could trust you, right? So I looked through your data a bit—just a bit. But I know you wouldn't help me like this if you were corrupt. You wouldn't care enough about the truth, about finding who really did this."

"That's right, I'm helping you because I still care about what's right, for God's sake! Yury, you don't understand—you don't understand everything that's happened to me." I broke off. Suddenly I wanted to tell him—to tell anyone, for God's sake, just to get it off my chest—about everything that had happened, about Celeste, the pressure of the gambling debts that followed, and then Jenny, and how she was the only thing that had seemed real since that night by the river, everything else like a dull dream.

Yury stared at me with those big, childish eyes. Could he be trusted?

But the risks were too high. I closed myself off like shutters drawn tight over a window. "Never mind, Yury."

We sat in silence.

"Just know," I said, "I've been trying to do what's right. I've been fucking trying." I couldn't stop talking, explaining myself over and over. I reached into a drawer and pulled out a bunch of crumpled sheets filled with the straight lines and neat angles of graphs. I'd burned the sensitive charts with my secret decisions, but I'd kept the charts for some of my other decisions. "Look at all these decisions. I weighed the options, made the calculations. The decisions I made make sense." I threw the papers onto the table, where they lay crumpled and limp, like the leaves of a dead plant.

Yury stared at me, clearly unnerved by my cryptic comments. He fiddled with his things on the coffee table, adjusting his phone so that it lay in perfect geometrical parallel with his tablet beside it, his fingers clasping tightly to control their placement. "I'm sorry, Frank, I'm sorry I ever suspected you. It's fine—it's all fine, really. We'll get this back under control."

"That's right. That's what I do best: keep things under control. Just give me some time to look into this next lead."

CHAPTER SEVENTEEN

After that conversation with Yury, I began to stalk Anton. A look into his data yielded nothing concrete, no obvious signs of payouts from Donaldson's network. I'd have to catch him in the act. I lurked, spied, and eavesdropped. And not just around the bank. I followed him to and from Sally Lane's, our twin shadows flickering on brick walls in the back roads of the Border. I followed him to sim sports bars, to grocery stores, to his apartment, where, behind the closed blinds on the bedroom window, he did God knows what with Jenny. After I saw that I slunk back to the Border, drinking Chem-7 until the early morning. Most nights got me nowhere.

One evening, Haru asked me to meet her in the basement of Randy Spillane's strip joint, a hotspot for traders. The bouncer seemed to know me when I walked up; he let me in with a silent nod. Clustered around tables, shadowy figures exchanged cash for weapons, stolen goods, pieces of paper, and bottles with no labels. A topless woman swayed on the stage at the back wall.

Haru awaited me in a bare, smoke-filled room with a red velvet couch. Wallpaper peeled off the back wall, revealing dirty cement behind it.

"You get the data?" she asked bluntly.

"Have I ever done anything but carry out your missions perfectly?" I said, taking a seat. "You know how I operate."

Her face, hazy behind the wall of smoke, showed no expression.

"The last time Heltatech updated the system was a couple weeks ago. December 16," I said.

"Frequency of updates?"

"Monthly. Next one's scheduled for January 16."

Haru asked all kinds of questions about the security updates. She absorbed the information silently, like a machine, without writing anything down.

"You ever going to tell me why you need all this?" I asked.

"That's our business."

When I got back to the main room, I spotted Anton at the back, one skinny elbow on the bar in front of the stage and a glass of familiar gold liquid in his hand. The stripper was peeling off her G-string right in front of him, but he paid her no attention, his eyes fixed on his Ruz.

Following him hadn't done me any good so far. It was time to take a more direct approach. I crossed the room and took a seat next to him.

His blood-shot eyes regarded me silently. I braced myself for more of his bullshit, but I quickly realized none was coming. He grinned, his teeth phantom-like in the blue neon, and surprisingly, his eyes were glazed with something that looked like happiness.

Could I have stumbled upon so rare a sight as a happy Anton? Few cracks ever formed in the impenetrable exterior of his gloomy frowns, his shroud of cigarette smoke and annoyance, those stone-cold eyes and hunched shoulders set like a gargoyle's. On the counter in front of him, a large stack of gold gleamed in the blue light. Maybe he'd pulled off a big heist tonight.

I pointed at the money. "Tonight a nice night for you or what?"

He smiled again, the expression strange on his narrow, skeletal face. Purple blotches showed on his neck. "Maybe." He laughed and slapped me on the shoulder. "Shit, Frank, we friends now? We friends?"

He was high out of his mind. Anton in a good mood reminded me of an angry gorilla wearing a shirt with a happy face on it—it was just too incongruous.

"Fuck," he said, "you and me, you and me, right? We haven't always been on the best terms, but we're good, right? Am I right?" He spoke quickly, words spilling out of his mouth like liquid.

"Sure we are," I said smoothly. Time to take advantage of his mood. I nodded in the direction of his glass. "That Ruz there, it's some pretty nice stuff. Never been as high as I was that night at Kay's."

"You were fucking lucky to get a taste of it."

"Would you sell some to me?"

Anton let out a high-pitched laugh like a banshee's. "No one sells Ruz."

I looked away from him and pretended to watch the stripper. The floor vibrated from the bass. After a while I said carefully, "Listen, I know you love all this real money stuff, but don't you ever wonder what it would be like to have Sentrac money? Don't you ever want some?"

Anton stared off into the distance, absent-mindedly swishing the liquid around in his glass. The mood shifted, darkened. He seemed to forget my presence. I'd never seen him look so lost. I recalled what Jenny had told me about the life he used to have, his past as a wealthy professional. It was just damn strange to imagine him wearing a suit to work in the Core, sipping Mabelle's at his desk, then coming home to his clean, modern apartment.

Anton didn't seem to remember that I'd even asked him a question. He was still looking ahead with those eyes fogged up like dirty glass. I wondered what went on in that Ruz-addled head, day in and day out. Were the highs of Chems and big heists enough to keep him going, to blind him to what he'd become?

"You know," I said, "you say no one sells Ruz, but it's funny—I've heard of Chems getting sold above ground. Some of the Sentrac money bigwigs have a hell of a weakness for them."

Anton's eyes, less jubilant now, flicked slowly back to mine. His face was still glazed with stupid happiness, but now his shoulders hunched a bit, a defensive posture. "What're you doing, buddy?" he said slowly.

Silence spread between us. Anton remained in that hunched posture, still and unmoving. A gap between songs left the room uncomfortably quiet.

"Don't nose around my business any fucking more," he said.

CHAPTER EIGHTEEN

I spent more time in the markets. Since I was broke I bought almost everything illegally. Doing jobs for Haru earned me cash. I traded. Saved up Chems. Late on the cold nights of January, I visited the darkest corners of the city: the basement at Randy Spillane's strip joint, the shadowy back rooms of bars and clubs, a run-down apartment building next to the train tracks crowded with skinny, strung-out traders who swallowed Chems like water. We travelled secretly; we knew the tech and the routes we needed to avoid data; we melted into the city and became a part of it, its second bloodline with a different rhythm than the pulse of Sentrac money. There were no phones. No tablets. Just names, faces, and an iron code of conduct that no one had ever written down but no one ever forgot. Violence was common. Your bank might get robbed any day of the week, and you might need to kill to defend it. Relations between the traders were structured by an unspoken hierarchy. I saw only the tiny corners of the markets; there were bigger figures out there, criminals much larger than Kay and Haru, but they were spectres I would never touch or see, shadowy figures that hovered between legend and reality. And every face I met held a sense of purpose, a quasi-religious conviction that change would eventually shake the city, that privacy, anonymity, and what they saw as freedom would return. They talked a lot about moving forwards, about bringing changes, but it seemed to me they wanted to go back- wards in time, back to medieval blood feuds, mob justice, and rigid hierarchy. And in those dark rooms and hidden corners, even I sometimes felt the thrill of living an invisible life with no one was watching, the guilty pleasure of complete, total privacy.

As December crawled by, ice crusting over the glass walls of my apartment, I almost welcomed loitering around Sally Lane's to spy on Anton. I had no money for the Indigo Palace. My apartment was cold and empty. But inside the bank it was warm, red, full of things, and isolated from the outside. And Jenny was there. I found her in Sally Lane's, and when she wasn't busy she'd take me down to the meadow in the back of the vault. She kept a lot of her things there in that clearing, including some archaic machine she'd refurbished. Sitting on the decaying couch, we passed long nights drinking and staring at the flickering faces of old televisions, running media on old systems she'd restored—a DVD player, even. We watched footage from the old games people used to play before sim sports, while the piles of things in the vault towered over our heads.

"You're so pale," she said one night, running a hand over my cheek. "And skinny. You been drinking a lot of Chems? They make you lose weight."

"I try to stay away from them as much as I can. Just—" I hesitated. Could I open up to her? "Just, let's say I've been having a bit of a difficult time with all this. With working for all of you."

"Identity crisis?"

"You know how I used to see things. Divided into two camps. Maclean taught me that."

"Maybe she was wrong."

"I mean, where am I now? Maybe I'm in the mud with the rest of the criminals, but what about the parts of me that are still good? I'm helping my friend, Jenny. I'm doing it because it's right, not because it'll benefit me in any way."

Jenny didn't answer. The video we were watching ended, and the television went dead. The mechanical light extinguished, she became invisible except for the red coal of her R&M, and the occasional curl of smoke lucky enough escape the dark.

Time passed. And all the while I lurked, spied, and eavesdropped, hoping to learn something about Anton. And then one night, I saw something.

Jenny had left me alone in the vault—she wasn't supposed to, but she sometimes did anyways if she had to run up to the diner to take care of something—and I was raiding one of my extra stashes of Chems. At the sound of bottles clanking in the distance, I froze, careful to make no sound.

More glass chimed. Someone was moving around in the clearing next to me, separated from my own area by a shelf and a wooden frame leaning against box. Through a narrow crack between the shelf and the frame, the back of Anton's head came into view. The nodes of his spine stuck out in his emaciated neck as he stooped down and placed a duffel bag and a crate on the floor, next to a few other bottles. He kept his Ruz in that clearing. The crate he'd put down was made of yellow plastic—the same crate he brought with him when Kay came to trade. He must've just met with her.

Anton paused. He looked to his right, then his left, standing up to scan the pathway. Then he turned around and looked straight at me.

I forced myself to remain motionless. Movement would give me away. The shadow of the bookshelf behind me should hide me. With luck, Anton would see nothing but darkness through that crack.

His eyes focused intently in my direction. He took a few steps forward. I shifted my hand towards my waist where I kept the Holt. A few feet away, he stopped, still staring. A strange expression came over his face: his eyes darkened, and his movements became awkward, every gesture self-conscious as he crossed his arms, leaned his weight onto one foot. He ran a hand over his jaw, feeling the patchy, scraggly stubble there as though noticing for the first time that he hadn't shaved in days. Then it clicked in my mind. He wasn't looking at me. The wooden frame in front of me had a mirror on the other side.

Anton's eyes narrowed, still sharp with an unreadable emotion. What went on in his head, at moments like this? What did he think when he looked at himself in the mirror? When he saw the rail-thin neck with veins running down it, the skin with the rough, weathered texture of old parchment, the eyes hidden by the deep shadows of his eye sockets? Still peering at his reflection, Anton pulled down the collar of his shirt just far enough to reveal his collarbone. It was grotesque, the bone protruding sharply from the deep recesses of his chest and neck. It felt like he was looking right at me. Just stay still, I told myself. His hand tracked to the middle of his white shirt, where a cluster of holes had formed in the threadbare fabric. And then his look changed, a new emotion flashing across his face. This one I could read. Anger.

He turned his back, lit an R&M, and sat on the floor with his arms around his knees. Smoking silently, he remained there for long minutes. Finally he extinguished his cigarette, glanced around a few more times, and turned back to the crate. He took a few bottles out and separated them from the rest, leaving them with the rest of his Ruz. Then he opened the duffel bag and shoved it full of bottles.

Wiry muscles straining in one arm, he threw the duffel bag over his shoulder and headed for the exit. I followed. Shelves and piles of boxes kept me hidden, and snatches of Anton's white T-shirt flashed through the cracks in the junk between us. After the door to the vault shut behind him, I opened it silently and slipped out.

The walk through the Border was wet. We'd had a patch of warm weather, and sheets of half-frozen rain all but obscured the streetlights, blurring the lines of Anton's silhouette ahead. His shoes were partly submerged by the water rushing along the side-walk towards the gutter. As the rain fell, it seemed to dissolve his figure into its currents, carrying him bit by bit into the sewers. His face turned sideways and caught the light, distorted by a streetlamp striking him at a long diagonal angle, and in that strange light his profile struck me: it reminded me of my own face. Streams of water ran off the ends of his hair and dripped down his cheeks.

When we arrived at Anton's apartment, he went inside and I crept around the back. Dull light shone through a first-floor window. Faded red curtains had been drawn across it, but a narrow crack ran down the middle, revealing their kitchen with dirty orange tiles on the wall. I stood a safe distance away and watched as Anton came into the kitchen. He put the duffel bag down on the table, then opened one of the cupboards and pulled out a cardboard box. He began pulling bottles out of the box.

A familiar orange stripe. The label read: IRON ENERGY DRINK.

Anton pulled a funnel from a drawer and placed it on top of one of the IRON bottles. And then, sure enough, he took a bottle of Ruz out of the duffel bag and poured it into the funnel.

It was him.

The rain hissed as it hit the pavement, and in the distance the electric signs of the Border blinked through the misty air. The city suddenly felt full of energy and potential. This was what I'd been searching for.

CHAPTER NINETEEN

I took the long road home, winding through the Border. The rain had slowed and frozen into wet snow, the odd flake falling and melting when it touched the cement. Fifty-Seventh Avenue was mostly empty, but unlike in the Core, even this late at night a few stragglers loitered in the streets. A man wandered by on my left, his hands gesturing to the shelves hanging from his neck, cluttered with plastic objects that wriggled and twitched like amoebas, like simple living things.

"Plastics," he announced solemnly. "Buy them. Put them on your shelf. Watch them. Leave them behind you."

In the yellow ring of the next streetlamp lay the glass remains of a broken observatory. Children scurried in and out of the empty shell, pretending that it was whole, still floating above the city and filled with tourists. Blue neon streaked along a jagged glass edge.

"Careful, don't play there," I called. Startled, they dispersed. It was too late for kids to be on the street.

On my left was a food stall plastered with two-dimensional images of French fries and sushi. A ring of customers stood with their backs to me. One of them turned around, and a hooded figure emerged from the group. A female figure with legs shuffling in baggy winter pants. Haru.

"Where are you coming from?" Haru asked in a quiet voice. With expert precision, her eyes swept over the streets, the nearby crowd, the traffic lights.

"Is that your business? I'm heading home from a friend's place."

Haru studied my expression, reading me to see if I was lying.

Abruptly, her eyes fixed on something behind me. She changed, tightening into a knot of tension.

"Walk with me and don't look over your shoulder," she said quietly. "You're being followed."

We turned into a narrow alley. Haru knew the streets even better than me—all the hidden walkways, the data-free zones. Suddenly we were moving faster, metal grates flying by under our feet. I heard it now too: the steps, gaining ground behind us. Muffled sounds trailed us through the alley. The awareness of a stalker possessed me.

Knocked to the ground by Haru—her strength astonishing—I hit the dirt behind a metal garbage bin. The skin on my forearms ripped against gum-covered pavement. Haru threw herself down beside me and fired around the edge of the metal, aiming at the man who'd followed us. The crack of the gunshot gave way to silence. There was no return fire.

Television sounds drifted from a window. Several buildings down, a washing machine churned. And somewhere beyond our metal shield, a man groaned.

Haru leapt up and disappeared, and I struggled to my feet to follow, blood leaking from my scraped forearms. A man lay slumped against the wall, breathing heavily with a gunshot wound in his thigh. Haru knelt over his body, yanked up his sleeve and exposed a tattoo on his forearm: a cluster of concentric circles, the outermost rings blue, the innermost red. When she saw the tattoo, her shoulders relaxed visibly.

"Hey!" A voice echoed from the end of the street. Three silhouettes appeared there, obscured by layers of exhaust.

Then Haru was grabbing me and sweeping me through the streets, sliding along the shadowy edges of the back roads. We passed brick walls, heaps of garbage, shredded rubber tires, doors with steel cages. Sounds gathered behind us where we'd left the body, but the darkness sheltered us.

We reached another alley and I followed Haru up a fire escape. At the top of the third storey, the stairwell broke off, replaced by steel supports propping up a decaying balcony two storeys above. She scaled the supports within seconds and vanished onto the balcony. I stared up at the mess of steel angles and poles sprawling in all directions. Sirens cycled in the distance.

"Get your ass up here," Haru whispered, the circle of her hood poking out over the balcony.

I began the climb. Freezing metal burned my hands. Snow fell steadily and melted on my jacket. It took me much longer than Haru to climb up. Her hand heaved me over the top, and she led me into an apartment.

"You better get in fucking shape," she said. "Guess your vitamins don't help you build any muscle. I climb up here all the time. Whenever I need to make a quiet entry. Front of this building's on a busy street."

We stepped into a kitchen with cracked green and white tiles. In a corner above a broken coffeemaker, a spider flexed its legs, and a refrigerator hummed in the background. Haru drew the blinds, shutting out the wintry light, and poured us full glasses of vodka. The apartment was small, and through a doorway I saw the corner of an unmade bed. Lines of lean muscle jumped to define Haru's narrow frame when she took off her jacket. Her hair fell onto her shoulders, the ends splayed out in a web of criss-crossed lines.

"You aren't worried about the cops finding that guy you shot?" I said.

"Him? He'd never fucking talk. He's not someone we need to worry about. I was worried at first, when I didn't know who he was."

"Right. You're not worried about him because he's just one of Kay's pawns."

If she was surprised at what I knew, she didn't show it. She lifted her drink to her lips and I did the same, mirroring her. Below my glass, a circular stain was forming, the newest addition to the army of rings on her tabletop.

"Kay and all her people have that tattoo," I said. "I saw it myself. And this isn't the first one she sent after me. I had one of hers following me last month too."

"Well aren't you a clever fucking detective."

"I think it's time I got a bit more information."

"Oh, is that what you think?"

She stood up, and when she peered through a crack in the blinds I glimpsed dirty windows across the alley, balconies with underwear flapping on strings. A sliver of light darted through the crack and fell on the tabletop. Instinctively, I moved my chair back an inch to remain in the dark. Screeching sirens faded into the distance.

"That's the second time I've caught Kay having me followed," I said. "Why would she bother to make me her business? Aren't I just some lackey getting you a bit of data?"

She didn't answer, still facing the window.

"I told you before, I think you need me for something big. And it seems like Kay might be in on it too. Least she sees me as important enough to keep tabs on me."

"Watch your fucking ego. Maybe you're not as important as you think."

"I'm not stupid enough to believe that."

There was a long silence.

Finally, Haru turned around to face me. "I tell you, Frank. One day it's going to come."

"What?"

She sat down again, drained the rest of her drink, and poured us more. "Change. The end of Sentrac. The start of something new."

Why had her mind gone there now? "Is this more about the independent economy you privacy lovers think you're building?"

"Jenny tell you about that?"

"Everybody yaps about it constantly. You can't spend two minutes with you people without hearing about it." I paused. "You pick a funny time to bring that up, though. Does your crazy plan for change have something to do with me? You saying I'm going to be involved in this? Because I didn't sign up for that."

Haru watched me for a while, then laughed, her muscular shoulders shaking. "You still don't get it, do you? What's going on. Aren't you the big man with all the data in the world? With those fucking eyes of yours? And yet, you can't figure this out."

"My eyes see plenty."

"Maybe you ain't as good a detective as you think. You don't know anything about what's going on."

She swallowed the rest of her drink and went to bed. That night, I slept on a blanket on the floor, half-drunk. It would be safer to leave in the morning, the police presence thinner.

CHAPTER TWENTY

Two days later Yury and I met at my apartment. While he played with his phone, over his shoulder I saw a barrage of ads for baby products: headbands with bows, pink jumpers, and stuffed animals.

"That's right," he said, smiling when he saw me looking. "It's a girl. The ads for baby girl stuff started coming almost the moment we found out."

I congratulated him but he didn't hear me, his gaze distant, captivated by the phone. The ads scrolled and scrolled, endless baby products tumbling down the screen. Lately, while we worked, Yury would suddenly get up and leave to call Akshara and check on her. When he talked to her his voice got an octave higher, and he spoke softly and quietly, as though nothing was wrong. How long he could keep up this façade?

Yury powered down the phone and tugged anxiously on the edge of his left sleeve, his forehead creased. "Please tell me you've got something new." His statement sounded almost like a plea.

Sipping a gin and tonic, I leaned back against the couch and grinned at him. "Big news, Yury. I've got him. The Ruz dealer."

His eyes widened, and his back straightened as he sat up taller, listening. I took a moment to enjoy the suspense and bask a bit in my victory. I'd had too few victories lately.

"Well?" he demanded. "Tell me about it!"

I took my time. Yury and I fell into a familiar dynamic. He waited eagerly for me to tell him the news I'd found, just like I had when we busted through the toughest parts of the cases we'd worked together. Yury usually had a hint of admiration in his face whenever he waited for me to break the news. The guy had talent, and plenty of it, but he stuck to the data, and sometimes that wasn't enough.

"What did I tell you about no loose ends, Yury? Stingsby says I'm a perfectionist but this is just being a good cop. Let me tell it from the beginning. First, I did some field work. I caught the guy in a bar when he was in a good mood, high and with his guard down. So I saw my chance. You know I'm always good at spotting opportunities, Yury."

"Get to the point, Frank! This is my life we're talking about."

"Next, I pressured him. Got him into a corner. Sure enough, he got defensive when I mentioned the possibility of selling Ruz. His face had guilt written all over it."

"And then?"

"But you can never let anything remain uncertain. You need certainty, Yury, you always need certainty. Absolutely no room for errors."

"This is not a fucking life lecture right now!"

"So I followed him home. But this time, I saw him pouring Ruz—pouring it right into those IRON ENERGY DRINK bottles, the ones Donaldson's always chugging from."

Yury's eyes brightened with intense focus. "Oh my God," he muttered, shifting with restless energy as he eagerly poured himself another drink. "So how do we nail him and link all this up, yeah? Link it all up to Donaldson?"

"That's the weird thing. I haven't been able to catch him selling anything. I've seen him taking the Ruz into his apartment and pouring them into the IRON bottles, but he never seems to take the IRON bottles *out* of his apartment to sell 'em."

"That makes no sense."

"But I've got it all figured out, Yury. You crunch this dealer—Anton's—data. I've looked at it before, but you, you'll look at everything—every fucking thing. That's how you operate. Any form of income in the past couple years might be Donaldson's way of paying him."

"Right, Frank, right, I'll start on that today."

"Meanwhile, I'll do what I do best. I'll go back to the Core Club."

"What? No. Look what happened last time when you went there Frank—you might get beat to death this time—for sure you wouldn't get out alive, for damn sure."

"When I followed Donaldson before, he went into the Core Club and came out for a smoke break with a couple of those bottles. Looks like he's getting them from somewhere inside. If I can trail Donaldson inside, then—"

"Oh," Yury said, "you're going *inside* the club now too?"

"If I can get inside, then who knows? This might be the missing piece—the piece that brings it all together."

"And how are you planning to get in?"

I recalled the man in the gray suit hunched beside the Core Club dumpsters, spraying the payment with vomit. "Last time I was outside I saw Jules Mercier coming out the back exit. He's a petty white-collar criminal I've dealt with in the past when I was a rank four and still working on small stuff like that."

Yury frowned. "Right, since rank four cases are just so petty, right? I mean, why does Stingsby even bother hiring losers like us?"

"If I can dig up something on Mercier, I can force him to get me into the Core Club with him. We need dirt on him. We'll look for fraud, tax evasion—small offenses."

"Got it."

Yury lingered in my apartment for a while, stewing and fidgeting like a swallow. The line on his forehead had deepened, and his skin was sallow like dead flesh. The rumpled clothes he was wearing—that was yesterday's suit.

"Have you been at the casino all night again?" I said.

"No! For God's sake, Frank."

We both sat, drinking, while I thought deeply. As I looked at him slumped there, I remembered that night I'd first brought him to the Palace, the night he'd worn those running shoes and that dusty plaid shirt. "Why are you doing this to yourself?" I asked. "You've got a bad penchant for lying, Yury. Why do you even bother hiding this stuff from me? I'm not your wife."

"Because I kicked the gambling—I gave it up, alright? Fuck. You think I'm the liar here, out of the two of us—me, and not you, right?"

I snorted and swished the liquid around in my glass, watching him. "Some people are capable of very elaborate lies, Yury. They can thread whole stories, put on an entire fake character, make you feel sorry for them."

He left shortly after without saying goodbye. I headed to Sentrac, ready to start searching through Mercier's data. The streets were crowded, and a man selling plastics jostled me with the shelves hanging from his neck.

"Plastics, cheap."

On his shelves, the little mechanical beings writhed with small, simple movements. I didn't understand why people bought plastics. Yury had one, and he said it gave him a sense of empowerment. I'd asked him why, but he couldn't answer. He didn't know.

"Evening, Frank." The security guard greeted me when I walked into the Sentrac lobby. As he spoke, he spilled a few drops of the coffee in his hand. On his chest was a button with a green checkmark. Mike's presence reassured me. He did need to buy some better shoes and tidy up that uniform—I'd often had to resist the impulse to brush some of those crumbs off his shirt— but I still had a soft spot for Mike. There was something calming about his careful diligence towards his job and his painfully earnest brown eyes. Mike probably didn't make a lot of money, and yet he showed up to work on time every day and took his job seriously, never missing a patrol.

"Hey Mike," I said. "How's Laura doing?"

"Laura's good, as always."

That was our little joke, a routine of sorts. Laura was a woman in his apartment complex he'd been interested in forever, but he never seemed to be able to bring himself to ask her on a date. The poor guy was painfully shy, like a teenager. He worked the night shift so I didn't see him often, but whenever I came in late I asked him how Laura was doing, every single time without fail. Mike, he never changed. He was there behind the desk at the same time on the same days, drinking his evening coffee at precisely 22:00. For him, time didn't bring change; it didn't sweep him along like it did the rest of us, carrying us from one spot to another like twigs in a river, carrying us so far we could barely see the spot where we used to be, way off and faded in the distance. Mike reminded me of my older self, before the traders, before Jenny, before Celeste.

When I arrived at my office after seeing Mike, the Yury case felt less perplexing than before. I would find answers soon. I knew that like I knew Mike would have his ham sandwich tomorrow at 22:00. Just like every other day.

Chapter Twenty-One

"Detective Southwood? I'm here representing the Indigo Palace. Can I come inside?"

The next day after work, a man stood inside the lobby of my apartment building, peering at me over the top of his glasses. He wore a stiff suit the colour and texture of wood.

"Guess I don't a choice," I snapped. "Just make sure your hands are clean, and don't mess anything up."

I led him into my apartment, telling him, "Take your shoes off."

"Oh, don't be concerned, Sir. I'm certainly one who understands the value of neatness."

I poured myself a gin and tonic without offering anything to him. He sat in my living room with an unblinking expression, wearing a yellow bowtie. His neck was thin and too long for his body.

"You're aware of your debts, I assume, Detective Southwood?" he asked cheerfully.

"I think you know I'm aware," I said, stifling the impulse to throw my drink in his face.

He pulled out a tablet and swiped the screen a few times. "To be precise, one million, twenty-four thousand and one hundred dollars is the amount." His eyes shone with delight. "Oh, and sixty-four cents." He sat neatly in his chair with his arms in perfect alignment with the armrests, his tie a clean vertical line.

"You have just over one month remaining to pay," he said. "It's my duty and obligation to give you a one-month warning."

"Listen, let me talk to your boss. He'll let me extend—"

"I can assure you there won't be any compromises made in this case. I was asked to inform you that this is a firm deadline."

I stared at him. His mouth widened into a smile, revealing small yellow teeth.

"Get out," I said.

After he left, I quickly swallowed two more gin and tonics. Everything in my apartment looked wrong, messy, out of place. One of the cupboards was ajar, a cloth had been left on the counter, and the heating vent droned too loudly in the background. Damn this place. Everything in it—every piece of furniture, every appliance, even the bottles of liquor in the cabinet—taunted me in the voice of a chiding parent, reminding me of my debts. I slammed the cupboard door back into its place.

But I knew how to improve my mood. I grabbed a bottle of sanitizer. Yes, things already felt better as I wiped the counters until they shone with lovely little diamonds of light, every germ annihilated, then the cupboards, the routine check to see if the jars of dried food were alphabetized, and then the best part, arranging the cleaning supplies under the sink, all those heavenly coloured bottles smiling at me from their proper places—but no, one of them was crooked so I rushed to adjust it, imaginary trumpets blaring in the background to announce my victory when I restored order, and finally, the bedroom, the closet with all its colour-coded shirts, the bed made just right and the pillows fluffed the way I liked them. Here in my apartment—here was order. Here was certainty and the knowledge that everything in the world was in its place. Nothing unexpected. Nothing but the known and benign and familiar. I allowed myself to pause and take in the warmth of that knowledge.

I pulled a bag out of a drawer, reveling in the sight of the neatly counted vitamins, carefully allotted for my evening dose. The yellow, blue, and red pills—I swallowed them one at a time. Vitamin D for strong bones, Omega-3 for dry eyes, vitamin A for healthy skin. Everything was in order.

Soon after, I threw on my jacket and headed out the door to find Jenny.

When I got to Sally Lane's, Jenny was alone. She told me Anton and Haru had gone to Kay's. She claimed they'd gone to trade, but her careless, casual tone—obviously fake—told me she was lying. Likely they'd gone to discuss whatever insanity they were planning, the plan that involved me.

We went downstairs, opened the door of the vault, and stepped into total darkness. All the lights were out. I fumbled with the switches on the wall, to no effect. Stumbling back towards the door, I tripped on a fallen coat hanger lying on the ground, lost my balance, and fell. One of the inverted chrome hooks of the fallen hanger tore a long rip in my shirt, just missing my skin. All around me, huge mounds of beaver fur were strewn across the floor like animal carcasses.

"This fucking mess drives me crazy," I said, picking myself up and thoroughly scrubbing the dirt off my hands.

Jenny took out her transfer scanner from Sally Lane's and turned on the screen. Her face glowed blue in the mechanical light, just like it had that first night in the Border. "I forgot the lights are out down here," she said. "Cedric's s'posed to fix it. But the fucker's too drunk."

"Well, I guess if you're down here with me, then I'm okay with it."

I hated the mess, but I didn't mind the darkness. It suited the vault better than the light. It suited the mess and the clutter, the blindness that overcame you when you ventured out into that maze of things and got lost in it. And it suited the feeling of privacy, too, the freedom and anonymity draped over the underworld like a veil, shielding it from all sight and judgement.

Jenny came and sat on a table near where I stood. Beside her, a heap of gold shone faintly in the electric light. She put the scanner beside her on the table, and the blue glow illuminated my stash in the corner. I took stock of my bank account.

Gold bullion, $3,000. Gold coin, $200. Holt-FR and ammo, $1,300. Three jars of hand sanitizer, $42. 375 R&Ms, $225. One plastic watch with dollar sign on the strap, $2—given to me by Jenny as a gift. Chem-7, $206,200—getting closer, but still not enough to pay my debts.

Lighting a cigarette, I shut the vault door and sat next to Jenny, drawn towards the warmth of her body. Smoke curled around us in tendrils, as though to shield us from sight. Tonight, she seemed different; she moved and spoke heavily, as though more burdened than usual.

"Your shirt's ripped," she said. "Here, wear this one instead. I'll give it to you."

She walked over to one of the shelves and brought back a yellow-and-white button-up shirt with palm trees on it. "Like it? I'll give it to you."

I cringed mentally at the sight of it. A hideous violation of all rules of style. As I reached out to take it, I thought longingly of the shirt I was taking off: a feather-light gray cashmere sweater, one of Aliano's most fashionable styles.

"Yeah, I like it," I said, changing into it.

I sat beside her again. "Since you're here and you've got that light on the transfer tablet, maybe you can help me get to the clearing at the back. I left my open Chems there."

"Drinking again?"

"I'm not hooked on them, alright? I just dip into them occasionally, when the need comes up. I do it out of necessity, that's all. Right now, I'm working on a tough case trying to help my friend. I'm worried about him. And I just can't crack this case. Normally there are patterns in the data. The data used to tell me the truth."

"But in the past, what you saw—the patterns—those were just the products of the Sentrac Optica. The products of your instrument."

I didn't know how to answer that. Instead I said, "Your eyes are red."

"Feels like they're red all the time, these days."

"That piece of shit husband better not be bothering you."

"It was nothing. Just a fight."

I shook my head. "He didn't touch you, did he?"

"Nah." She fiddled with a bracelet—one of those cheap plastic things Anton always got her. She stared at it for a moment, then a frown darkened her face, and she flung it into the piles of junk. It vanished into the blackness. "I'm just tired of it," she said. "All of it."

Her winter boots clanged against the legs of our table as she swung her legs back and forth; she seemed animated by strange energy, a mix of anger and excitement.

"He doesn't deserve me," she said.

She shifted her body closer to me. The piles around us seemed to loom and sag, as if about to topple over, and the vault looked alien, the gold beside us jarring with the blue of the scanner. In the distance, the gentle whirring of robotics rose and fell as the cube floated in circles, cycling through its random movements.

The silence changed, became heavier. Now she was staring up at me, eyes flicking back and forth between me and the door. Her face had changed; all her reserve was gone, the barriers she put up when I was around, and in that strange blue darkness she seemed abruptly and startlingly real, as if she'd shed some kind of shell and left it lying on the floor. Something had changed between us. Things would not be the same afterwards. She leaned towards me, bringing her familiar scent of coffee and cigarettes, and brushed her lips against mine. Her body tensed at the contact. She drew back for a second to look at me, then we kissed without stopping. Her hands around the back of my neck gripped me almost painfully tightly, the same way she held all those trinkets she hoarded—those scarves, plastics, and pieces of faded jewelry.

For a minute I was apprehensive, not ready to believe that this was happening and convinced that it might stop at any moment. But soon my misgivings faded and thought gave way to a simple animal need. It blinded us and it made us into basic beings, simple living things like those plastics the vendors sold in the streets. Her tongue met mine and shaking started up in her body, little tremors of nervous energy. I started to pull her onto my lap.

She drew back, her face flushed, and glanced at the door. "Cedric might come in."

"Forget him," I said desperately. If we stopped now then something terrible would surely happen, some undefined thing that hung in the surrounding darkness and threatened us.

"No one can see," she said. "He'll kill you. Anton." She stood up and gestured for me to follow her into the piles. "No one but us ever comes to the back."

I followed, my pulse thudding with adrenaline, and she held out the scanner so that it illuminated a thin strip of ground in front of us. Shadowy masses floated by on either side as we moved slowly, cautiously, edging further into the blackness. The fresh memories of the few minutes we'd just shared pounded in my head, and my mind raced with the strange fear that we would never reach that meadow—if we just could get there then this terrible waiting would be over, but it continued to feel far, far in the distance.

Two hands fanned out abruptly against my ribcage. Jenny had spun around so quickly I almost bumped into her, and the light of the scanner, now pressed to my side, splashed onto my shirt. On the hologram of her upturned face, her brows were tense with confusion.

"I'm married."

In the sinking moment that followed, I suddenly remembered I was wearing a shirt with palm trees on it.

I didn't say anything, glued helplessly to the spot. The shadows around us seemed to solidify into walls and edge closer.

"I made a formal vow. There were legal documents. I swiped my fingerprint on them."

"Never mind the legality of it."

She stood still, the whites of her eyes shining. "Are those the kind of things a cop should say?" But she didn't move away, her hands still on my chest and our bodies pressed close together.

The drone of the robotic cube was louder now, and I realized that it was dangerous to fumble around like this, because we wouldn't be able to see that cube coming in the darkness. Distantly, I remembered an urban legend Jenny told me once about a man whose head was pulled clean off his body by that cube. The myth held that after he died, his ghost could be seen wandering around the site of his death, headless and utterly blind, with no way to see where he was going.

Jenny melted into the intimacy, the closeness. Her hands moved over the contours of my chest and shoulders, as though seeking to know the lines and shape by touch. The droning grew louder in the distance. That cube might float into us any minute. Slowly, her face changed, became more decided.

"Come on," she said. "I want to keep going." She grabbed my arm and pulled me onwards, and we stumbled blindly through the mess.

When we reached the meadow, moths fluttered overhead, fighting to get closer to the blue light Jenny held. The space overflowed with her things, the couch covered with clothes, fabrics, magazines. We swept most of it to the ground, but we were rushing and we didn't clear all of it, fabrics and papers still strewn around us as I followed her down to the couch. When we kissed again she pulled me down, right up against her. I ran a hand up the smooth skin of her thigh and her skirt bunched up to her waist. The scanner's idle screen switched off and left us in total darkness. We were blind; we couldn't see each other at all, but the darkness was a welcome deletion of everything outside our small and selfish sphere of existence. I pulled off her shirt and shifted my hand to her breast, and her body softened against me as the nervous tension drained from her muscles. She must have given up worrying whether someone came in or found out. Fumbling in the dark, she moved her hand down the front of my pants. Blind and oblivious, we started making love there in the mess, the dirt, and the clutter. Scattered papers and fabrics tore underneath us.

She climaxed quickly, and I followed a while after. For a moment as we lay there spent and lifeless and pressed against the mess, it felt as if we'd become part of it, that we'd melted into the clutter and disorder that was the vault.

Afterwards I held her and she sat leaning against me. She turned the scanner back on so we could see each other. For a few minutes after her limbs were motionless, the muscles relaxed. I touched her forehead and loosened some of the hair that clung to the sweat on her skin. The longer strands fell out of the way but the small, finer curls remained stuck there. When I saw those fine curls I was struck by a deep wave of feeling for her.

But soon her fidgeting started up, the glances at the shattered glass on the floor, the nervous clasping at a piece of Anton's clothes that I hadn't noticed was still on the couch. I peeled off a shred of paper plastered to the sweat on my arm. There was no escaping this junk. Just once, I wanted to see her without all of it around. I could never get to the core of her, not with all this in the way.

"You shouldn't stay here," she said sadly. "I don't know what time he'll be back."

"Can't I stay a little longer? You don't owe him anything, I keep telling you."

I was speaking to someone who didn't really hear me.

"Let me stay with you," I said.

But she was firm about it. There was no arguing with the inevitable arrival of Anton and his Holt-FR. We followed the thin beam of the transfer scanner back to the door, and I left alone.

CHAPTER TWENTY-TWO

I waited until the office was mostly empty, then got to work on my plan to infiltrate the Core Club.

Jules Mercier—Personal Account. R&Ms, $35. Thirty-Second Street Pub, $70. Core Club Café, $397. Beef-Time Burgers, $18. Goddamn these men with terrible eating habits. A slug like this had probably never taken a vitamin in his life. Thirty-Second Street Pub, $82. Steven's Beer and Spirits, $44.

No surprises there. Pretty much all his income went to booze. The night I saw him coming out of the Core Club, he'd been so drunk he'd vomited all over the alleyway. And the guy had a history of petty crime. It shouldn't take too long before I found some new dirt on him.

Footsteps sounded in the hallway, and I quickly wiped away all my searches. Those steps were unmistakeable. Quick and purposeful, the familiar black leather oxfords on the linoleum. I opened some of my Donaldson files and pretended to take notes on them.

Stingsby appeared in the doorway, throwing a trench coat over his bony frame. "Here late again, Southwood?"

"Yeah, boss." I was surprised to see Stingsby approach me. He'd been avoiding me ever since our encounter at Gibson's Pub. When he saw me in the hallways, he put his hands in his pockets and drew himself up, standing straighter as though to make himself look taller, more put together. Stingsby's professionalism was iron-clad; he didn't lose control often, and he didn't forget it easily if he did.

Stingsby and I made eye contact, and he tensed like usual, drawing himself up. "You're still working on Donaldson?" he asked.

"Making good progress, as always."

He brushed a speck off his trench coat. "Southwood, I know there's a lot of red tape, but we damn well need to keep things moving. I want a hard deadline. When are you taking Donaldson to court?"

My mind spun to make all the necessary calculations. It could take another week to dig up enough dirt to blackmail Mercier. Finally I said, "Three weeks." Anything more than that would be suspicious.

Stingsby hesitated, then nodded. "Three weeks, then."

Country music twanged from a digi-jukebox as I stepped into Thirty-Second Street Pub, the air smelling like fried food and sweat. I wove through the customers hunched over their tables and made my way to the bar. I'd have to wash my hands after spending time in this dump. It was the kind of joint that served up drunks until they were hedonistic shells on the floor, slugs lubricated in the slime of their own vomit. When white-collar vermin developed a habit of drinking until they passed out, they sometimes frequented holes like this one—places where none of their co-workers would see them, where their wives wouldn't find them sprawled in the dirt outside. But a data detective saw everything.

There he was at the bar. Jules Mercier, the very man I'd come to see, slumped on a stool wearing an oversized suit. This guy had money, and yet he chose to wear something that fit him that badly? Men with no style put me on edge. It was no surprise to see Mercier here. It wasn't hard for predictive analytics to foresee when an alcoholic would frequent one of his favourite watering holes.

I slipped onto the stool beside him and ordered a gin and tonic with two lime wedges. When I sat down he didn't glance up. He looked like a corpse bent over his beer, his eyes fixed on the sim sports screen behind the bar. He held himself with a strange mixture of arrogance and wretchedness. From what I remembered, he was a man who would make a show of holding the door open for a woman any day of the week, then cheat on his wife an hour later.

After the bartender dropped off my drink and moved away, I said quietly, "It's been a while, Mercier."

His face turned towards me. Deep-set eyes and a thick moustache, hanging over his upper lip like the fringe of a rug. His body tightened up like a spring, and I could feel his eyes scanning me for weapons, even though they didn't move.

"I don't need a D72 to get what I want from you," I said. "I've been taking a look at your data. Back in the day it was tax evasion, now it's fraud—turns out you're a man who does the works, huh?" I pulled out my Sentrac portable and showed him the screen. "This look familiar to you? I've got more than enough on your latest fucking scheme at Larson & Wang to put you behind bars."

"You dirty motherfucker," he said under his breath, beads of spit flying onto the bar.

"You can say that if you want, but you'll wake up tomorrow looking at five years in prison. Or, if you want me to keep this quiet, you'll answer my questions."

He turned back to his beer, forcing his face into a steely mask that showed no expression. His breath reeked of alcohol.

I jerked my head in the direction of an isolated corner table, and when I picked up my drink and headed towards it, Mercier followed. As we slid into the shadowy corner, a blanket of stale darkness settled over us, the country singer whining in the background. We blended in just fine, and no one looked at us strangely. That was convenient, and yet it also bothered me somehow.

"August Donaldson," I said. "His data says he loves spending money at the Core Club. And so does yours."

"I don't know a fucking thing about Donaldson."

"And when Donaldson's at the Core Club, he loves spending time in that VIP room. You know, the one with the special entrance, around back. The one you jackasses think the cops don't know about. And I've seen you leave from there too, after you have your fun with some of the prostitutes down there, the ones your wife might like to know about." That last part was an educated guess, but a bluff could pay dividends.

Drops of beer trickled onto his suit. The bottom of his moustache was wet with beer. "So you followed me around," he said. "That's your job, isn't it? Stalking people, watching them fuck whores, your dick in one hand and your fancy binoculars in the other—what d'you call them again? Big data programs?"

I didn't answer, my eyes narrowing.

"And who are you, Southwood?" he said, slurring his words as he took another drink of beer. "You a man who's never paid for sex, had an affair, committed a fucking crime?"

"That's bullshit," I said, my voice too loud. "You and me, we're nothing like one another." I was helping Yury to balance the scales. And after this one deal, I'd be out.

In the background, the country singer serenaded us with his hideous, whining voice. The two of us drank in unison. The dim light shone on our suits, made of nearly identical fabric.

"There's only one difference between us," Mercier said. He pointed a finger at my chest, the spot where the insignia would be if I was wearing my uniform. "That's the difference. Nothing else."

My hand clenched into a fist under the table. "Just start talking, you fucking slug. Donaldson. You see him spend time with anybody down in that VIP room? Talk to anybody?"

"No. He came alone."

"Oh, then I guess we're done here." I drained the rest of my drink, put down the glass, and slid towards the edge of the booth. I took my time, collecting myself and getting ready to stand up.

"Alright," Mercier said, "there was Sara Figueira. That woman from his company—I saw him with her sometimes. He was fucking her."

I sighed. "Not good enough. I already know about her." I stood up. At a nearby table, a drunken heap glanced at me, the whites of his eyes glowing like pearls. I started to walk away. I'd only taken three steps by the time Mercier cracked.

"Jay," he said, almost too quietly for me to hear. "I've seen Donaldson talking to Jay."

A sheen of sweat shone on Mercier's forehead now.

Slowly, I slid back into the booth. I waited for the eyes of that drunk to unfix from me—waited until those two glowing pearls were extinguished, his head slumped face-down again, and then said, "Go on."

Mercier stared at me with desperate eyes. "They'll kill me. They'll kill me if you let this get back—"

"Jay who? Don't waste my time, I'm telling you."

"I don't know his last name. I've just heard him called Jay and that's the fucking end of it. A blond guy, young. And there's his spot—his spot, he always sits there, in the booth left of the bar. I've seen him talking to Donaldson there."

"Talking about?"

"I fucking told you he's sitting in that spot with Donaldson!"

"You haven't given me a goddamn thing to go on and you know it."

He sat, trembling, and drank. Finally he said, "They're both in the ring."

"The ring?"

"That's what they call it. A network. I think Donaldson's in it. And Jay."

Glasses clinked in the distance, mixed with human voices that sounded far away. The stale air was suffocating.

"Are you in the ring too?" I asked.

"No."

He wasn't lying about that. I'd checked his data and found no connection to Donaldson or Figueira, not one pattern except frequenting the same club.

"How do you know he's in the ring?" I said.

"I think he helps them with money laundering. I've heard them talking about research grants, charity donations, and laundering fees."

Fake charity donations—a classic laundering trick. I'd seen my share of companies who "donated" money to a fake charity, then the charity pumped it back out as "grants" or "research money," washed clean and tough to trace.

"You know the name of Jay's company?"

"No."

I pressed him a while longer, threatened him with everything I had on him, but I didn't get a thing. He insisted he knew nothing else, and if I'd read him right, he was telling the truth. When I finished my questions, I sat for a while, thinking.

"New plan, Mercier. You and me, we're gonna have a night out together. You're getting me into that VIP room."

CHAPTER TWENTY-THREE

Standing in front of the mirror, I put on my new gray Aliano suit I'd bought in the markets, ready to blend in with Mercier and his ring of petty criminals at the Core Club. And yet when I saw myself in the mirror, I hesitated. I looked just like him. Like Mercier. The gray suit, the hairstyle—they were like his when I saw him that night outside the Core Club.

Suddenly I wanted to erase my reflection, wipe it right off the mirror. Even the suit I was wearing I'd bought with dirty money.

I left the bathroom and slammed the door shut behind me.

Soon after, I met Mercier at an intersection.

"You keep your distance from me tonight, alright?" I said. "We have to pretend we're buddies, but we're not. Don't talk to me, and above all else, don't touch me."

"Just keep your mouth shut. If you blow our cover, both of us are dead." His speech was already sloppy, the smell of alcohol trailing him in a cloud. He walked beside me encased in a huge trench coat with the collar buttoned right up to his bloodshot eyes.

We made our way down Tenth Avenue enveloped by the city's Babel yell: the bellows of drunks, laughter, and the occasional darker note of a taunt or threat, aggressive men jostling each other. The lights of the city looked beautiful but distant, strung along the lines of the orderly web that was the city, its strands made of wireless networks and sensor sightlines stretching out long and deep into every street. But that orderly network had gone cold, as though it were far away from me.

Mercier and I turned down a familiar alley, and the voices receded into the distance. When we reached the rear door, the alley was silent. Mercier entered his code. The new face on the Expo-Screen would disguise me.

The door swung open, revealing a new bouncer. He glanced at Mercier, then at me. "Another one of your guests, Mercier?" he said.

"Business partner," Mercier said.

In the pause that followed, music pulsed from downstairs. The bouncer looked me up and down.

"If you're with Mercier then get in," he grunted.

We passed through a doorframe with peeling red paint into a dark hallway. Music rose up from below, shuddering in the floor and walls, shuddering in my chest until it replaced my heartbeat with its own, darker beat. Last time, I'd watched this place from outside, trying to see into the depths of this sick heart without going inside myself. But that was impossible. There were no windows here—no rear windows, only doors, and to see into the depths, I needed to go inside myself. The rear door shut behind us. The sounds of the city and the lights of its grid vanished.

I followed Mercier down the staircase, thick, moist air rushing into my lungs. The stairwell led us to a corridor, long and curved and lined with doors on both sides. Most were closed, sounds drifting through the wood as we walked by. Raised, angry voices from one door. Laughter from another. Female cries of pleasure. The hallway wound onwards, twisted like the veins of a human body.

We arrived in a crowded, velvet-carpeted room, hard neon pounding from the ceiling. I followed Mercier across the room and took a seat at the bar, just as a G-string fell around the ankles of the woman dancing on top of it.

"Double gin and tonic with two limes," I told the bartender through the pair of neon-drenched legs swaying on the counter between us. "Mercier's got my tab."

As the bartender passed me my drink, I surveyed my surroundings. It was incredible. The room was fucking full of them. The super-rich, those dark swarms of Sentrac money, all of them drenched in it, dirty with it like the suits at the Indigo Palace. Data bigwigs, corrupt cops, CEOs, all the high and mighty from the Core basked in their playground, crowded around square tables heaped with glasses, their bodies melting into plush leather sofas, naked women on every counter. At the back of the room, neon circles spun on an electronic wall in quick, random movements. The crowds, the grime on the bar, the moral filth all around me—it was hard to breathe, the air full of the dirtiness of these people. The crowd writhed and pressed, threatening to swallow me and make me one with it.

I'm just in this to help Yury, then I'm out. The thought made it easier to breathe.

Help Yury, then I'm out.

Help Yury, then I'm out.

Help Yury, then I'm out.

My drink was already empty. "Another," I told the bartender.

He brought it, then poured a beer for the man beside me, a drunkard slumped on the bar with his head rocking back and forth on his arms. A profusion of thick orange hair sprouted from his scalp, but his face wasn't visible.

My gaze tracked to the booth left of the bar. Empty. "That's Jay's spot?" I whispered to Mercier.

He nodded.

"You said he and Donaldson are here every fucking Saturday," I said. "If they're not, you'll pay the price."

"They'll be here."

We waited and we drank. I should've stayed sober to keep myself sharp, but each drink made the crowd feel more distant, more separate from me. Mercier sat, hunched and red-eyed, and drowned himself in liquor along with me. The music thudded as customers came and went, but Jay's booth remained empty.

"Another gin and tonic?" the bartender asked over the music.

I nodded. A new stripper replaced the old one on our bar, dark hair shaking all the way down to the small of her back when she danced. Her hair looked like Celeste's. Absent-mindedly, I started ripping label shreds off an empty bottle on the bar.

"You like Rosie, huh?" the bartender said, making me start. He was smirking at me over my heap of empty gin and tonic glasses. "She's one of our best."

Rosie was climbing down now, sitting on the bar with one high-heeled leg on either side of me. She ran her fingers over her bikini top.

In the corner of my vision I saw Mercier shaking his head, his eyes narrowed into slits. "Filthy hypocrite," he muttered.

"You can see the rest in the back," Rosie said. "Two hundred dollars."

I hesitated. "Maybe some other time," I forced myself to say. "I need to talk with my friend here."

My eyes turned to a new scene: Jay's booth, now occupied by a thin man sandwiched between two strippers, sipping a drink with his dress shirt unbuttoned halfway to his navel. One of his companions ran her fingers through the blond shell of his slicked back undercut.

That would be my Jay. None other than Jason Shutter, the richest man in the country, heir to the legacy of Aaron Shutter, a recently deceased genius of big data tech. The Shutter Gardens, down on Eighth Avenue by where Maclean had been shot, had been built in honour of his father Aaron Shutter and the institute he'd founded for data research. Since his death, his son Jason had taken over. Jason kept his public persona pretty private, which is why Mercier didn't recognize him—when you owned huge portions of the information in the country, you could find ways to keep your profile quiet—but I knew his face. I'd lost money to Jason Shutter at the Indigo Palace Gemini tables more than once.

"Jay!" the bartender shouted over the music. "The usual?"

Shutter heard the question and his head turned towards us. He nodded at the bartender and then paused. His eyes fell on me. But the screen did its work; he scanned me up and down then looked away, turning his gaze to something behind me.

A wave of the familiar smell of Ruz came next, washing over me from behind. Donaldson glided past me towards the booth and took a seat across from Shutter. The back of Donaldson's shirt read: FIGHTING FOR ANIMAL WELFARE ACROSS THE GLOBE.

"Show's over girls," Shutter said, shooing the women away. A waitress brought drinks and the two men appeared to exchange greetings, but the music drowned out their conversation. Before I could figure out a way to get closer, they stood up and headed towards the hallway with the chambers.

As Donaldson and Shutter passed by me, only a few inches away, I spotted the nearly invisible blotches on their necks, the faint yellowish hue of their skin. They headed down the hallway, entered a chamber about three doors down, and shut the door behind them. Damn.

My mind groped for a solution. I scanned the hall with the chambers and caught sight of an open door beside Jay's and Donaldson's room.

"Mercier," I said under my breath, "how thin are the walls here?"

"What?"

"Don't try to pretend you haven't been in one of those rooms with one of these strippers before."

"You think I pay attention to the walls when I'm in there?"

I turned back to the hall. An employee sat on a stool near the entry to the hallway, keeping an eye on the traffic through the chamber doors. I'd have no excuse to go in there alone. I glanced up at Rosie dancing on the bar, an idea starting to take shape.

"Rosie," I said, standing up, "I changed my mind. I'm convinced."

She turned her head, flipping her hair over her shoulder with one hand. "Two hundred dollars, then."

I slapped Mercier on the shoulder, ignoring his muttered curses. "My friend Mercier here, he's got my tab. Charge it to his account, alright?" I laughed.

When Rosie and I walked down the hall together, the employee barely glanced at us.

"In here," I said, turning into the room beside Donaldson's and Shutter's.

She shrugged and followed me into the chamber, a dark cell with a single disintegrating couch. The couch was pushed up against the wall separating our room from Donaldson's and Shutter's, and in the middle of the wall behind the sofa was another door connecting the two rooms, tightly shut and secured with a digital lock. The rooms must have been adjoined at some point. The connecting door was painted red, long cracks stretched across the wood.

Treading cautiously in the moist, stale air, I approached the couch and inspected it. A dark stain. Sticky white pools of human residue. Maybe I could still back out of this.

But then Shutter's voice drifted through the door in the wall, just loud enough for me to hear him over the distant pulse of music. "We've already had to talk once before about you getting greedy, August."

I forced myself to sit down on patch of sofa that looked cleaner than the rest.

"We're all friends here," Donaldson said, his voice unsteady. "Are you talking about that extra money I was funnelling on the side? There's no connection between that and the ring. I did that on my own."

"You did that without asking us and you got caught for it. The fact is, August, soon you'll be going to fucking court for that."

"That's all fine, just fine—my lawyers will take care of it. It won't put you at risk. None of you. I swear it, friend, I swear it. There's no way they'll find the rest of it. They'd have to know about Sara helping me to find it."

"Maclean found out about the rest of it."

"We already dealt with her, right, friend?"

Vermin. That was the only word I could think of to describe them, talking about Maclean that way. I fucking knew they'd killed her. I'd known it from the beginning.

Donaldson's voice started up again. "And—and the new detective on my case is just a rookie, a nobody who doesn't know a damn thing about the bigger picture—"

Rosie tapped a device in the corner of the room, and blaring music pounded from an overhead speaker.

"No music!" I shouted over the noise.

Staring at me, she switched it off. "You want me to dance without music?"

"Yeah—that's right, I just like the quiet. I've got a thing for the quiet. And be careful not to touch my face. Just another pet peeve of mine." She wouldn't be able to see the Expo-Screen, but she might be able to feel it.

With a sigh, she started swaying to imaginary music, her hips and ass shaking in unbearable silence. I shifted awkwardly. She seemed not to notice the faint voices; she was on the other side of the room and lost in the slow, swaying movements of her dancing.

"Maclean may be gone," Shutter said, "but I don't like the idea of you going to court, with everything you know in your head."

There was a pause. Then muffled sounds floated through the door. Dull scraping, a thud, a cry of pain.

"Don't try to run," said a new voice. Another man seemed to have joined Donaldson and Shutter.

More thuds. The sounds were nauseating. The awareness of the stains around us swelled in my head. Rosie was swaying back and forth just a few inches in front of me. "That's fine," I said, looking away from her. "That's enough. I've had enough." It was hideous, the sight of her dancing while those sounds came from the next room. More grotesque thumps floated through the door behind me.

"I think I drank too much," I said, standing up and clutching my stomach as a flash of nausea crippled me.

"Fine. You're still paying." She strode out of the room.

Donaldson spoke between gasps. "Jay, friend, you know me, you know me. I'm not going to say a word in court. Not a word. On my honour, and you know me, you know I—"

A crash and the rasp of choked breathing.

"Give me a good reason why I should let you live."

"I'll give you two million—"

Faint, dull thuds drifted through the door. The door shook and rattled when something fell against it. I knew it when I heard it. Those were the sounds of a man dying.

It was quiet.

"Two million wasn't enough," Shutter said. "He was too dangerous to have around, going to court like that. He got greedy and he paid the price. You take care of this body."

I hurried out the door into the hall and back towards the exit. God only knew what else was happening in those chambers, each its own private cell in the dark labyrinth of this basement. The pumping bass receded as I made my exit through the rear door and stepped into a thick white sky. Shreds of snow swarmed like flies under streetlamps. The night was mute, the whiteness muffling the noises of the city. As the head of the Institute his father founded, Jason Shutter owned the digital gardens down on Eighth Avenue. I recalled standing in the yellow ring of a streetlamp at the scene of Maclean's murder, smoke refracting the light of a nearby sign that read: SHUTTER GARDENS.

CHAPTER TWENTY-FOUR

As I walked down the hallway at work on Monday, deep voices resounded from my office.

"Always a shame to meet under these circumstances, Detective Hays."

No one could mistake the commanding bass of Commissioner Gareth Stingsby. It flattened you. It knocked you onto your back so that you watched him speak from the floor, the black leather oxfords shining an inch away from your face, and above them, the thin waist and tall figure ascending upwards until it receded into the overhead halogen, beaming down like a beacon from heaven.

I was frozen. A mannequin in the middle of the hall, one foot in front of the other. Perez blinked at me over her glasses. I needed to act normal. Whatever happened, I couldn't let on that I'd been at the Core Club on Saturday. If I did, I'd have to tell them about Yury and why I was there. And that I'd been hiding it from Stingsby.

My feet were moving again—forwards. A pair of men slid into view behind a mahogany doorframe that rolled by in slow motion. Stingsby leaned on the corner of my desk, arms folded over his chest. He was speaking to a homicide detective with bushy orange hair and eyebrows.

"Southwood." Stingsby's greeting came with the customary crushing handshake. "You remember Detective Hays?"

I nodded at the orange-haired cop and said, "Homicide, right? We met outside the crime scene of Maclean's murder."

His eyes skimmed over me without recognition. "Sure. I'm in charge of that investigation too."

"Gotta situation on our hands this morning Southwood," Stingsby said. "Hell of a fucking mess. Here at Sentrac Bank we dedicate our lives to fighting crime, then this happens. Sickening."

"What happened?"

Stingsby continued. "Last night, August Donaldson and Sara Figueira, his manager from Fullston Big Data Tech—both of them, dead."

"The two of them were found down by the river," Hays said. "Both of them had an eye stabbed out. Their company was a major leader in big data. That must be why they were targeted."

A phone rang somewhere in the distance.

"Shit." That was all I could muster.

Orange eyebrows squirming on his forehead, Detective Hays said, "That's right. Glass right in the eyeball. Disgusting." Hoarse laughter spilled from his mouth.

"This is no joke, Hays," Stingsby snapped with a shake of his head. He turned to me. "This is the end of your case. Homicide's taking over. They want full responsibility, but they'll need you to send everything you found on that funnelling scheme Maclean had gotten started on. That's all you found, in the end?"

For a second I couldn't speak. Detective Hays' hair. It was exactly the same colour as the thick, orange hair of that drunk sprawled face-down on the Core Club bar last night.

"Right," I forced myself to say, "that's all I found. I'll send the data this morning." If I told Hays I knew any more than that, I might well find myself in the ditch like Donaldson with glass in my eye.

When they left, I crumpled into my chair and put my face in my hands. So this was the ring's next move. Not only would Donaldson not risk going to court, his case was also out of my hands now. If Hays was corrupt, then the ring had successfully taken the case from me and put it under Hays' control instead. Hays had probably been the second man in that room, the one who'd killed Donaldson with Shutter. Things were getting complicated, out of control. I thought about giving up and telling Stingsby to see if he could help us. But Jesus, I couldn't betray Yury like that.

I needed to talk to Yury.

But for some reason, he never showed up at work that day. As the office grew more and more crowded, phones rang, Stingsby grunted commands, assistants rushed back and forth with coffees in hand, but Yury's desk remained empty and still, separate from the currents of rush and business. He didn't answer any texts or calls. I should have gone and seen him after work, but I was too afraid of what I might find.

I couldn't face it—whatever was waiting for me at Yury's apartment. Instead, I fled to my stash of Chems.

Jenny took me down to the vault, where she stood leaning against the table where I kept my Chems. Her ruby fingernails held an R&M in one hand. She looked so different lately: the red in her cheeks, the new calmness that subdued her anxious fidgeting, and even her teeth seemed whiter. It had been two weeks since we started sleeping together. A few days after that first night, I'd walked into the vault and Anton's stuff had been gone. In the spot where one of his piles used to be, a patch of the floor stood out from the rest, cleaner and less dusty than the surrounding pavement. That circle of emptiness remained there like a stain, a reminder of his presence. All his bottles had been cleared off one of the tables, revealing the circular marks on the wood underneath them, marks that would never fade.

"I don't owe him," she'd said when I came in. "I don't owe him." She'd repeated that a few times, as if startled by the realization. Her wedding ring was gone, exposing a band of skin paler than the rest. She moved more lightly than before, humming to herself as she bustled around the vault arranging her precious things. She never told me exactly what had changed her mind.

"What did you tell him?" I'd asked her then.

"Nothing. Just that I'm leaving him."

He must know. How could he not? My intuition told me that this wasn't the last time I'd see Anton. I needed to watch my back. But I wondered if he'd even have it in him to try anything. Back when I saw him at the diner, on those nights when I'd first started going there—he'd seemed real then, but the Ruz had slowly faded him into nothing. He had become the rainwater running down the hill behind Sally Lane's, a muddy stream that snaked its way down to the gutters, then the sewers. Maybe he could find a new day job at some other run-down diner in the Border.

Jenny ran the Diner alone now, on reduced hours. Every night we met at her tiny apartment at the Border. I invited her to my place but she didn't want to go. "I'd rather be here," she said. "I don't want your money." Out on the front lawn, garbage was heaped up again like it had been the night we drove by here on our way to the Stack. The garbage drone might never come. The city had forgotten this place. At Jenny's apartment, we kept the blinds closed, and the place was tiny, three-hundred square feet of carpet so crammed with her treasured possessions that its contents almost squeezed out through the crack under the door. We cleared a path through the stuff so we could get from the door to the bed. We didn't talk much. Things always happened very fast: we met and exchanged a few words, then started undressing each other, rushed and uneasy as though someone was about to stop us at any moment. It left us drained and exhausted, and sometimes, as we lay together too tired to speak, I wondered why we'd rushed so much. But by then we were already falling asleep. When she slept she was even more beautiful, all that heavy makeup washed off and her body completely still, as she finally let herself rest from all that fidgeting, pacing, and worrying.

I gave Jenny a kiss. "Thank God—it's good to see you," I said, and meant it. Then I reached for one of the bottles beside her.

"Don't," she said. Her hand caught mine just before it touched the bottle. "No Chems tonight. Just for one night. Don't."

I hesitated. The warmth of her hand on mine inspired a fleeting desire to lift her up onto the table and make love to her like we did on her desk a few nights ago. But thoughts of Donaldson's murder and Yury's absence intruded, and a wave of anxiety jarred uncomfortably with the fantasy. I pushed the desire aside and picked up the bottle instead.

"You don't understand," I said. "It's just tonight—I need to have a drink tonight. Unbelievable things are happening at work right now, fucking unbelievable things."

"You've been drinking too much."

I was already pouring myself a glass of Chem-7, my mind turning rapidly as it continued to grapple with Donaldson's murder. Pacing the space in front of the table, I said, "They're corrupt, Jenny."

"Who?"

"The police. People at Homicide. They've been blaming their dirty work on privacy fanatics. And they did it for Maclean, too. They blamed her murder on the fanatics."

"That's what you're surprised about?" She sighed. "Oh Frank, this is already obvious to everyone but you. Is it so hard for you to realize that the police are corrupt?"

"Yes, it's fucking hard." My voice came out loud, bouncing off the walls of the vault and echoing back.

She shook her head, extinguishing the rest of her cigarette. She eyed the glass of Chems I was holding. The new light of excitement had left her eyes.

"Listen, I'm sorry I snapped," I said. "It's just—things are turning upside down. I'm not even sure about myself anymore."

"Sometimes I'm not sure either."

My pacing quickened. The bitter taste of the Chems seared my throat. "I used to think I was different from the criminals. There were rules I wouldn't cross. But look at me. I've broken every rule. Legal rules. And us, we broke the moral ones too."

Jenny listened quietly as I continued.

"But," I said, "I still have some rules. Yes, that's right. I don't cross certain lines. I don't kill people, for one."

I didn't know why I couldn't just keep my mouth shut instead of revealing all my private thoughts. Maclean's legacy had to mean something—the principles she'd taught me, that night she'd set me straight with slash and line. Maclean had to have left something behind.

"What would happen if you did cross that last line?" she asked.

I barely heard her, my mind racing now that it had caught onto some thread. "Yes," I said, "I'm also helping my friend, Yury. You don't know him, but I'm helping him because he's innocent and he's on the hook for something he didn't do. That's important, see? See?"

After all those words poured out of me, we were quiet for a while. Eventually Jenny left the vault while I remained there. I just needed to think.

I drank for hours, lying sprawled in the meadow while thin clusters of smoke hung in patches around the sofa and nicotine burned in my lungs. Since I started drinking Chems, I'd gotten even paler, my skin like ash with blue veins standing out against the white. And I'd lost weight. My arms were so skinny the bones on my wrists stood out in round knobs. And now every morning I woke up coughing until I spat out chunks of blood and phlegm in the bathroom sink. Bits of my hair had fallen out, and that bald patch on my jaw had become even more noticeable.

I imagined myself suspended in the clearing: just the innermost part of me, bare and naked, vulnerable and amorphous, like a single-cell organism or those plastics the street vendors sold, ready to dissolve, to die, at any moment. Ready to be laughed at. To be humiliated, like that night in the alley outside the Core Club. But the more I drank, the more the liquid hardened around me in a shell, hid my insides, made me unbreakable. The liquid gave me a second skin, just like my uniform used to. I remembered how much I used to love that uniform, but now it felt like any old layer of fabric, thin and impermanent, vulnerable to holes.

I let an hour slide by in heaven. But after a while little cracks started to form in my shell. I tried to cling to the feeling a little bit longer, but it slipped through my grasp. I needed something. Something else. I didn't know what, but I just needed something.

Up the narrow stairwell, then a flood of red light. A giant twirled a shotgun and drank heavily from a bottle, laughing in sheer jubilation while a horse's mane twisted down his over-muscled frame. The tattoos jarred with the equestrian flesh and the long snout, the bared horse teeth. At the other end of the room was a female figure inside a crackling gravitational field that drew me in. I took a few steps towards her.

"Don't come over here," she snapped. "You know I hate when you get like this."

The sphere around her sprouted a thick black outline with a diagonal line streaked through the middle, the paint still dripping.

"I'm not that high," I said.

"It's only been two weeks. You're already like him. Just like him. This is the same thing."

The same thing. Her words became the numbers that pounded in my head as I counted my money over and over, back down in the vault. Ten thousand. Eleven thousand. This made things better. I stacked the gold into neat piles, the ends lining up perfectly. One rectangle slipped out of place, and I jumped to fix it. Twelve thousand. Thirteen.

But things still didn't feel right. There was dirt all over the jewelry I stored down here. I stumbled to my feet and scanned my surroundings; there must be something I could use to clean it. There, a bottle of something—what did it say? I was too high to read it—but this looked like cleaner. I poured some on a scarf and started polishing the jewelry.

I cleaned and scrubbed and polished, my movements clumsy and blind.

I stopped for a second. Images crowded my head. Yury's empty desk. Hays's laughter when he talked about Donaldson's murder. The way I'd look in that mirror—just like Mercier.

I cleaned and scrubbed and polished.

I cleaned and scrubbed and polished.

I cleaned and scrubbed and polished.

I woke up with the taste of vomit in my mouth.

"What happened?" I said.

I was lying in bed next to Jenny at her apartment in the Border. She lay on her side of the bed, tucked between the wall and me, the way she liked.

"You passed out." She pulled my hand out from under the blankets and held it in front of my face.

"Jesus," I said. My palm had been rubbed raw, the skin partly scraped away, purple and discoloured.

"It's from the chemicals you were using. That wasn't cleaner. You were in there scrubbing for hours until you finally passed out and I found you."

I leaned over the side of the bed and coughed up phlegm and blood into her garbage can. I tried to roll onto my side to see her better, but bumped into a pile of magazines. Jenny's hoarding had intensified lately, and she continued to pack her apartment to the brim with all sorts of things. The never-ending labour of hoarding exhausted her. But when I asked her to get rid of some of them, she snapped at me, carrying them away protectively.

"Why d'you do it?" she said. "Why d'you get so high all the time?

"How can I even begin to put it all into words? Everything that I used to believe has fallen to pieces."

Jenny's eyes were red. She fell asleep beside me with a few of her belongings still surrounding her: a book, a scarf, a bracelet—the remnants of the things that used to circle around her like Saturn's rings and protect her.

CHAPTER TWENTY-FIVE

Finally, I worked up the courage to go to Yury's apartment. On the way there, gray daylight faded in a dirty sky streaked with pollution. Empty benches lined the sidewalks, and pigeons fought over scraps, scattering as I approached. When I touched the screen to ring Yury's buzzer, my fingers were unsteady.

A familiar apartment with soft carpet. Yury was on the couch, and behind him a door was ajar; through the crack was a room that looked bright and freshly painted. The walls were painted pink.

Yury wasn't wearing his glasses, and his eye sockets were deep caverns. In the dim light of the apartment, one long sliver of light fell across his chest. It came from the fridge, left open a crack and softening the silence with its hum.

"Yury," I said.

He didn't answer.

"Yury, your fridge is open."

Finally I went to close it myself, and the room grew darker. But by the time I got back to the couch, the yellow sliver had returned, the hum creeping back to its original volume.

"Your goddamn fridge is broken. How can you stand that?" I ached to fix it myself, but I didn't know how.

Yury spoke suddenly. "This thing, Frank. It's bigger than we are."

"No. We can get everything back under control. We can fix this."

"We're done Frank."

"No, we've definitely got something. Last night I got into the Core Club, and I saw Jason Shutter—"

"They know about A. Chawla Consulting. I'm looking at jail time. Liu found it yesterday."

"But I've got a lead, Yury, it's fucking Shutter Gardens—"

"It's not as bad as it could be, Frank. Stingsby's helping me out. He can get me a plea bargain. Just three years, if I confess."

"You can't do that."

"Why?"

"Because it's not the truth! You lying in court now? You're a fucking detective!"

"That means nothing. You still believe in all that bullshit, after this many years on the force, after what's happening right now?"

"If you're innocent, you're not going to jail. We'll find the real culprit and they'll pay. That's the law."

"Even you're corrupt, Frank. I'm not sure exactly how or why. I don't want to know. But you are."

Glass shattered against the wall where I'd thrown my drink, the shards sliding down to the floor with a chorus of soft chimes. Yury and I sat in silence.

Finally, I calmed down enough to speak. "I heard them kill Donaldson last night. He was murdered in a back room of the Core Club." I told Yury everything I'd overheard last night.

"But this morning—Homicide, they said they found him near the river, with Figueira. The privacy fanatics . . ."

"The ring has people in Homicide helping with this cover-up. The same detective that was in charge of Maclean's case is now in charge of Donaldson's too. If they set up his murder to look like it was done by privacy fanatics, they may have done the same for Maclean." I took a few heavy breaths, then continued. "Just tell Stingsby to hold off for a bit while you think about it. Give me a little more time. Shutter Gardens, Yury, Shutter Gardens. It's going to be there."

"What's going to be there?"

"I don't know—'it'—just 'it' is gonna be there—the fucking clue, the key to it all! The piece of data we're missing. I told you I saw Shutter down in that basement dealing with Donaldson. I looked at the data, and it looks like the ring has been using the Shutter Institute to help launder money for them, with Jason Shutter taking a cut of the profits while he's at it."

A glimmer of hope flickered across Yury's sagging face, but I could see him struggling to restrain it. "Problem is," he said, "the Shutter Institute's mostly legitimate. They have thousands of donors and research grants, most of them clean. How're you going to single out the corrupt ones to identify more companies in this network?"

"Shutter Gardens is where the Institute honours their donors. And here's what I think. The gardens would be an ideal place for criminals to meet. It's huge and full of hidden, isolated areas. It's a public place with no entry fee to leave a record. And Shutter owns it. He'd know plenty of data free zones and he'd have control over the security. Maclean was killed by the ring leaving Shutter Gardens, and the glass in the eye was a cover-up. They killed her because she saw something at the gardens that she shouldn't have."

"How do you know?"

"She was investigating Donaldson when she was shot, and I saw her body. She was just outside Shutter Gardens, on that path everyone takes as a shortcut when they come in and out of the gardens. The way she fell, it looked like she was walking away from Shutter Gardens when they shot her, and she wasn't wearing her uniform. She went there under cover."

"So you think she found out about the ring too?"

"At first I thought she only knew about the small stuff Donaldson was doing on the side, but last night I overheard them saying she'd found something to lead her to the ring, likely to the involvement of the Shutter Institute. And when she went to Shutter Gardens to see what she could find, she saw something. A face, maybe. Two people meeting."

"If she knew about it, why wasn't it in her notes when you took them over?"

"That I don't know. But I think there's something there, in the gardens. I know it, I fucking know it, Yury, just give me this one last chance, and everything's going to be okay—alright? Understand me?"

He sat silently while the fridge hummed, still ajar. Finally he said, "Stingsby wants to know my answer about the plea."

"Stall for a bit." On my way out the door, I added, "And fix that goddamn fridge."

That night I went to Kay's warehouse to pick up. She wasn't in her usual building; instead, a woman led me to her in another building in the factory complex. The trading took a few minutes, and soon I was on my way out again, carrying a crate of bottles under one arm.

Machinery hummed in the background, and on a conveyor belt on my left, mechanical claws picked up bottle-shaped pieces of glass, glowing red with heat, and swept them from one spot to another, where metal clamps closed around them to solidify their shape. The procedure—the way that glass was moulded from raw matter into patterns and shapes—reminded me of data processing, but for the first time I noticed how violent it was: the hellish heat, the brute force of the machinery, the cruelty with which the materials had to be treated to mould them, twist them into shape.

Continuing down the narrow walkway beside the conveyor belt, I passed side-rooms filled with traders, stacks of money and goods piled between them. Some distance ahead, a man walked in front of me. On his left, the bottles shuttled obediently along the conveyor belt, streaming by the man in pairs of two, identical and uniform like twins.

I stopped moving. The unsteady gait of that man ahead was unmistakeable. His familiar stick-thin figure swayed back and forth like the feeble antennae of a half-dead insect, and in his hand was a bottle of gold liquid. A heavy-looking bag had been thrown over his shoulder. Anton.

He disappeared into an alcove on the right. When he turned his body sideways, I noticed something wrong with his face. One cheek gleamed with unnatural brightness, and the shine also trailed down his shirt like the gleam of a sticky substance. A shudder of disgust went through me. This man was vermin.

I couldn't pass by that alcove without him seeing, but the exit to the building could only be reached by going forwards. I would have to wait. I slipped into a space in between two pieces of machinery near the alcove.

"What the fuck, man?" said an unfamiliar voice from Anton's alcove. "You wanna make a deal like this and you come in here looking like that? What is this?"

"I'm jus' fine, so lay off me, fuck," Anton said.

"What's on your face? Is that puke?"

That must've been the shiny substance crusted over his face and shirt. How brittle Anton's body must have felt whenever Jenny had embraced him, as though she touched the fleshless bones of a skeleton. How brittle he must have looked when he came into Sally Lane's night after night with some new trinket for her, laying his feeble offerings at an altar beneath her feet. I thought of the way Jenny had described his old self before he lost everything. I saw him healthy and muscular, dressed in a suit as he walked into work in the Core, then hurried around after work shopping for groceries, buying his milk and breakfast cereal, showing up at his dentist's appointments and making small talk with the receptionist. But the images were too absurd, too far-fetched. They faded quickly.

"Honestly," the other man said, "I'm a professional. I've got standards."

"I said lay off me! I'm offering you one and a half mil for fuckssake."

In the pause that followed, metal clanked from inside the alcove, the sound of a bag being placed on a table.

"You may be a sad motherfucker, but your money's still good," the man said.

"I pay y'when he's dead, alright? Jus' lay off me, lay off me."

"You bring the file?"

"Here."

The sound of shuffling papers.

"Really?" the man said. "A private eye?"

"Thas' right."

"The risk's higher with a private eye, of course."

"Well I'm payin' you enough for't."

"I know this face. Isn't he one of yours?"

"You jus' do y'fucking job, alright? I said lay off me."

"When you want it done?"

"You wait till I tell you. Not yet. We still need 'im for somethin'. I'll tell you when it's done. Y'get the rest of the money then."

Strange energy began to burn under my skin. That first night at Sally Lane's, when the squares from my spreadsheet had lingered on Anton's face—how I wanted to go back to that, to pull his flesh through those steel lines—that was what I'd been training my whole life to do, wasn't it?—to put data through the grinder, break it and bend it into shape like those bottles on the conveyer belt across from me, beaten and melted and destroyed until they conformed to the patterns, the shapes set out for them by the massive machine that presided over their existence. Anton deserved it. He deserved worse.

The other man left the alcove and turned down the hallway in the opposite direction from me. Not long after, Anton stumbled out and followed.

I fell into pace behind him, unnoticed. He swayed in front of me, his path winding and obeying no pattern. Then he staggered, lost his balance, and fell heavily. His head smashed against the conveyer belt with a dull thump. He crumpled onto the floor and lay there without moving.

I stood over him.

Everything was sharp with detail. The fine hair on the back of his neck, the scar that made a bald patch on his head—that was the exact spot where I could put a bullet. The Holt was under my jacket. Exultation rose in me as I thought about what I might do to him. The machinery droned in the background but now it sounded like music, like shuddering breath that moved in time with the quickening rhythm of my heartbeat; yes, surely I'd been training my whole life for this, to grind the numbers back into the grid—all those nights I'd stayed up with the Sentrac spreadsheets, the graphs, bright stains of data lighting up my screen, the rush when the errant numbers caught my eye, the corners of my office sharpening when I spotted them, those numbers slipping from the spreadsheets, just waiting to be ground back into the grid. Anton was just a scrap of data, an unruly number. He had strayed outside the lines.

How simple it would be, my thoughts sang in my head, to shoot him right now. Whatever half-baked threat he was making would dissolve on the spot. He'd never come back to haunt me. I could be with Jenny without worry. And look at him. It would be nothing to extinguish the faint flicker of life that was left in him. No one would know the difference.

The Holt was under my jacket, I thought again, more urgently this time. But my hand wasn't moving towards it.

It would be so easy. But that thought sounded fainter now; it no longer resounded in my head. New thoughts were beginning to push through in my mind. About Maclean's dogma of slash and line. The need to stay in one camp and never stray into the other.

I didn't kill people. There were still some lines I didn't cross. Maclean had taught me something. If I allowed myself to cross that line, soon there would be no lines left. Adrenaline still made the light streak along the edges of metal crates, but the sharpness was fading, replaced by a void of emotion.

Anton was unconscious, blood leaking from his forehead. That was a nasty head wound. He would need to get to a hospital right away. He'd already vomited tonight before I saw him. In the wasted state he was in, if left unconscious like that with the head wound, with no medical attention, he might never wake up. He also might vomit again and choke on it.

But in the position he was lying in—on his side—he would never choke on his vomit. He would have to be lying on his back for that. And he was clearly visible on the floor there, where someone would surely walk by, see him, and get help. If he could get medical help, he'd likely live.

I glanced over my shoulder. No one was around, and there was no surveillance here. The thought empowered me. This was data-free space, where no one would see me. No data, just two people with no one watching them.

Quickly, I dragged Anton's body off to the side where it was hidden behind a piece of equipment. Then I rolled him onto his back.

My stomach cramped as I hurried out of the building, sensations falling upon me with incredible clarity. A wedge of moon hung over the horizon. Cold air chilled the saliva on my lips. Certainly, I hadn't killed him, I told myself. I would never do that. There were lines I didn't cross. His fall had been a tragic accident, and what I'd done—those were just the details.

PART THREE: SHUTTER GARDENS

Chapter Twenty-Six

On my way to Shutter Gardens, wearing the Expo-Screen, I took a shortcut through the walkway where Maclean had been killed. The spot where her body had been found looked utterly unremarkable. Just a patch of indifferent pavement next to a dumpster and a man in chef's attire, sitting at the back of his restaurant smoking a cigarette.

I passed through the front doors of Shutter Gardens easily. There was no admission fee, which made my job easier. And it would also make it easy for criminals to meet here off the radar. Shutter gardens was vast, full of long tunnels and isolated, sheltered spaces. I'd watched Shutter from a distance for a few days, and I'd noticed that he sometimes visited the gardens in the early evening, around when it closed—right around the current time.

Tropical leaves waved across my path as I entered, a fan of green, holographic vegetation. My legs passed right through the leaves. The rest of the world was erasèd as the digital foliage closed in behind me and concealed the exit. A cactus flickered on my left, and behind it, a trellis of flowers scaled the wall.

Dark paths stretched out deep into the gardens. Leaves shifted in a false wind, but they made no sounds. I took the path farthest to the left and began to wander, wondering where I was going, what I was looking for. Maclean must have found something here before she died. Something worth killing for. I drifted through the dense forest, scanning the deepest corners and recesses.

A mother and a child walked by me as I turned into a mountain pasture. Cone-shaped conifers rimmed the edges of an oval clearing, waving with thread-like stalks of grass. There was a pond with a flat, motionless surface. A dragonfly skimmed the holographic water. As I wandered deeper into the gardens, leaves shaking soundlessly overhead, a thought began to take shape. I would find it here. I would find the missing piece of data that would set things to right. The data that would bring order to this chaos, that would make the patterns in the Optica make sense again. It would put an end to the nonsense. I would save Yury.

I was sure of it.

After a long stretch of wandering I came to a path that had been boarded off. CLOSED FOR RENOVATIONS, read the hanging sign. In the surrounding area, I saw no surveillance cameras like there had been in the previous sections of the gardens. There were no footsteps, and there was no one around.

I slipped through a gap between the boards and the wall. A long, winding tunnel led to a coral reef, an enclosed pocket hidden deep in the gardens. The air was alive with fish shoaling overhead and seahorses that swam through me. As I rounded a bend in the reef, I heard no sounds and saw no humans, but somehow I sensed the presence of a person, another living, breathing body waiting behind this bend.

I stuck close to the wall of rocks beside me and entered a clearing that opened onto a fake underwater expanse. A shark-shaped shadow circled in the distance. False sunlight filtered down from the ocean's apparent surface, vaulting far over our heads. And there—some distance away, a person sat on a bench, half concealed by a shoal of bannerfish.

I moved forward slowly, and the figure grew larger. But their back was turned to me. I couldn't see the face, but it looked like a woman, a hint of long hair showing between the swarms of fish. On the ground beside her lay a crate full of bottles with the label: FOCUS ENERGY DRINK. I took a few more steps.

With a flash of movement, the shoal of fish dispersed, startled. With a metallic click, I was at gunpoint. The woman had spun around and she was pointing a pistol at me. It was a familiar black Russell.

For a minute I said nothing, terror crackling like radio static in my head.

Finally I said, "Jenny, it's me. I'm wearing an Expo-Screen." I hoped that she would recognize my voice. I didn't want to say my name in case we were under surveillance.

Her skin paled. Behind her head, a jellyfish inched towards the sunlight, weaving through hanging ropes of kelp. Her eyes, wide and tinted green by the underwater sunlight, looked like those of a stranger. They couldn't be the same eyes I'd seen that night in the dirt and darkness of the vault.

"What the fuck are you doing here?" she said in a shaking voice. She didn't lower the Russell.

"Jesus, I'm working on a case. What's going on? Would you put that gun away?"

Her skin paled further. "What case?"

"I can't talk about it here."

"Fucking talk. This is a surveillance-free zone."

"How do you know that? What are you doing here?"

A sudden realization seemed to strike her, and she fidgeted anxiously, her gun still pointed at me. "Someone's gonna be here soon. You've got to leave. Now."

I couldn't bring myself to move, frozen in place.

"Go to your apartment," she said. "Stay there and don't fucking leave. Don't talk to anyone."

The coral reef, then the rest of the gardens, then the street bled into a blur as I moved without thought, overwhelmed with fear from an unknown source. A car screeched its horn. Music thudded from a truck streaking by and shoulders jostled me as I shoved through crowded sidewalks. The night looked strange and confusing. The letters of neon signs stuck out oddly in the dark and seemed illegible, threatening me with their nonsense. I didn't understand what I'd just found at the gardens, but whatever it was, it was a destructive force, something that would make me come undone. I'd found the clue I was looking for, but it didn't help me understand things. I'd found the data, but when the pieces all fit, what they showed me made no sense.

Chapter Twenty-Seven

As I waited for Jenny at my apartment, I thought of the day I decided to join the data police. On the surface, it had been a quiet and unremarkable day, but something had clicked. Something had made me certain this would be my career.

After college, I drifted for a little while, unsure what path to turn down next. But one morning, I woke up with a headache and the smell of gin on my breath, my mind reeling with shadowy memories of squandering big money on an expensive party the night before. I glanced at my tablet and a webpage was still open, one I'd been looking at yesterday: information about careers in the data police. It was something I'd been thinking about lately, but not seriously.

To clear my head, I left my apartment and trudged to the park, nursing a coffee. An ugly morning was dawning, a haze of clouds shedding gray light on gray concrete and my gray mood. I settled on a bench across from an elaborate vertical garden scaling a wall. Intricate arrangements of leaves and flowers stretched skywards and filled my sight, vines twisting between ferns and the long waving leaves of spider plants. But order had been imposed on the overgrowth. The differently coloured leaves had been pruned with ruthless precision into groups and patterns, into smooth lines and geometrical shapes, a diamond of red flowers in the centre. As I looked up at that mass of growing, living green, the throb of my hangover subsided and gave way to a sense of lucid clarity. Such complexity, distilled into such simple structures. The unruly organic life had been crafted and controlled, moulded into geometrical arrangements. Thoughts began to form in my mind, some new knowledge taking shape that I couldn't yet verbalize.

Rustling leaves on the edge of the garden startled me. A human shape came slowly into view from around the corner of the wall. He wore a broad straw hat and he had a hunched back, his gloved hands working with care and steadiness to prune the garden's overgrowth.

I put my coffee down on the bench beside me and watched him make his slow, meticulous progress along the wall. I was overwhelmed by a sudden, deep respect for him. Now that I looked closely, I saw that there were tiny imperfections in the garden, one little shoot of new growth growing on a string of ivy, straying from the clean lines of the shape where it belonged, a wayward tendril of a spider plant, one brown leaf wilting in a patch of green. The gardener and the garden were locked in a constant struggle. The leaves grew; the gardener cut them back. The leaves grew; the gardener cut them back. And so it would continue until the day he died, when another would replace him. The patterns in nature were not there on their own, waiting to be discovered. The gardener created them.

I sat, watching him work, for hours. By the end of the day I knew I wanted to make patterns like that gardener did, patterns that were the products of my art. I would make sense out of forensic data, out of the unruly mess of life. I wanted the eyes of the data detective, the ones that could see the answers in the Optica that no one else could.

As I continued to wait for Jenny, that memory was already glazed by nostalgia, distanced by the awareness that it was firmly in the past. If I returned to visit that garden again, it would be overrun with greenery, wild and irregular. The gardener was losing the struggle.

After I finally buzzed Jenny into my apartment, she rushed through the front door taut with nervous energy, her eyes darting around the room. I reached out to touch her arm, but she jerked away. She was shaking underneath the jacket.

"Goddamn you," she said. "Maybe I fucked you, but don't think I'll go easy on you if you cross me."

"What are you talking about? And first, are you sure we weren't recorded earlier? On surveillance camera?"

She looked worn. Broken. "No surveillance in that area, I told you. That's why we meet there."

"Who?"

She said nothing.

"Just tell me what's going on," I said.

There was a long silence, and she stood shifting her weight from one foot to the other.

"I'm ashamed," she said quietly.

I sat down on the couch, and she followed, but settled herself on the opposite end from me.

"Jason Shutter," she said finally. "Were you at the gardens because you're investigating him?"

"Yes." It was partly the truth. "What do you know about him?"

"I meet him there sometimes. He told me it's a safe place to meet. The fucker owns the place and keeps that area free of surveillance. He doesn't want to risk any footage getting made there, even by his own people."

"Why do you meet him?"

"To deal with him. I sell him Ruz. And the others. Donaldson too." She pulled her hands up into the baggy sleeves of her leather jacket and brought her knees up against her chest.

"You deal with him?"

"I fucking convert, you get it? How dense are you?" Her eyes flashed with anger. "They gimme Sentrac money for it. I'm not proud of it, okay? I believe in the project. In rebuilding, in independence. But I didn't have a fucking choice."

I couldn't reply right away.

"Don't tell the others," she said. "Haru. Kay. They'll kill me."

"What about Anton?"

"He knows. He helps me. He gets the Ruz for me, pretending it's all for him. Then I sell most of it to the ring. He helps me—he always has, see? He still gets it for me even now that I left him, so he can help keep me alive and out of jail."

That explained Anton's defensive behaviour when I'd prodded him about Ruz, and the night I'd seen him pouring it into the IRON ENERGY DRINK bottles.

"Why do you do it?" I asked.

"So I don't go to fucking jail, alright! Remember that night, when I told you about Anton's bribe, the one to keep me out of jail? I told you they made me do something else besides the bribe, too. That officer we bribed, he was in the ring. Him, Donaldson, Shutter and a few others had gotten hooked on Ruz a while back, see? The fuckers had been getting it from Kay's lover, before she found out and killed him. That cut off their supply. They needed a new source. They made me agree to be their supplier, if they'd let me go free."

Pieces began to fall into place. If the gardens were a point of negotiation for the ring, then Maclean got shot for seeing something, just like I thought. But why hadn't any of this been in her notes, if she'd started to find evidence about them?

"Jenny," I said slowly, "who is the officer you bribed?"

Her head jerked to face me. Strain showed in the lines around her eyes. "You think I'm gonna tell you that? That'd endanger me. If you investigate him—if you keep on investigating Shutter, even, it might implicate me. I've accepted dirty fucking money from the ring. I might go down with them."

Jenny remained where she was, lost inside the baggy jacket with her hair splayed out on its faded shoulders, the ends tangled and broken. "I'll kill you if you betray me."

If the method that the ring had used to pay Jenny also led me to the member of the ring who was framing Yury, the same evidence I used to convict him might incriminate her too. Now that I knew about Jenny, a crucial piece of data, the end might be near, just around the corner—what we'd sought for so long, Yury and I.

Jenny was still looking at me, her expression softening. She edged towards me. "Look, I—I got angry, I know. You fucking scared me showing up like that. But I know you wouldn't expose me. You'll find some way to drop the Shutter case." She smiled faintly. "And of course, I'll shoot you in the head if you sell me out."

What Jenny didn't know was that this was no ordinary case. Yury's fate might be on the line. Incriminating her might set an innocent man free. My mind reeling, I held her and ran a hand through her hair, combing my fingers through the dry, tangled ends. Her body relaxed a bit, but her legs still fidgeted, crossed tightly.

"Your heart is beating so fast," she said.

"You won't tell me who the cop is? You don't trust me?"

"I do. But I still don't want to tell you."

She could choose not to tell me. That was fine. I would figure out who it was myself tomorrow, when I looked into her data. I think she knew it, too, and her not telling me, that was out of principle. But it was my right. I was the data police. Yury was probably at home right now, waiting for me to come back and tell him about Shutter Gardens, drowning his doubts in online gambling and hard liquor.

There was nothing more to say, so we went to bed then, letting Shutter Gardens fade to the background temporarily. The Forest shone through the glass walls of my bedroom, staining both of us green. Plant-life waved on the screens: simple living beings, moving on a virtual surface. Things were lucid here. My apartment was empty, free of the clutter in the vault. Nothing was in it. And in that nothingness we were closer than ever before.

Soon night had fallen, and I left the bedroom for water. When I returned Jenny was sitting in front of the window, right up against the glass, wearing nothing at all. Here on the twenty-eighth floor in the heart of the Core, the view from my windows was commanding.

"No one can see me," she said when she heard me come in. "But I can see them. Not very close up, but I know they're all down there."

"I don't even need curtains. I don't know why I even have them."

"Usually I'm the one being seen, down there with everyone else. This feels different."

"I don't know what you mean."

I wished she'd come back and lie beside me. Eventually she did, but she slept on her side facing the window, her back turned to me.

I stayed awake in the emptiness staring out my windows. Not far in the distance, a steel crane sagged crookedly across the white and yellow lights of the city. The windows of a private apartment building glowed just far enough away to make it hard to tell what was happening behind the glass. As the night stretched on, those squares went dark one by one. My breath tightened in my chest as I watched. I wouldn't be able to bear it if all the windows went dark. I didn't want to feel like the last one in the city who was still awake.

For a moment my thoughts drifted to Anton. What had happened to him after I left him there? Was he still alive?

But I couldn't let that distract me. If Jenny had been paid through an outlet that linked her to others in the ring, that payout strategy could be crucial evidence to save Yury from jail, if he was innocent. But whatever that method was, Jenny would have been paid out with it too, many times over the span of years.

The Optica would find the patterns. It would mine the data, until it did.

By the time Jenny began to stir in the morning, I was already up and dressed in my uniform. Small, gentle movements rippled the thin layer of sheets covering her body. She brushed the hair from her face and sat up, foggy-eyed.

"You want coffee?" I asked.

"No."

I busied myself packing up for work, shoving my phone into my pocket, straightening my tie.

"I hate seeing you in that Sentrac get-up," she said.

"This uniform used to mean so much to me."

"You need to give it up. Just give up on the data police. They're corrupt."

I didn't say anything.

"Frank."

"What?"

"You're going to have a choice. You're going to have a chance to disrupt it. The data police."

I looked over my shoulder at her. She was leaning against the headboard, clutching the sheet wrapped around the restless outline of her body. Uncertainty filled her dark, beautiful eyes. The air thickened as the gravity of what she'd said began to register.

"What are you talking about?" I said.

"I—I shouldn't be telling you, but I don't care. You aren't supposed to have a choice. The others—they won't give you one. But since lately, since we started. . ." She stopped for a moment, watching me anxiously. "Just all of a sudden it didn't feel right to me. What we were planning to do to you. I—I wanted to tell you early, so maybe you could try to find a way to hide, if you didn't want to do it. I wanted you to have a choice, see?"

I'd suspected something like this of course, but that was different than knowing it. More pieces were coming together, as what had once been disparate strands of suspicion and shadowy possibilities now began to gather and shape themselves into something certain. The information they wanted about the firewall. Kay's and Haru's intense surveillance of me.

I resumed getting ready for work and forced myself to speak in a level voice. "Whatever you're planning you better tell them to give it up. It's impossible. You're not big enough to make a dent in Sentrac security."

"We're big enough. You got no idea how many people have been involved in preparing this. You've seen only a corner of the markets."

"I need to get to work. We'll have to leave separately. It would be dangerous for us to be seen together."

Standing in front of my window, I watched her exit the building. She looked very far away as she blended into the human traffic, twenty-eight storeys below.

Chapter Twenty-Eight

The cement flew by under my feet on my way to Yury's apartment. I'd looked into Jenny's data, and the Shutter Gardens case was solved. Yury was innocent.

He lay on the couch when I came in, a tower of dirty plates on the coffee table, another on the kitchen counter. The apartment smelled of stale food. No lights were on, and only Yury's tablet, propped on his chest, illuminated the room.

"Leave the lights off," he snapped when I switched one on. "My eyes hurt."

"You fixed your fridge," I said, sitting across from him. "Thank God." Things in here felt better now. The electric hum was quieter, and no sliver of yellow sprawled across Yury's chest this time. Through the open door next to the couch, the baby's room was fully set up, full of furniture, toys, and clothes.

"You find something today?" he asked. "We need something good here, quick, Frank. I'm hitting nothing but dead ends. Stingsby wants to know my answer about the plea."

"That's what I came to talk to you about."

"You've got something?"

"No. I came to talk about the plea."

Yury looked at me with confusion in his large, childish eyes. Faint sounds drifted from behind their closed bedroom door. Akshara must be resting in there. Yury had told me that she'd still been feeling ill lately. The gentle rumble of a passing subway shook the floor of the apartment, and the screeching wheels of a bus drifted through the window, followed by the roar of an engine, the hum of busy urban motion.

"I already told you everything about the plea," Yury said. "Stingsby wants to know—"

"You can tell him your answer. Your answer is that you'll take the plea."

He sat up straight. All traces of exhaustion had disappeared from his face, the lines in his skin hyper-sharp, the white dots of light in his pupils shining.

"This is a dead end," I said. "We're too small, Yury. Too small for this."

The fridge hummed in the background, a mechanical heart-beat. His face told me that he couldn't accept this yet. Before now, he'd said every day that it was hopeless, but he didn't really believe it. Now that he was faced with certainty, he would fight it, fight it with everything he had.

"Why?" he demanded. "Why now—why would you just fucking give up like that?"

"Because I have nothing. And so do you."

"You can't just stop looking!"

"I'm not going to look anymore."

He argued more, but eventually I left him there like that, left him to sit helplessly in his apartment while the certainty of his future grew and swelled until it swallowed him. By the time I hit the sidewalk I was moving fast—I had to get out quick before Akshara came out of that bedroom, pregnant and showing now like she was last time I saw her, dark streaks under her eyes—and Yury would never know why I couldn't help him; he wouldn't understand, but Jenny, she was just trying to save herself when she broke the law; she was forced to sell the Ruz to Shutter, and she was too young to go to jail for ten years; she couldn't go to jail because I had a feeling that it wasn't right, and what I'd just done had made that feeling into reality. As I hurried through the streets, the signs I passed bled into a blur, too much movement in the words that slipped by one after another until they seemed to fall apart, the letters turned upside down.

Last night, when Jenny and I met in my empty apartment and there was nothing there: that was what Yury would never fucking understand—it was the reason why I did it, the key to it. It was the sweat and the heavy breath and the simplicity of being a living thing. I did it for her.

I did it for me.

An ad flashed overhead, selling data customization services for the home. A smiling man went about his day while all his appliances operated automatically, serving him eagerly, customized to his schedule, preferences, and needs. The ad read: ALL ABOUT YOU. Across a wide sky, a mauve dusk darkened into black. Traffic moved smoothly, and I moved alongside it, swept through the streets like a shred of data in a city of sensors, a needle in a haystack.

Earlier that day, I'd found the answers in the data. Because finally, I'd known where to begin.

Jenny Stiles—Income and Expenses. Paycheque from Sally Lane's Diner, + $910. Groceries, - $46. Internet Bill, - $79. Clothing, - $92. Paycheque from Sally Lane's Diner, + $910. Lucky One Gemini, + $440.

A Gemini win. Except that Jenny had told me, that night at Sally Lane's, "I don't gamble. A girl like me can't afford it." This whole time I'd known her, she'd been getting Sentrac money from the ring, and yet she'd hardly ever spent any of it. She kept on living in that run-down apartment. Why? Maybe she felt she didn't deserve it.

The account for Lucky One Gemini came next. *Lucky One Gemini—Income and Expenses.* Jason Ortiz—loss, $2,000. D. M. Samson—loss, $300,500. Cynthia Jackson—win, $150. Jenny Stiles—win, $440. Jason Ortiz—win, $1,500. Juan Carrera—loss, $1,270, 000. August Donaldson—win, $2,800,000—

Donaldson. He'd used this Gemini website as an exit point. It was a real Gemini server, but it must've been run by accomplices helping out with laundering on the side.

Jumping to my feet, I paced my apartment three times before I could sit again. I'd failed to see the larger picture until now. The grand narrative. Donaldson, Jenny, the detective who'd accepted Anton's bribe years ago, A. Chawla Consulting—they were all connected, all part of a massive criminal machine.

I continued poring through Lucky One's Gemini's data. Jenny Stiles, win—$2,100. Sarah Ricci—loss, $770. Lee Ng—win, $1,200. Jenny Stiles, loss—$235. It was genius, really, the way they'd smuggled Jenny's payments in slowly, in little chunks, even throwing in a loss here and there to keep things realistic. Then my eyes caught on the next line.

Gareth Stingsby, win—$140,000.

I sat there for a long time before I could proceed. I sat for what felt like hours. In the background, the sounds of my apartment building went on as always—voices from the neighbours' apartment, the pitch rising and falling as they moved through an argument—but the noise just sounded like nonsense. I couldn't take my eyes off that one line of text: Gareth Stingsby. That knowledge—the world felt too small to contain it; it was a tiny sliver wedged a little bit deeper each minute into the straight lines and sparkling white space of spreadsheets, the patterns of data mining, the clean empty rooms of Sentrac Bank.

When I looked further into Lucky One Gemini's account, it turned out my boss gambled on Lucky One Gemini all the time. And guess what? He usually won.

And with a little more digging, I even found Anton's bribe from three years ago. Since I'd been searching for a current drug dealer, I hadn't looked far enough back into Anton's data to see the massive bribe he'd paid out to Stingsby through Lucky One Gemini. I'd seen Lucky One Gemini in Donaldson's account and Shutter's, even Hays when I checked his accounts briefly, but the website had blended into the thousands of gambling purchases they made all the time, at all sorts of venues. It didn't look suspicious right away. I'd seen Shutter and Donaldson myself at the Indigo Palace and I knew they were addicts. We were a gambling nation.

I couldn't give them Stingsby without giving them Lucky One Gemini. And I couldn't give them Lucky One Gemini without giving them Jenny.

The night after I told Yury to take the plea, I couldn't bear to go home. I couldn't bear the cold hardwood floors underfoot, the clean counters and alphabetized jars and smell of disinfectant.

The cleanliness was a mockery of itself. The haven of my apartment was like a doll's house, a plastic toy filled with parts from an assembly line, manufactured by the million and shipped to houses across the city.

Instead I found myself sitting on the hill outside Sally Lane's with numb fingers and my breath freezing into ice on my scarf. The streets at the base of the hill bustled with a winter festival. Children milled about with cotton candy, their shrieks and laughter layered on top of the rumble of engines, the screeching wheels of a bus as it slowed to a halt. Couples with shopping bags walked in and out of the boutiques in the Core, moving like threads that wove together the patchwork scene of happiness, the stitching that bound it together. On my left, a path wound down towards the river, where I'd confronted the man who'd followed me that one night. Where only a crumbling fence separated the path from the dark current of the river below. Why did I want to let myself fall over that fence right now, until I tumbled into the river and it swept me away? When I'd beaten that man by the river, it had been because he was one of the criminals, but now, there was no way to the deny it, I was one of them too.

The scene before me shifted as a street performer began to draw a crowd in the festival. People clustered around to watch, and the children's laughter softened into the hushed voices of attentive listeners. I imagined Yury in an orange prison uniform, sitting across from Akshara while she showed him pictures of their daughter on her phone. Then I imagined Stingsby coming and going through Sentrac, the lines on his face hard and unbending as he gave orders to his detectives, prepared for press conferences, helped throw people in jail.

In the sky, the air tight with cold, the tiny glass circle of an observatory floated above the city. As the scene of happiness unfolded in front of me, it was as though I watched from that observatory, far above what I saw and decidedly, painfully, distant.

CHAPTER TWENTY-NINE

"Since I didn't know there was a corrupt cop at Sentrac, I had no reason to suspect Stingsby at first," I told Jenny when we were alone in the vault. "But I should've started putting two and two together back when you told me about the bribe."

I'd decided to tell her part of the truth about my Donaldson case, including that I'd looked into her data. She'd known that I'd probably look, but she also trusted me not to sell her out. And I could tell the anxiety had been eating at her. She'd known my investigation involved Shutter and she'd been afraid my case would expose her. To put her mind at rest, I'd told her I was dropping the case with Shutter and Donaldson. But I didn't tell her about one thing. I didn't tell her that Yury was being framed, that he was going to jail now while his sick wife was about to give birth to his daughter alone. Jenny was tired of feeling like she was in debt.

"But once I found out about Stingsby by looking at your data," I said, "I looked into Sentrac's own spending records, and I found out someone had been stealing money from Sentrac Bank itself. Stingsby had been pumping money into the ring, using a data technology account only the forensics department had access to."

Stingsby had set up the frame for Yury just in case someone ever found the money he'd been funnelling out of Sentrac. He'd set up that frame with the art of a professional, so that it would lead to Yury as a dead end, without exposing his network. With Yury set up like he was, about to plead guilty to taking the money, finding A. Chawla Consulting wouldn't lead them to Stingsby.

I would've had enough to start building a case for proving Yury innocent. Since I'd found all these people connected through the same online gambling website, since I'd known about these Sentrac payments, I could've helped him. It wouldn't have been easy, but it would've been worth a try.

"Did Stingsby kill that cop too?" Jenny asked. "The one who died outside Shutter Gardens the night I met you?"

"That's right. Maybe Stingsby didn't pull the trigger himself, but he must've been behind it. He might've warned the ring Maclean was coming. Maybe she told him she was going there to investigate. They killed her because she'd started to find out about the ring, when she was investigating Donaldson."

"If she knew about the ring then why wasn't all that in her notes when you took over the case?"

I thought back to the weekend when the case got transferred to me. Stingsby had stepped out of the car into pissing rain on the night of Maclean's death and said, "Go home, Southwood. You'll start the Donaldson case on Monday."

"He altered her notes," I said slowly, thinking it through. "Over the weekend, before he transferred the case to me, he must've used his authorization to read through them and take out whatever Maclean had found. If she'd started to find the first traces of the ring like I had, she may even have told him what she'd found and that she was planning to go to the gardens. The two of them were close. He probably had the sniper waiting outside for her."

"Why didn't you tell Stingsby when you first found out about the ring, too?"

I hesitated. "I wanted to make sure I had something concrete first." A few more lies between us wouldn't hurt. I couldn't tell her about Yury.

And then there had been the day Stingsby had come to my office, warned me not to go beyond the data—undoubtedly to discourage me from finding anything extra. I'd told him I'd only known about Donaldson's small stuff on the side. That lie I'd told to save Yury had also saved my life. And there'd also been Stingsby's dismissive wave the night Maclean died, outside the crime scene. "Fine. Southwood can wait here," he'd said, as if I'd been a worthless rookie tagging along. Stingsby had underestimated me. He didn't think I'd find it. And if I hadn't followed Donaldson and learned about his affair, maybe I never would've.

"Is there any way you can nail Stingsby without implicating me?" Jenny asked.

"There's no way." I turned my back to her, lit a cigarette, and poured another glass of Chem-7. Now that Yury was about to plead guilty to the charges of A. Chawla Consulting, Stingsby was safe. That's why Stingsby had helped him get that plea bar-gain in the first place. I'd been drinking steadily the past few days, since I spoke to Yury, since I found out it was Stingsby. A dark-ness was settling over me.

"The data police—the whole system is a fucking failure," I said. "On the outside, it looks impenetrable. A city of sensors, collecting data on everyone, keeping a vice-grip on crime. But under the surface, the system is brittle. Weak. It's easy to manip-ulate it. Easy to avoid surveillance. To steal." Easy to set up a frame, too.

"So you're just going to let Stingsby go free, then?" she asked. "Just let the data police keep running, corrupt like it is?"

I drank more, angrily. "I can't fucking touch him. Even if I put Stingsby away, the corruption runs deep into the data police. I've been following Stingsby today. I've even seen him talking to Ryan Green, commissioner of another branch of the data police. This is bigger than the financial department, bigger than Sentrac. They've got people in Homicide too. The detective working on Maclean's, Donaldson's, and Figueira's murders."

Jenny said nothing, and I drank in silence.

"That fucking slug, Stingsby," I muttered after a while. "After Maclean's and Donaldson's deaths, they blamed it on pri-vacy fanatics."

"I know."

"No, you don't understand what this means," I said, pacing. "Everything was wrong—I was wrong, for fuck's sake, wrong about everything. I thought I could read body language. I thought I understood how people work. How everything works."

"A lotta people think they understand how things work."

"And goddamn it, that fucking Stingsby—I can't believe him. One night I saw him at Gibson's pub after work—and now that I think about it, he must've been waiting there for me, just waiting for me to walk in—and he acted so angry and disturbed about Maclean's death. He completely tricked me."

"The fucker's a dirty snake."

"Jesus, he probably ran predictive analytics on me! He could've easily crunched my data and found out I'd probably go to Gibson's Pub at that time. I always do after work. Stingsby never goes to Gibson's. He was there waiting for me, just waiting to put on that act and throw me off."

"All this used to mean something to you. The law."

I said nothing.

Spidery threads of smoke drifted from the sofa where Jenny sat with an R&M in one hand. Her face became grave, and the first hints of dread ran through me as I realized what she was about to say before she opened her mouth. I wished she wouldn't say it. I'd been avoiding thinking about it these past few days, overwhelmed by everything else.

"Maybe you're ready then," she said. "To disrupt the data police with us."

"It's crazy, whatever you're planning. It isn't going to work."

"It's a virus," she said, her voice quiet. "It will seriously damage digital money."

"Bullshit." I took two rapid swallows of Chem-7. A fog of intoxication was starting to consume me, dulling the fear her words were provoking. A glaze darkened my vision, details fading fast.

"You'll need to make a choice soon. They're going to come for you."

She was right about that in more ways than one. I had only a few weeks to pay my gambling debts, too.

"Frank," Jenny said. The tone of her voice had changed. Her eyes had changed, too, now shiny and filled with some kind of emotion. "There's something else I didn't tell you yet. You were so occupied with this when you came in, I couldn't find a place to say it."

I waited.

"It's Anton. He—" She paused. "He's dead."

Jesus Christ.

"Dead?" The word came out awkwardly. I struggled to put a blank expression on my face.

"He took too much Ruz and hit his head. He crawled into a corner after he fell and passed out there. Eventually he died."

She came over to hug me, her eyes turned up to mine and filled with sadness. Then she buried her face against my chest. Wetness stained my shirt. I held her and didn't say anything, my mind racing. Relief. But also some kind of sinking feeling, a heaviness tinged with something very nasty. It had been an accident. I needed to remember that.

That night I drank until I'd almost forgotten what Jenny told me. When I got home and stumbled into my kitchen, I saw my phone lying on my counter. Impulsively, I grabbed it and opened my contacts list. I stared at the screen, my finger over Yury's name. After the news he'd gotten recently, he might be doing something reckless. Maybe the Indigo Palace, maybe worse. If I called to check on him, at least it would put my own mind at ease.

I put the phone down without calling. I was too drunk and high to speak to someone, shut off in the foggy cell of my own existence. And it didn't matter anyway. I couldn't help him now.

Chapter Thirty

When I sobered up in the morning I slunk out of bed with a headache, made coffee, and turned on my tablet. Thoughts of Anton haunted me, but even more pressing was the fear. Fear rose up violently with my crawl into wakefulness, with the first cloudy streaks of light outside my windows.

Could I run?

Could I evade both the vast webs of privacy fanatics and the police, who'd no doubt be looking for me and assuming I'd skipped out on my gambling debts? I had no connections. No way to get any kind of fake identification. Nowhere to go.

I began combing through newspaper archives on my tablet. JOSHUA WALKER, I typed into the search bar. Dozens of articles came up, and I clicked on one, dated from five years ago. The headline read: DATA DETECTIVE JOSHUA WALKER ESCAPES JAIL IN EXCHANGE FOR TESTIMONY.

> Detective Joshua Walker of the financial data police was released from jail on Thursday and given witness immunity, in exchange for critical insider information about a planned cyber-attack at Sentrac. Walker had been jailed on multiple charges of assault, extortion, and bribery, crimes committed during his collusion with a network of organized criminals. Police have revealed little information about the case, including the planned attack and its prospective perpetrators. . . .

The details were exactly as I remembered them. Walker had gotten involved in something that got too deep to back out of easily, just like I was. At the last minute he ducked out and confessed. Desperate for his testimony, the police gave him immunity, and they got him out of town. He disappeared. Left the country and got a new identity so his fellow criminals wouldn't find him. With the information he gave, the police made multiple arrests. The people he'd been working with went to jail, and they stayed there.

I'd already done it once with Yury. I'd put the person I was working with in jail. I could do that again. Maybe Stingsby could even help buy me time on my gambling debts. In my mind I saw an image of red fingernails clasping vertical bars, the steel pillars casting harsh shadows on her skin. I'd need to try and find a way to get Jenny out, too. Maybe I could bargain with them.

But no. There were complications. There was the sickening idea of making a deal with Stingsby, the man I still had to watch every day, striding into the office wearing his pristine suits, his D72 in its holster, the hints of scarred skin showing on his wrist underneath his sleeve. And there was Hays, and others like him, walking free and running this town with their vice-grip of corruption.

What the privacy fanatics were planning couldn't be done, at any rate. Not a cyber-attack of this magnitude.

But the uncertainty, that small gnawing chance that it just might be possible. The vast networks of traders that extended deep into the city like they did. The money they had. The resources. I imagined the fallout from the collapse of digital money, the fiat economy rent to shreds, the arteries of Sentrac dollars slashed open and tattered shreds of data floating like confetti, all the patterns rent to pieces and falling like feathers in a zig-zag motion, the cold fingers of a national apocalypse spreading through the country. The Core in shambles. The blue circuits of Sentrac money dried up and dead, the Indigo Palace an empty shell, and the streets overflowing like the vault, voices fighting between staccato gunshots and cries that rang out like sirens. The guns, those ropes of machine gun ammo in the underground bank, they were the only thing keeping that money safe. And I thought of the darkness that rose out of people when they knew that no one watched them, recorded them, held them accountable. That feeling of empowerment when I'd looked down at Anton's passed-out body and realized there was no data, no one watching us. Life would be lived like a perpetual Gemini game, everything run by chance.

I watched, a helpless observer, as my mind slowly begin to grapple with the decision, somewhere beyond my full awareness or control. Experiences, memories, thoughts, and emotions began to stir, then settle like particles of sand. I saw Stingsby standing outside Maclean's murder scene on a November night, blue light from the police dome staining his white hair and eyebrows. I thought of the calm that came over Jenny when she lay still for just a little while, the small curls stuck around her hairline. The gardener pruning those leaves, all that complexity made simple. Who knew where all those particles of thought and memory would settle? It might be like the moment when I'd decided, with abrupt certainty, that I would send Yury to jail. Though the awareness had come suddenly, my mind had been toiling on the choice throughout the day, as I went to work looking at Jenny's data like an automaton, my eyes craving designs and certainty. And when it was all laid out for me, I stood up and paced my office. A few feet away, Perez tapped one of her heels into the ground, the soft sounds echoing through the office. I stood still and silent for a moment, and as those quiet taps broke over me, I knew, suddenly and with certainty, that I would send Yury to jail. There was no connection, no logical link between that moment and the decision I made. I wanted it to have meaning, for there to be a narrative behind my choice, for that moment to be significant. But it wasn't. That was simply the moment when I became conscious of my choice. And it was random, random like the leaves of a garden that no one had pruned in years.

I tried to draw up one of my charts, but the moment I touched the paper, I felt sick.

In the evening I went to Sentrac to gather some additional data about the deal Stingsby had made with Detective Walker.

"Evening Frank," a familiar voice said when I walked into the lobby.

"Mike," I said, nodding at him. "How's Laura doing?" But even this little routine with Mike on his night shifts brought me no pleasure. It felt more like a formality. But of course I still

needed to ask him how Laura was doing. It would be blasphe-
mous not to.

"She's great." He smiled, sipping his coffee. "Hey, I just saw
the news before I came here. The latest story about the Yury
Sokolov fraud case that Liu shut down. And I was thinking, you
know—we're lucky to live in the time we do. Nothing gets by
you."

I looked at Mike standing there, smiling and dumping sugar
into his cheap coffee, and suddenly I was amazed by him. Mike
made comments like this all the time—he praised the data
police often—but now, with everything going on in my life, I
simply couldn't comprehend it: how did Mike go on this way,
day in and day out? How could such a simple being exist,
untouched by the complexities of life? I had an absurd urge to
cling to Mike, cling to him like he was the last thread of safety.
I wanted to throw myself at his feet and beg him to stay exactly
the way he was.

But instead I just said, "Thanks, Mike."

CHAPTER THIRTY-ONE

The traders came for me the next day. Cedric appeared in Sentrac Square on my lunchbreak, wearing his pin-striped suit. As he approached, the clock in the centre of the square threw a dark streak of shadow over his figure, and he looked huge and monstrous, a half-formed shape lumbering towards me. I glanced around for a way to make a quick exit, but he was already taking a seat on the fountain beside me.

"Come to the bank at 22:00 tonight," he said, his gold incisors flashing. "Just routine business."

No, my mind pleaded silently. Not yet. I wasn't ready to decide.

I didn't go to the bank that night. I sat at home with my phone in hand ready to call Stingsby. In the end, I did nothing. One thought kept me sane. Even if they tried to force me to carry out some kind of cyber-attack, I could always back out. They'd likely need me to go into Sentrac itself, and they wouldn't be able to send anyone in with me. Security was too tight. Once I got inside, I could always call Stingsby.

On the way home from work the next day, they came for me again. About a block away from Sentrac, I sensed the presence of someone following me. I quickened my pace; he did the same. A glance over my shoulder revealed a tall man in a trench-coat half a block back. A stranger's face with aviator sunglasses. He walked quickly, his stride sharp with attention and purpose. I rounded a corner. He followed.

Breaking into a run, I shouldered past a man and spilled his coffee, hot liquid searing my arm. Faces turned to stare. I stumbled around a sidewalk sign in front of a coffee shop and knocked it over. I veered left onto Eighteenth Avenue. Elbows, shoulders, and faces crowded on all sides. A bicycle swept past on my left, its bell ringing shrilly. I tried to let the crowd swallow me. Maybe I could lose him in the pedestrian traffic. I needed to stick to busy streets, where they couldn't take me openly. If I went to my apartment, they would come for me.

The man was still behind me, closer than before, his feet pounding the cement. He was moving fast. The corner of a glass skyscraper flew by as I turned onto another bustling street, lungs burning. Crowded images streaked by. Racks of dresses, purses on the ground, the yells of the street vendor as I cut through his merchandise. My stalker's feet thundered behind me.

My feet stopped moving. There, standing a short distance ahead, statue-like and unmoving, was Kay, one hand in the pocket of her leather coat, where the bulk of a concealed weapon was visible. The crowd flowed around her like liquid as she stood, still and untouched by its currents.

Panicking, I jerked my body to the right without thinking and slipped into the first alley I saw. Footsteps sounded behind me. I stumbled over a piece of junk metal. Pain exploded in my foot. Noises clamoured from stairwells overhead as feet clattered against metal.

I neared the end of the alley. Against the brick wall before me, Haru stood holding a gun. They knew these streets top to bottom—knew them without data, through sight, sound, feeling, and instinct—and they'd corralled me like a sheep.

She fired. My shoulder stung, and the alley wavered and blurred. Shadowy figures began to close in on me, but they were already fading into blackness.

I regained consciousness tied to a chair in a wide indoor space, my head still thick and foggy from the tranquilizer. The air was thick with cigarette smoke. As the world slid into focus, I recognized the webs of aluminum pipes hanging overhead. It was Kay's warehouse.

The hazy figures of Haru and Kay flickered behind the smoke, sitting across the table from me. Kay's long fingers tapped on the table next to her gun. "I don't think I can do it, Haru," she said quietly. "I can't put it in his hands."

"Have to," Haru said. "We need his eyes."

"But this hopeless, weak man. I think he's the wrong one."

"He's the only man we got."

Kay stood up and paced. She turned her back to me, exposing the tattoos across her shoulder-blades. A desolate, sandy landscape stretched across her back from shoulder to shoulder. In the centre, and cutting up into her neck, stood a tower, and a spiral staircase wound around the outside like a string. The tower looked familiar; I couldn't place it, but it raised vague intimations of chaos and confusion.

I looked at Kay and said, "You're the one that's been having me followed lately. I saw your man's tattoo, both times. The same one you have. Just fucking tell me what all this is about."

Haru nodded at Kay. "Bring it out."

Kay placed a small black box on the table. As she put it down, she moved defensively, protectively. The box was made of sleek, jet-black chrome, and it was a perfect cube. Its shape reminded me of the blue cube that circled the vault, its movements random and its sensors blind to humans. I could almost hear the drone of its mechanical movement.

Kay opened the box. She drew from the inside a tiny gray rectangle and placed it in front of me. "A virus." She spoke quietly, eyes fixated on the rectangle. "The product of years of work. The information you got us only helped us through the final stages."

Even though I knew this was all bullshit I found myself unable to keep my eyes on that rectangle for too long. It looked dangerous to touch.

"We gotta borrow your eyes," Haru said. "Go into Sentrac, with this hidden on your body. Access the Optica. Open the file-sharing network. Transfer the virus—a standard skin transfer. We've done all the work. Your part—it's just one swipe of your finger."

"This won't work," I said. "There are fucking backups. It doesn't matter what this virus is, what it does. You'd never find all the data centres, corrupt all the backups. This won't destroy digital money—"

"Not single-handedly." Haru cut me off. "But you know what digital money runs on? What keeps it working?"

"What?"

"Faith."

"Faith?"

"You heard me. Sentrac money, it's a religion. It works because people believe in it. It's nothing but a bunch of numbers, a bunch of data—it's got value because the government and Sentrac say so. Because people believe in it. They accept it. They use it. Every time you buy something with Sentrac money, any old bullshit thing, you're pledging your belief in money. Why d'you think we absent ourselves on principle? We don't wanna make that pledge."

Kay lit another cigarette. Her composure had returned, and I marvelled, as always, at the powerful sense of calm that followed her everywhere. Her muscular shoulders sloped gently down from her neck with no tension in them, she leaned against the back of her chair without a hint of awkwardness, and her free hand, resting on the table, remained completely still as though frozen.

"If you take away the faith," Kay said, "what you're left with is what you actually had all along. Nothing."

"Nothing, Frank," Haru said. "Get comfortable with it. The virus can only take out the system a little while. Few days, maybe. But its effect on trust, that'll be powerful. The strength of the virus is in the fear. People will panic. They'll realize the nothing that they've had all along, then the motherfuckers will flock back to gold and real wealth, hoard it like crazy, fight over it. This is how it's been, time after time in history, every time a crash hits, every time people stop believing in money. And more than that—people will stop trusting the data police."

I didn't answer.

"Just think how many people are discontented. They hate the data police. The Church of Sentrac's on its way out. The rich are drowning in money. The Core and the Border getting farther and farther apart every day. We've got the energy. We just need to get it started. We've got a toxic religion on our hands, so we're going to get a new fucking religion."

"So you're planning to try and cause a national apocalypse, then?" I asked.

"Apocalypse?" Haru put her hands behind her head, leaned back, and looked up at the smoke of her Vintage curling in the air above us. "Jesus. The apocalypse happened ages ago. Let me tell you this. An apocalypse is slow. It creeps up and it's all over you before you even know it happened. Whoever it is that gets to define when an apocalypse happened, they got a lot of fucking clout, I'll tell you that."

"And if I refuse?"

"Death. It's simple. No blackmail this time. You may think you can hide but you can't. There are too many of us."

A simple but effective threat. I knew suddenly that even if I drank every night, gambled my life away, wandered through the Border looking for risk, at the core I was still a simple living thing, desperate to breathe, eat, live. But Stingsby might be able to hide me if I backed out.

"After you put through the virus," Haru said, "go to the corner of Twelfth, where our people will be stationed. The virus takes exactly three minutes to take effect. When everything is done, you won't need to worry about you. You'll become invisible, like one of those ghosts people talk about."

"If I don't show up for work tomorrow, that'll raise alarm bells."

"That's why you're going tonight."

Jesus.

"At 22:00."

There was nothing to say.

"Just get yourself ready," Kay said.

They left me in a back room, the door locked from the outside. Noise clamoured outside in the hall. Voices shouted. The metallic sounds of guns being loaded. For half an hour the noise rose to an apex, then slowly began to subside. Quiet came next. It was the quiet that made me nervous. People were moving out.

Getting ready for violence. After an hour had gone by, the scraping sound of someone opening the lock broke the silence.

The door opened and Jenny stood behind it. Her coat was unbuttoned, her hair stringy and unwashed. As she stood there, I saw, for the first time, the startling richness of her imperfections. The uneven patches where her red nail polish had chipped away. The tiny lines around her eyes, capable of immense expression and shifting with her mood. The purple circles under her eyes. I'd never seen any of this, not in the darkness we made love in, not in the plain light of day either. The way I looked at her now, my eye made no adjustments; it didn't search for patterns or try to alter the details; it simply let them be.

She shut the door behind us and I held her. "I'll go with you," she said, looking up at me. "After you put through the virus. We'll leave the country. Wherever they take us, we'll have to live a small and simple life."

A simple life. I thought of the endless small, repetitive acts that would stream by, day in and day out, and constitute my existence. We would make a home somewhere remote, fill it with food and furniture and plants and blankets and other simple things. We would talk, eat, sleep together, fall asleep, wake up again, and then repeat. At the beginning, the days would slide by in contentment: our physical attraction would engross our attention and shut out the need for more complex things. We'd have plenty to talk about. Our past lives, of the ordeal we'd been through, then what books we'd read, what kind of food we'd eat that night, who would clean the kitchen next—and so on, until the topics became smaller and smaller, more and more meaningless, sliding into nothingness. It would be a reduction to the life of a basic being like the plastics sold on the streets. But shouldn't a human be a more complex thing?

I thought longingly of my old life, the thrill of ambition and trying to move up in the ranks of the data police, the incredible complexity of the search for patterns in huge expanses of data. The constant searching after more—more money, power, prestige, more challenges met and overcome.

Jenny was looking at me, waiting for my response. The awkwardness of the moment deepened. So many things needed to be said, but to try and express my thoughts would be to distort them, cramming something unwieldy into the unnatural shape of words. Deep silence grew between us as what might be my last chance to say something to her slipped away.

Flustered in the silence, she repeated herself. "We'll have to give up some things."

I nodded then, and she looked like she understood something by that. She told me it was time for her to leave. The brass buttons on her coat were fastened up right to her neck, and she was covered up again, shrouded and distant like she used to be. The fabric enclosed her like those layers of clutter that followed her everywhere, hiding the core of her.

Kay and Haru loaded me into the back of the stealth van. They passed me a handgun. I was still wearing the uniform since I came from work. As the van rolled into motion, time moved strangely: quickly at first, then slowly. In the distance, cranes hung in the sky, making strange angles in the night. The traders would drop me in a safe location some distance away from Sentrac. Then I would walk, followed closely in case I tried anything.

Road after road swept by in silence, and the industrial buildings of the Stack rolled by our windows. Cars passed by calmly in the street, shuttling passengers about their routine business. Assembly lines of innocent people filed by on the sidewalks, and I wished they would sweep me up and carry me with them to their dentist appointments and grocery shopping, their desk jobs and petty marital squabbles. The streets of the Core grew closer, neon streaking along the edges of a glass skyscraper as we entered the harsh, brightly lit streets of the city centre, flashing with advertisements and electric light. The city was functioning like it always did: the workings of an orderly network, the pulse of data-directed traffic, the sensors that monitored and recorded, the circuits of a vast system. A system that was beautiful in its symmetry. But there was frailty underneath it. Below the orderly exterior lay deep fault lines and terrible flaws—flaws that could not be fixed.

We reached the Core. Faces streamed by our windows, though none of them could see me behind the glass. Distantly, I wondered when, precisely, I had become a criminal. Was it when I put Yury behind bars? When I moved Anton's body? Or earlier, when I stole data for Haru? Was it when I paid for Celeste's surgery? Did it go even further back, still, to that first night I'd bought things for Celeste to steal, desperate to see her again?

I climbed out of the van and set out on foot, moving swiftly towards the main streets. One last time I wanted to walk in time with the traffic, in time with the city's rhythms that might be altered soon. The people and things on the street looked utterly normal, and though I didn't know why, that pained me. A couple dawdled on the sidewalk ahead. A child played a video game in the back seat of a car. In front of me, a beggar crouched on the sidewalk, his blind eyes upturned and his sign reading: ANYTHING WOULD HELP.

I reached Sentrac. The doors swung open to welcome me into the wide space and vaulted ceilings of the lobby. A familiar sight. As I walked past the security desk, I heard a voice I knew well.

"Evening, Frank," Mike said.

It was the night shift, after all. Mike was leaning back against the security counter with a coffee in hand, his belly sagging over his belt. I nodded at him, adrenaline warping the lobby, details hyper-sharp. Crumbs straggled in Mike's moustache. His jaw moved silently as he chewed on a ham sandwich.

"Evening, Mike," I said.

His face turned to follow me with interest, but I kept walking. Mike wouldn't do his nightly patrol until 22:30. He was the epitome of routine and regularity. The elevator arrived, and the plain, empty square shuttled me upwards.

No one was working in my section of the office. There were all the familiar sights: the rows of tiny trees in pots, Yury's desk, cleared out now, the chair where Perez sat every day, tapping her heels into the linoleum, the cubicle where I'd spent my early years, struggling to climb in the ranks and impress Stingsby. All those little things that had mattered then more than anything else. As I walked, I could almost see the Sentrac data being unravelled, the steps of data processing working in reverse, the patterns of data mining undone, the target data, still processed, normalized, and made uniform, and then at last, the raw data, stripped to its barest form.

I entered my office. The quiet inside the room was not total; the ventilation system hummed and electricity droned in the overhead lights.

I turned on my interface. INITIALIZING, the screen read. I opened the file-sharing network. I swiped my finger on the data upload pad. Sentrac put all their trust in their cyber-security, the best in the world. But the fanatics had put everything they had into this virus, the resources of a vast network of the angry and the discontent, festering and growing in number throughout the city.

The skin transfer took place instantly.

It was done.

"Frank."

The voice came from the hallway. A man's voice. The sound sliced into me as if the fabric of the room had been slashed open. I had three minutes to leave the building. Distantly, the thought of my cold silence earlier, with Jenny, crossed my mind.

I took a few steps. The mahogany rectangle of my doorframe slid by slowly as I stepped out into the hallway.

Mike stood in the hall, in between me and the elevator. He looked very simple, his arms dangling at his sides, the crumbs still in his moustache. That button with the green checkmark was pinned to his chest. He was no longer eating or drinking his coffee. Like all the security guards, he carried a D72 at his waist. His brown eyes shone in the halogen, in the bright light too sunny and businesslike for the scene that was unfolding.

"Yes?" I said. I heard the stiffness in my voice and longed wildly to call the word back into my throat. My voice betrayed me.

"Just doing an early patrol."

Goddamn his thoroughness. Damn his love of the data police and of his job. He shouldn't be here. Not until 22:30. This broke every pattern in the book. Patterns couldn't be trusted.

"Is something wrong?" he asked.

I paused. More seconds passed.

"Nothing's wrong. I just came in to finish submitting some data for a case."

But when I spoke, his face grew warier. My voice confirmed his fear—that terrible voice coming out of me, hideously flat and false, revealing me beyond my control.

"I don't know," Mike said slowly, his eyes like two small beads of glass, fixed on me with an unreadable expression. "Are you alright, Frank? You didn't ask me about Laura when you came in. You've never done that before. And something just seemed wrong with you."

"I'm fine."

He shook his head, eyes narrow. "Something's wrong. I can tell. I know you."

"Just move out of the way." My voice held no emotion. I spoke as if stating a simple fact. Less than two minutes remained.

"Move out of the way."

He didn't budge. More precious seconds slipped by.

I took a step. His hand shifted towards the D72 at his waist.

My hand moved quickly, without thought. The crack of a gunshot, still loud even with the silencer. Mike fell onto his back.

He lay still. It was silent except the soft drone of the ventilation system. The soles of Mike's shoes faced me, the toes pointed outwards slightly, tread marks on the rubber soles cut neatly in diamond shapes. A patch of gum stuck to his left shoe. Behind those shoes lay an unmoving heap of man, one arm sticking out awkwardly. I glimpsed what a simple thing a person was: just a slipshod assembly of flesh and bone, so easily stripped of its complexity. He'd been a simple man, and now he was a simple thing.

He remained motionless. His chest did not rise and fall. And yet his body looked unharmed, as if he'd simply passed out. But when I stepped over him towards the elevator, I saw the small red hole in his forehead.

I wanted to see Jenny again, and I wanted to live. I did it for her.

I did it for me.

At the end, that was what it came down to. All of it. Yury. The bribery deal. This virus. The traders lived for themselves, lived for their own gain and their own will, their own greed and lust to live and thrive. And so did I.

When I reached the elevator there was less than one minute left. A moment of silence as I sank back down to earth. The doors opened. I began the walk through the lobby. By the time I approached the front doors, security had noticed something had happened. Someone had heard the noise or seen the surveillance footage.

"Hey!" someone cried as I reached the doors.

But I was already outside, cold air rushing. Within moments I was carried away by the hands and bodies of strangers that swept me into a vehicle. The traders had not backed out. They were here and they would help me get out. Movement jolted me as I found myself in the backseat of some vehicle, all the windows blacked out. I let the current of chaos sweep me along to an unknown destination.

Anton had been just one step in a bigger narrative. I'd been reluctant to kill him outright, holding back from shooting him because I'd been afraid to extinguish the tiny, living thing some-where inside of him that was the core of him, because under-neath everything we'd built—the houses, tech, the city of sen-sors, laws and regulations, the traders' code, all their gold money and hordes of possessions, the philosophies, codes of politeness, the institutions and languages—underneath it all lay simple scraps of life that demanded to breathe and live, like those plastics the vendors sold in the streets, like the night Jenny and I had spent in my apartment when there was nothing in it, nothing but the green light of the Forest staining us the colour of plant-life. I had-n't been able to admit that I'd extinguished that life with Anton. I'd had to tell myself it was an accident.

But I'd extinguished it now. This time, there was no ambi-guity. Somewhere out there, Mike lay on his back in what had now become a crime scene. He was still a heap of flesh, but soon he would become an outline, lines drawn in white chalk on the floor. And even now, there was nothing inside him.

In the chaos of the next few days, many would feel the way I had when I'd stood over Anton in a room with no surveillance: just two people with no one watching them, free to do whatever they wanted. Things in this city had become uncertain. But what Haru had said earlier tonight was true. An apocalypse was a matter of opinion.

Acknowledgments

I have received an incredible amount of support in writing this book. My partner, Jonathan, provided me with invaluable editing of my entire novel and helped me throughout the journey of writing my first book. My parents and brother have been immensely supportive of my creative endeavours and offered editing help as well. I am also amazed by how much support I've received from the writing community, and how many writers collaborated with me in reading and revising this novel. I'm grateful for the insightful beta reading of Kristine, Justin, Irina, Calder, and Katherine M. I'm also grateful for David, who created a productive and positive community for writers to support one another, the Toronto Sci-Fi and Fantasy Writers Group. I received fantastic editing support from my Front Street Writers Group—Michelle, Freda, Andrew, Peter, John, Jason, Justin, K.M. McKenzie, Wayne, Julia, Yale, and Adam—as well as my University of Toronto writing group—Katherine S., Margeaux, Philip, and Joel. I also appreciated the additional reading and editing support from Catherine and Clayton, Sophia, Rawi, Joanne, Melissa, Jonathan, Joe, Rob, Rahul, and Kat. I'm grateful to work with NON Publishing and Chris Needham, who have been fantastic to work with.